Richard Hahlo is an actor and teacher at Exeter University, and the University of California, San Diego. As an actor he has worked in schools, community centres, repertory theatres, West End theatres, the Royal Shakespeare Company, and the Royal National Theatre. He is an Education and Training Associate at the Royal National Theatre and has facilitated drama development work for groups in theatre, education and business throughout Britain. He has also led workshop programmes in many parts of the world, including South Africa, Japan, Poland, the Czech Republic and Switzerland.

Contact Email address: dramevents@hahlo.dircon.co.uk

Peter Reynolds is Head of Department of Drama: Theatre, Film and Television Studies at the University of Surrey Roehampton and an Education Associate of the Royal National Theatre. He was one of the founders of the Leverhulme-funded Shakespeare and Schools project at the Cambridge Institute of Education, and has published on Shakespeare, performance and pedagogy. He has led workshops throughout Britain.

Contact Email address: peter.reynolds@virgin.net

W·D

Dramatic Events

How to Run a Successful Workshop

RICHARD HAHLO
AND PETER REYNOLDS

faber and faber

First published in 2000
by Faber and Faber Limited
3 Queen Square London WC1N 3AU

Printed & bound by Antony Rowe Ltd, Eastbourne

The extracts from *The Cherry Orchard* by Anton Chekhov,
translated by Michael Frayn, are used here by permission
of Methuen Publishing Ltd.

A CIP record for this book
is available from the British Library

ISBN 0–571–19161–4

For Ali, Lucy and Esme,
with my love and admiration.
R.H.

For Joshua.
P.R.

Contents

Acknowledgements

Mike Alfreds, Chris Barton, Lois Beeson, Kevin Cahill, Geoffrey Church, Sue & John Driver, Jenny Harris, Dorinda Hulton, Peter & Fay Hahlo, Peter Hall, Jane Hepper, Tim Joyce, Phyllida Lloyd, Michael Mackenzie, Les Read, Kimberley Reynolds, Rick Scott, Hetty Shand, Joseph Smith, Peter Thomson, Kate Valentine, Carole Winter, Exeter University Drama Department, the Market Theatre Laboratory Johannesburg, Royal National Theatre Education, Royal National Theatre Studio.

Plus all those people we have worked with over the years, especially those too numerous to mention whose ideas and exercises have been absorbed into our own and this book. Thank you.

Introduction

My first experience of working in the professional theatre was in an unusual setting: the far end of a pier thrusting out into the North Sea. I was the assistant stage manager for a summer season of variety, one of a company of twelve. We struggled twice daily to win, and then hold, the attention of a holiday audience lulled, after hours resisting the icy 'breeze' off the sea, into semi-consciousness by the comparative warmth of the theatre. Given the nautical location, the company also had to work against the competing demands for their attention coming from wind and water. The small wooden auditorium was situated almost at the tip of the pier with only the lifeboat station between the stage and the sea. 'Swooping out of the blue – oo – glad to be alive, nineteen sixty-five!' bellowed the six chorus girls as they energetically high-kicked their way across the stage in fish-net tights strong enough to hold bigger fish than us, and 'guaranteed' to last the season. The regular thumping of their feet on the boards almost disguised a deeper, more insistent vibration from below, as waves knocked hard against the delicate ironwork of the pier's legs.

There were six dancers, two comedians, a soubrette, and – the undoubted star act – a quick-draw artiste. His job was to cajole usually reluctant members of the audience to exchange the security and anonymity of their places in the auditorium for a temporary seat on the stage. There they would pose, at first awkward and self-conscious, but later relaxed and comfortable in their part, as he quickly drew their likeness on a huge sheet of white paper. Their drama over, they would return to their seat, clutching the already-crumpled and smudged likeness. Watching this nightly from the wings, the tension I always felt arose from my lack of conviction that he would succeed in actually getting someone from the audience to go on to the stage. What would happen if he failed? He never did, but on some memorable nights he practically carried his subjects on to the stage, so apparently unwilling were they to take part in our show. Crossing that invisible line between their space and ours almost always appeared traumatic, but once they had been persuaded to join in, the reality of the experience, as opposed to the anticipation of it, became memorable.

On some nights the whole place seemed to be trembling, whether with excitement or the elements it was hard to tell; but although I was excited by the energy generated by the event, and the audience was voluble and appreciative, a niggling adolescent thought often occurred to me. Although the seaside audience always appeared to enjoy what was (aside from the pantomime at Christmas) probably their annual dramatic event, the effect on them of our shared experience was, I suspected, transitory and fleeting. I wanted it to mean more to them than that, but I knew that it never would or could. Soon they would head back down the wooden deck of the pier to their boarding houses, and subsequent nights would be spent in either the pub or the television lounge; while we usually went straight to our digs, too tired to contemplate further entertainment. What we had shared was what Shakespeare called a 'holiday humour', a brief and sometimes intense but ultimately unimportant diversion from the reality of their world of work.

Over thirty years later, all kinds of live theatre, not only that still happening on the end of our few remaining piers, sometimes seems to me, if anything, even more socially marginal and unimportant. Theatre no longer seems to matter to most of us. So, in the light of this, why write a book which makes a claim for the potential centrality of theatre, or at least of certain dramatic events, to everyday life?

One part of the answer to that is to invite the reader to reflect on a paradox: although live theatre continues in rapid, some say terminal, decline, the desire of many young people to study how theatre works, and to become actively involved in dramatic events, has never been greater. In England, A level Theatre Studies has for some years been the fastest-growing A level of all, and is now enormously popular among people who, for the most part, have little or no knowledge of, or even interest in, regular theatre-going. They are not drawn to the subject because of what they have seen on the amateur or professional stages of contemporary England; nor, despite the claims of cynics, are they attracted by the illusory glamour of the actor's life. What draws them, and ultimately holds them, is the fact that the mode of study itself offers a different quality of experience from that of more conventional academic subjects. The syllabus requires not only the familiar academic skills of reading, writing and private study, but also a way of working that is collaborative and cooperative – students work *together* to make performances. Their core learning experience is not solitary, but social, and therein lies its attraction and strength.

This book offers ways in which the social and educational nature of theatre workshops can become more widely experienced, valued and understood. They are already well established in education, and businesses too are rapidly discovering their potential value in management training. As the active learning experience provided by theatre workshops is more widely acknowledged, and as their popularity grows, so too, the authors believe, will the demand from individuals and groups to experience these dramatic events for themselves. Perhaps, in the new millennium, theatre workshops will become a new form of popular drama. As an alternative to sitting in a theatre watching actors at work creating characters, all kinds of people, not just students, will learn to fashion their own dramas in spaces where there is no division between performer and spectator. After all, to operate successfully as a performer in the contemporary theatre requires a high level of skill. You cannot simply go on to a stage and expect instantly to be able to play King Lear convincingly. However, it does not require any particular skill, training or knowledge to become involved with others in exploring some of the issues in *King Lear* in a theatre workshop. Of course, seeing such great plays performed by actors will remain for some a key cultural experience, but an active involvement in negotiating some of the play's issues – age, family relationships, loss of power, etc. – offers a powerful, equally valuable and above all accessible alternative or parallel experience.

The exercises and stories contained in this book are based on the authors' experience of working with thousands of people of different ages and backgrounds, actors and non-actors alike. It is designed to be a useful resource for an experienced workshop leader, and to encourage other readers either to lead a theatre workshop for themselves or, at the very least, to take an active part in one, perhaps for the first time.

The dramatic events described reflect our experience not only of the professional theatre, but as workshop leaders in a wide variety of situations. These range from a London prison to a township in South Africa, the boardroom of a large international company, countless school classrooms, and the rehearsal rooms at the Royal National

Theatre. These events, and others like them, were usually not intended to be a preparation for theatrical performance by professional actors. They were held in order to provide opportunities for non-actors, young and old, to develop personal and social skills, while at the same time enjoying a personally and professionally significant and useful experience.

Workshops are the embodiment of experiential learning, where people will often learn better by practice rather than by being asked to take in information passively. Students wanting to comprehend a play are often more engaged by a structured approach to staging some part of it. Teachers hoping to widen their knowledge of a theatre practitioner respond best to being engaged practically with the body of work. Many people in the business community are well aware of theories of communication and presentation, but may shift their ingrained patterns only as a result of practical exercises that allow them to try out different ways of behaving.

Any good workshop will stimulate the participants to release their energy, to free their body and their voice, to listen, to think, to be creative, to engage in focused exchanges with other people, to take risks and to watch others. None of these benefits is unique to workshops, but what a workshop particularly offers is a concentrated occasion which condenses larger issues into a manageable participatory event. A workshop should promote collective learning, where a group of people spend time together using certain materials and, more importantly, each other as resources to explore ideas through interaction.

This book itself is a concentrated form of workshop practice and experience, which hopes to offer a clear route taken from a landscape of exploration. For any workshop, effective exercises and processes need to be drawn together, and most importantly of all the workshop leader needs to offer a narration through the prepared plan which gives the participants the opportunity to learn and develop. We hope that each chapter that follows, as well as offering useful material, allows the reader to reflect on the practice presented and how it might be made to work with a group of people.

To make a workshop *work*, whoever leads it and whoever takes part must be prepared to play their part. Although we often play different personal roles in the dramas of everyday life, we do not generally have the opportunity to play an active part in public events. Only on rare occasions, such as the funeral of Princess Diana, are ordinary people able to come together to mark, with sometimes awkward but moving rituals, an event which temporarily unites them. Weddings and funerals apart, the old public ceremonial occasions regularly afforded by organized religion, where people spoke, sang and listened together, and knew what to do and how to do it, are almost gone. We now risk losing our collective knowledge and skills in how to behave with one another in public, and activities that once felt comfortable and reassuring now often appear alienating, even threatening. Of course, theatre workshops cannot by themselves fill the void in society left by the current scarcity of public ceremony and meaningful social rituals. However, they do represent one of the few genuine opportunities open to people to come together in order to enjoy and profit from the kind of shared experience they represent. At their most basic, theatre workshops remind us of the fun to be had from social play. They can help us relearn social skills. Beyond that, individuals can benefit from opportunities to practise and recast the myriad roles expected in the dramas of everyday life.

What now follows in this introduction is an account of various events, all in their very different ways dramatic and public, which were chosen in order to illustrate some of the opportunities as well as pitfalls involved in theatre workshops. They are written from the point of view of the workshop leader. There were, of course, as many other perspectives on these dramatic events as there were people who made them happen. The authors shared a common bond of dread before the event: a fear of failure and the public humiliation that would follow. Doubtless some of the participants had that same fear, but there would have been many more for whom the opportunity to work collaboratively was embraced with alacrity. For those readers who have never taken part in a theatre workshop, these narratives offer clues to what can go on in them, and why. For those who have experienced workshops for themselves, either as leaders or as participants, these stories will, the authors hope, strike a chord of recognition.

Johannesburg

In the piercing light of a South African morning, I find myself in a crowded, shabby office that doubles as a meeting place. The fieldworkers drift in, speaking mostly in Xhosa or Zulu, breaking off briefly into English as they are introduced to me, before folding themselves into the furniture or on to the floor. We wait to see if anyone else will show up. I awkwardly try to make conversation that amounts to very little. Can they understand my accent? How much English do they speak? Are they just uncomfortable with speaking to me?

Eventually I follow the fieldworkers off through an adjacent building that is being noisily rebuilt around us to a dusty room, mostly full of old chairs. Here they sit in silence, looking at the floor or staring into space. I am feeling very nervous, totally unsure what to do next; they are guarded and uneasy. The sound of nearby drilling cuts into the strained atmosphere.

This is the new South Africa soon after the election of Nelson Mandela as President, and to mark the end of the cultural boycott, the National Theatre Studio has taken a group of thirty-one actors, directors, writers, designers to take part in workshops with their South African counterparts. The group is conspicuously high profile and includes Richard Eyre, Ian McKellen and Antony Sher. It is all very exciting, but how is it going to work, making contact with all the different groups of people we are to meet, and how will they respond to these 'experts', most of them white, from London? By the time I step off the plane my trepidation at what lies ahead is rapidly mounting.

My main purpose is to work with the fieldworkers based at the Market Theatre Laboratory in Johannesburg, to share practice on using theatre with the wider community. Shortly before we were due to leave London for Johannesburg news came through that the fieldworkers had held a meeting, and there had been significant opposition to the idea of people parachuting in from London intent on working with them. I could understand their point of view, and wondered whether indeed we were about to involve ourselves in yet another episode in the long history of cultural imperialism. I was unsure that I had anything useful to offer them. I had worked with community groups in Britain, but would that have any relation to the world of the townships? The fieldworkers are young actors and directors, who go to the townships outside Johannesburg and beyond, where, despite deprivation, hardship and the struggle to get by, theatre groups flourish. The groups usually meet at the end of the day to rehearse, in schools, community centres and in one case an abandoned and dangerous factory. The fieldworkers go to work with them to offer advice, direction and support where needed.

After receiving some reassurance about our intentions, the fieldworkers resolved that they would meet with me so that we could explore how and if we might work together. There I sat in the makeshift workshop space on that first morning, looking into a sea of faces none of which returned my nervous smiles, and I could only guess at what was going on inside their heads. My mind had slowed down, as in the moments before an accident, and I could feel a rising panic. I felt way out of my depth, in a culture I knew almost nothing about. What should I do? My attempts at starting a discussion dissolved into nothing, and I was sensitively conscious of imposing myself upon them. The very real prospect of my abject failure to make this situation work re-entered my mind, and with it my complete humiliation in the full glare of our visit.

It was evident that I had to do something quickly, take the initiative and begin some activity. As at the start of so many workshops, I asked them to walk quickly around the space; but on this occasion, rather than following the instruction with half-hearted compliance, they were immediately off, charging around the room as if their lives depended on it! I then outlined a simple variation of a game of tag, which they played with undivided concentration, before finally giving way in an instant to tremendous outbreaks of laughter. The tension had cracked. We played a game of keeping a ball in the air, which they threw themselves into with fearless commitment before moving on to some quick improvisation exercises requiring speed of thought and the ability to be completely alert.

These simple exercises conducted in the first half-hour made an immediate difference to the atmosphere of the event. By sharing enjoyment and the common purpose of making theatre, the cultural preconceptions between us began to fade and we were able to make contact. We continued to play together throughout the day, and the fieldworkers showed an amazing ability to be in the present, completely letting go of the concerns that could possibly have bogged down this unprecedented encounter. Their earlier reservations were suspended, and they were happy to be there, playing and learning. It was clear to me that these were people who were hungry for information, ideas and the chance to experiment and explore. They had been starved of contact with the outside world by the old political system, and as they overcame any initial mistrust of me and of what I represented, they were willing to grab the opportunity for new experience. This led the way into what the best workshops should always be: an opportunity to play, exchange ideas and exercises, and share the enjoyment of making a dramatic event together.

The Prison

You enter HMP Brixton through a narrow entrance set into the massive, high, razor-wire-topped walls that surround the prison. Once you have successfully established your identity and reason for being there with a prison officer in a cubicle behind bullet-proof glass, you pass through an electronic door, and then a metal detector, before finding yourself in a cramped, sparsely furnished, overlit visitors' waiting-room. From there, on a chilly autumn morning, I waited to be escorted through the prison to the gym, where I was to hold a workshop in preparation for an extraordinary forthcoming dramatic event: a performance of *Hamlet* by prisoners and prison officers. The initial workshop was my first experience of what was to be a lengthy spell inside for a number of people from the Education Department of the Royal National Theatre. The setting on that first morning was inauspicious, to say the least. The gym was large, with a low ceiling and, like the waiting-room, it was overlit. It was also cold, smelling faintly of sweat and disinfectant. As I waited anxiously for the arrival of the participants, a couple of prison officers watched, mildly amused spectators of my obvious unease.

When the thirty or so participants entered the space, they immediately split into small groups and made for the walls, where they leaned back against the climbing-bars and looked at the floor. The most difficult time of *any* workshop is the first five minutes, when the participants are usually feeling anxious and even hostile – when the workshop leader, and sometimes the majority of the participants, wish they were anywhere but where they are. I began the two-hour session as I have begun almost all the workshops I have led, by asking everyone to move away from the walls, walk around in the space, and ignore everyone else. After a few minutes of shuffling self-consciously around, trying with varying degrees of success to suppress laughter or mask contempt, they were asked to look carefully, without ceasing to move, at the building and the equipment in it. They had to see if they could find anything new in a space that most of them knew well, but had experienced in a very different context. They should, I explained, choose an object and then focus on it while keeping moving and trying not to draw the attention of others to what they had chosen to look at. They should, I explained, look at it as close up as possible, as well as from a distance, and from different angles, all the time trying not to draw other people's attention to it.

There was no particularly sophisticated rationale behind this simple activity; it was designed to encourage the men to begin to use the space together, to lose a fraction of their inhibition, to concentrate, and to do something that literally filled up the daunting empty space of the gym. It was going well, but not for long. I was working to a pre-planned strategy in which the next stage of the introduction involved shifting the focus from objects to the other people in the room. 'Performing is all about looking at other people and also about *allowing yourself to be looked at – feeling comfortable knowing others are looking at you*,' I said with emphasis as I walked around the space, moving in and out of the group. But when they were asked to look at one another as they continued to move through the space, it didn't happen: a quick stolen glance, perhaps, but for the majority even that was asking too much too soon. They studiously avoided eye contact. The instruction was an insurmountable obstacle, and the energy and enthusiasm that had begun to replace collective unease quickly evaporated. It was a foolish mistake, a failure on my part to think ahead, to anticipate and plan properly. I subsequently managed to rescue the session and restore confidence, including my own, but it was a close-run thing. It served as a reminder that, however experienced you are, it is still easy to overlook something obvious about the group with whom you are working, with potentially disastrous consequences.

The initial reluctance of the prisoners to look at one another remained a major obstacle that threatened subsequent attempts to build a company and to perform effectively. In the macho world of prison, nowhere more graphically symbolized than in the gym, to look another prisoner in the eyes constituted a provocative challenge, an action most prisoners avoided assiduously. A lot of future workshop time was given over to exercises designed to build confidence and trust, and eventually the men were able to use their eyes as well as their bodies and voices to communicate. The workshops, finally, gave them, as it were, permission to look at other people. It was one of the major achievements of this entire dramatic event.

In that situation there were massive social tensions to be negotiated resulting from men being locked up together against their will, and from their collective mistrust of people in authority. Getting the men working together to put on a play was seldom easy or straightforward; it was never simply a matter of them somehow managing to lose their inhibitions. Rather they were able, after a time, to suspend some of them in order to open themselves to new experiences and new potentialities. Those prisoners were eventually able to enjoy the luxury of looking at other people and feeling comfortable when their gaze was returned. They then connected looking with speaking, thereby giving their words (and Shakespeare's) much greater weight and conviction; they began to use language, most of them for the first time, with authority and skill. If, in the course of a workshop, *any* group of people – teachers, students, business men or women – experience such new or different awareness of themselves in relation to others, that has to be positive. If they also discover skills they never knew they had, that can provide the fuel to enhance and enrich their subsequent performances in the home, the workplace and the street.

The Hotel

I once ran a workshop for teachers of English at a small hotel in the Lake District. The space allocated was normally used as a lounge and contained lots of heavy draylon-covered easy chairs. On the floor was a thick, swirly carpet, and the walls displayed a collection of sporting prints. A large picture window looked out on to a spectacular view of the lakes and hills, and on one side of the room there was a clear glass partition separating it from a corridor. A flimsy, transparent white nylon curtain partially covered the glass. Although a suitable space in which to read a novel, or take a nap after a heavy lunch, it was far from ideal for a theatre workshop. There wasn't much space in which to move about, feet sank into the carpet, making any movements feel awkward and restricted, the view from the window was continually competing with everything else for attention, and the glass partition gave the whole room the feel of a goldfish bowl.

As they gradually came into the room, the teachers headed straight for the chairs, and looked as if they were going to stay in them for the rest of the day. None of us knew one another, and although one or two people were talking, most remained silent, staring out of the window. It took all my nerve to ask them, finally, to get up, take off their coats, push the chairs back against the walls, and start the session.

Perhaps prompted by the sound of desperation in my voice, just as the prisoners had done, they obediently began the first simple exercise of walking around the room, looking at the objects and also the people in it. As they did so, they couldn't avoid noticing not only those in the room, but those just outside it. To our dismay and discomfort, an audience had formed to observe our tentative first steps through the gaps in the curtain. Four of the hotel staff, including the chef, were lined up in the corridor, with bemused expressions. Dramatic events did not apparently occur often in this quiet corner of Cumbria, and we were proving a mild diversion to the normal business of the day. I waved them away, and they went with a collective smirk, but not before the teachers had experienced one of the things they doubtless dreaded most: the horror of public mockery.

It was the worst possible beginning to what, from the moment I saw the space, had always appeared a lost cause. There was no alternative – the only larger area was the car park – but at the very least I should have got in there early and *moved* the chairs. As luck would have it, the subsequent work did not fail, and the group managed to come to terms with their surroundings, with one another, and with me. However, the experience taught me never to underestimate the importance of the space in helping or hindering group work, and above all the absolute necessity of privacy. It is hard enough to come to terms with strangers, and build a cooperative unit, but it is impossible if this process is being observed by those who have no investment in the outcome. So if there are any rules about running workshops, one has got to be that there are no spectators.

The Conference Centre

I was wearing the standard-issue casual loose-fitting trousers and denim jacket that would be instantly acceptable backstage in theatres all over the world, but which made me feel decidedly self-conscious as I waited in the business-class departure lounge at London's Heathrow Airport. I nervously eyed my smartly suited fellow travellers while trying to conjure up some projection of how they would respond if I were to exhort them to put down their financial papers, mobile phones and complimentary coffee, and join me in the adventure of a theatre workshop.

The resulting nightmare was fortunately interrupted by the imminent departure of the flight to Frankfurt. Not much later I found myself being shown into the functional room of a gleaming conference centre, to be met by a similar-looking array of the international business community I had just encountered at Heathrow. Only this time it was no dream: I really did have to lead them in a theatre workshop.

For the purposes of a business conference the room was large, but for a theatre workshop it was too small. It was also stuffed full of tables, chairs, overhead projectors, and a lifetime's supply of bottles of mineral water and bowls of imperial mints. My first objective was apparent: to get the people to move as much furniture as possible out into the corridor. This proved a tremendous success! It was a clearly defined task with a definite goal and, being a conference of engineers, they set about it with admirable efficiency and well-organized team-work. Soon the room was clear and for a fleeting moment there was a collective glow of satisfaction at a job well done. Then, as we all stood uncomfortably in the denuded room, the horrible realization came upon them and me that we now had to start a very different kind of activity. There was nowhere to hide, no chair to sit upon and no conference pad on which to scribble intelligent-looking notes. I was about to lead them in a session looking at 'Personal Awareness and Communication', programmed by an enlightened human resources manager whom I now noticed out of the corner of my eye looking visibly panicked.

The reason for emptying the room was not just that we needed more space so that people could physically move around, but to take people away from their 'props'. In the daily course of interaction with our colleagues, friends and families it is wonderful how many displacement activities we devise to deflect and avoid clear communication. The rituals of tea and coffee, the shuffling of documents, the swivelling chair behind the desk are all well practised in order to give us something to do, and to put up a smokescreen between us and the rest of the world.

The workshop the company had paid for was designed to explore how we are and how we communicate when we take away some of the behavioural habits we cling to. Hence the rules of no furniture, no outward acknowledgement of job titles, and no dressing to confer status deliberately. At the start of our session the effect on the delegates was disconcerting as we drifted into a circle, avoiding each other's gaze. Everyone looked awkward, and I thought: How do I get these people, most of whom have probably never done anything like this since the playground at primary school, to start to let go of their carefully crafted modes of self-preservation?

In the excruciating clumsiness of those opening moments I doubted that it could be done. These were engineers at a conference on 'Managing Change', most of whom had English as a second language and looked as prepared for a theatre workshop as I was to construct a suspension bridge. I asked them to move around the room and to look at it. It gave them something to do and meant they could avoid looking at each other for a few moments. They had to walk, stand still, and then carry on walking in response to a series of signals from me, which started to vary in time and pattern. Next they had to use their bodies physically to form a series of shapes (a triangle, a square, a question mark) as a team without anyone talking. Now they were looking at each other, communicating and – just as in shifting the furniture in the room – engaged on a clear task, only this time they were stretching their resources for communicating, because the driving power of spoken language had been removed.

One exercise fed into another, keeping them busy and engaged, and before very long they were holding extended eye contact as they considered issues of status in everyday communication. They explored different types of body language and participated in status-based role-plays, highlighting interaction in the workplace and beyond. At the conclusion of this workshop they seemed amazed at how quickly the time had passed. They were sorry that it had to end and that they needed to get back to the 'serious' business of action planning. Of course, just as in the primary playground all those years ago, they had enjoyed the opportunity to play. In the two-hour space of the workshop they had let their habitual guard slip and, if only temporarily, opened their protective shells to discover a cooperative experience that, instead of leaving them, as they had feared, hopelessly exposed, had given them a light, engaging and positive feeling.

The School

Many of the most rewarding workshops that I have done have been in schools. It can be difficult to plan them in advance if, as is often the case, you don't know the students and you have a limited time to work with them. The school will usually have requested a particular workshop

– in my case often one on a Shakespeare play – and will have stated the age-range, likely number of participants and how long the session can last.

When you go in, you inevitably take with you not only your plan for the session, but a whole set of expectations and possibly prejudices about the students and the school that may or may not turn out to be either accurate or helpful. In my experience, one of the most common errors is to underestimate the ability of the students to cope with the work. Another is to assume either that they will be 'difficult' i.e. they will 'misbehave', or the opposite: that they will be a doddle! If you go in assuming the latter, you may be in for a surprise.

I was asked to run a two-and-a-half-hour workshop on *Romeo and Juliet* for Key Stage 3 (fourteen-year-old) students at a suburban school just outside London. I had not worked there before, but had heard from colleagues that it was a very well-run, highly organized and academically ambitious school with an overwhelmingly middle-class intake. The students, it was said, were well behaved, respectful of authority and 'highly responsive'. As I approached the gates down a long, tree-lined avenue, and entered the building, I was immediately struck by two things: the neat and tidy appearance of the students in their uniforms, and the calm atmosphere of the entrance hall and corridors. I felt immediately reassured. The class teacher was waiting for me and I was taken to the hall where the workshop was to take place. There I was introduced to the thirty young people who were also waiting for me – sitting quietly on the highly polished floor. Then I received my first surprise of the day: having introduced me, the teacher apologized, made an excuse, and left. It does sometimes happen that class teachers cannot take part in a session because of pressure of other (usually administrative) work, but in my experience it is rare to be thus abandoned. However, I thought little of it and set about the first part of my plan of work – the warm-up.

I got the students to their feet and asked them to take off their shoes. This provoked some hilarity and blushes, as the very varied state of their undershoe wear was revealed. I then began, as usual, by asking them to walk around in the space. Their walking quickly became jogging, then running, and finally sprinting to all corners of the space, threatening in the process the safety and security of everyone! I was startled by the explosive energy the exercise had unleashed, and by the speed with which this superficially well-mannered and disciplined bunch of adolescents was now threatening to run out of control. It was certainly not the usual response to this standard opening exercise, and the last thing I had expected in this location. I brought the session back under control, but only by yelling at the top of my voice in a most undignified fashion and for a very long time. Having succeeded in penetrating the wall of sound thrown up by their manic squealing, and after getting them back sitting on the floor, looking distinctly flushed I pulled out one of my 'life belt' exercises and threw it at them. They had, I quickly explained, to shut their eyes tight, maintain total silence, and then imagine a blackboard on which were projected the numbers 1–5. The numbers had to be imagined as coming on to the board in sequence, and if any other images intruded, they had to begin again. It worked – just – and the few minutes of silence that followed gave me the necessary time to recover my equilibrium, think of another way in which to re-encounter the space and the group, and begin a more constructive approach to the workshop.

The problem was, I subsequently realized, that, as far as the students were concerned, the hall was associated with the authority and control that the school exercised over them. It was normally used only for whole-school events such as assembly and prize-giving, and not for the kind of purpose that I had designed for it. The absence of the teacher was also unusual, and certainly contributed to their initial euphoric release. The school itself took an approach to drama that tended to focus on textual study rather than on any kind of practical exploration. Consequently, my initial approach was as much of a surprise to the students as their response to it was to me. I had failed to anticipate their possible responses because my plans had been built on the assumption that these were well-behaved middle-class students who would do exactly as I told them. The possibility that they might threaten a state of near anarchy and leave me looking and feeling alarmingly superfluous to requirements had never entered my head. The lessons I learnt were to try to keep an open mind, not to anticipate what the behaviour or attitude of a group of students might be, and certainly never to do so on the basis of the reputation or location of the school. I also learnt the value of being, as the jargon has it, 'flexibly responsive': however carefully I had prepared my workshop in advance, I should always be ready to ditch the plan and improvise. As it happened, the workshop achieved quite a lot of what I had hoped for, but only after I had dropped some of my planned exercises and substituted more structured, tightly controlled activities than those I had originally planned.

Wherever the workshop takes place – school, conference room, prison, hotel or rehearsal room – and whoever takes part, once the initial problem of the space has been overcome, the creative energy of the group can be unlocked, and an event which is both affirmative and celebratory can begin. Those taking part, especially if it is a new experience for them, have to be encouraged to get to a point where they can begin to take small but significant personal risks, and prick the bubble of inhibiting self-consciousness. The workshop leader, unlike the quick-draw artiste, won't physically or even metaphorically have to drag spectators into active participation; but she or he will inevitably gently need to persuade and cajole sometimes reluctant spectators into positions where they can become active participants in making a dramatic event of their own. Once that happens, theatre begins to work on them and they can begin the risky process of, for example, publicly exploring what their voice sounds like, and what it might be capable of. They can look critically but not judgementally at themselves, how they sound, stand and walk, how they appear to others and how others appear to them. They may begin to make physical contact, to touch and be touched without any threat of trespassing, or transgressing what is acceptable to the group. They can begin to feel comfortable with looking someone in the eye, and allowing their gaze to be returned. Above all they are ready to start on an often lengthy but ultimately satisfying journey of personal and social exploration.

1 Getting Started

When a group of young children enters an empty space, irrespective of whether that space is familiar or unfamiliar to them, they immediately see it as an opportunity waiting to be exploited. They spontaneously rush about to all corners of the room, shrieking and laughing at the joy of having room to move freely – to release their energy – all this within a space that appears to them to be an open invitation to decide for themselves how to behave. Adults coming into a large space tend to behave in an entirely different way: instead of claiming the space by immediately moving freely within it, they gravitate to its furthest extremes, standing still, backs to the walls, eyes and bodies betraying anxiety and hesitation. To them the open space represents a problem; individuals feel exposed, and if there are any chairs available adults will grab them, eager to take the opportunity of inhabiting a confined space where they can cautiously wait to see what will happen to them.

Why is there such a marked difference of behaviour in this situation between adults and children? Obviously the self-consciousness of the former has a lot to do with it, but there is something more. Most adults are unfamiliar travellers in the landscapes of public spaces. When, occasionally, we find ourselves in a cathedral, a sports stadium or a theatre our behaviour is highly regulated by convention and protocol. We are not normally encouraged to wander freely in that space, but instead to occupy a limited part of it (we don't go on to the pitch, or the stage, and we aren't encouraged to sit on the altar). 'Our' space, and our role within it, is different and separate from that of the players, priests or actors. All of us know (roughly) how we are expected to behave and what our role is. However, when we first enter the unmapped space of a theatre workshop we do not normally know what is expected of us. Unlike a church, a theatre or a stadium, the space is not clearly demarcated by lighting or architecture that might help us. The function commonly associated with the workshop space (it could be a school hall, a scout hut or a rehearsal room at a theatre) gives us conflicting clues as to how we should behave within it. It is almost certainly going to be unfamiliar; or at least, if it is familiar to some people (it may be their school hall), the familiarity arises from a very different context in which they play a very different role.

In order to cope with the new space and the as-yet-unknown demands of the workshop, we immediately begin by establishing the symbolic limits of our territory, our personal space. If we insist over the next few hours on policing that territory rigorously, keeping others literally and metaphorically at arm's length, then opportunities for sharing the possibilities of what the group can achieve in that space are going to be severely curtailed. Far from making use of the time and space the workshop presents to relax and open up to other people, if we are not careful, our instinctive fears will close it down. The workshop leader has to devise a strategy for meeting the challenge to personal space represented by the workshop. If he or she fails, far from liberating the participants as it does their children, the space will disempower them by heightening self-consciousness and feelings of inadequacy about how to behave socially.

Preparation

We shall look here at the basic setting-up of a workshop and the vital business of getting started. Subsequent chapters look in more detail at particular areas of workshop material and practice.

Personal Space: 'Don't Crowd Me!'

Adults have few opportunities of acting out any part of their lives in large spaces, whether indoors or outdoors, public or private. Our homes, offices and places of work are relatively modest in size, filled with objects such as tables, desks and chairs that make the space feel even smaller. We are very sensitive to what we regard as our personal space, our own room, office, desk, even 'our' seat on the bus or train to work each day. If that space is invaded – say our home is burgled or something as trivial as our seat being taken happens – we may feel personally violated and angry. That feeling is multiplied many times over in prison. In Brixton prison, where even the lavatory doors have two-foot gaps at top and bottom, the men attach enormous significance to their few jealously guarded moments of privacy. Helping them to share the limited space provided in the prison for rehearsals of *Hamlet* (rehearsals usually took place in the prison chapel) was always challenging.

All of us, in whatever situation we live and work, have an even more personal and intimate symbolic space that we jealously guard. If you imagine a spotlight shining down from somewhere immediately above your head, the pool of light it spreads on the floor around you is analogous to that intimate space. This is the area you reserve as your territory, into which intrusion is normally unwelcome. The size of the area is fluid, but the bigger you make the pool, the more personal space you feel you need. In situations where individuals feel comfortable and at ease in the company of other people, they will have a smaller pool and allow others to come physically close to them. In other more formal situations, and at work when individuals are on their guard, the pool extends sometimes by a considerable distance. Perhaps its existence is tacitly recognized by one of the more familiar gestures of greeting exercised in a formal setting: the handshake. When you move to shake the hand of another person, what you are doing is extending your hand outwards from your body to signify the edge of your personal space. There, in the boundary between your space and that of others, you meet and greet strangers. Where greater intimacy and corresponding trust exists – for example, when people genuinely hug one another – the pool may dissolve entirely.

Checking out the Room

Given that the nature and size of the space chosen is always going to be significant, if you are planning a workshop, start by checking out the space you will be using. Then at least you will know what to expect, and have immediate answers to those small but significant first questions, such as: 'Where are the lavatories?' 'Can we get a coffee?' You may also avoid some of the initial problems of having to get people up on to their feet by ensuring in advance that, if there are chairs in the space, you move them, to prevent them from becoming the day's first obstacle. If the space is overlooked, try to find something – a curtain, blind, anything in fact – that will help make it more private.

Space and Numbers

You should try to find out the approximate number of people expected so that you can anticipate the warm-up exercises, and plan accordingly. To make a generalization, twenty is a good number for a workshop. It enables everyone to feel they are an integral part of the event, and there are sufficient numbers to feel safety as part of a group. As the numbers go down, people sometimes feel too exposed, as there is nowhere to hide; below ten the energy starts to drop off, and it can be hard to get people motivated. Above twenty, people can start to drift to the edges and opt out. In schools you will often have to work with a class size of around thirty, but as a workshop leader, whatever the size of the group, you have an obligation to work constantly to include all the participants. That is the difference between a rehearsal and a workshop. A director can get interested in a scene that involves two actors and may keep everyone else waiting around all day in case they are needed, whereas a workshop leader should strive to keep everyone on board all of the time. It is obviously preferable to have an even number, for pair and group work.

If you have any choice in the space to be used, remember that you will need sufficient room for people to move around freely, preferably without any feeling of being cramped. In the early stages of the workshop people will need to feel that they do have their own personal space; and later on, even when the boundaries of that space are removed, you will often have the group working in smaller units, where each will need some space in which to work. Obviously the size of the space should also reflect the number of likely participants. It is equally problematic if a group of, say, eight has a hall the size of a football field, as it is if a group of twenty-eight is crammed into an average-size school classroom.

Clothing

Make sure those who are coming are told in advance what kind of clothing is appropriate. It is a near-hopeless task to get people moving freely if they are wearing clothes that restrict their movement, or if they are nervous about getting them dirty. Some clothes would simply be inappropriate: you don't need or want individuals to stand out from the rest; you want them as far as possible to blend in with one another.

Timing

It always takes time with a new group to break the ice, lower their initial resistance, and reach the point where they are receptive enough to do good work. Even when you are working with a familiar group, it still requires a focused warm-up to bring them together and make them ready to work. Don't make the mistake of dispensing with the warm-up altogether, even if you have less time for the session than you would like. Occasionally there will be pressure from the group to do this, to get on to the 'real' work as soon as possible, but it should be resisted. The warm-up is always necessary, because the beginning of any workshop is like going through an 'air lock', moving slowly from a highly pressurized environment to one in which the pressure is radically reduced. It helps people clear away some of the daily clutter that they bring with them into the workshop and which needs to be ditched if they are to establish the necessary focus on the work in hand. People also need the rite of passage it represents. A workshop might last a day, two days, a week or even two; but to achieve anything – that is, work which has some tangible development – a minimum of two hours is probably required. In schools the time available may be shorter, and if you are new to the group it will be hard to make much progress in less than a double lesson (about ninety minutes). As a regular teacher it is (usually) possible to structure a series of connected workshops over single lessons.

The timing of individual exercises is very difficult to predict in advance. Sometimes work that you expect to last for hours is over in minutes and you are left floundering because you don't have enough material. There is also a temptation, especially if you are nervous or encountering a group for the first time, to keep them constantly busy, so that you rush through the programme, and although it may seem lively and full of variety, it lacks depth. There is a fine balance involved in knowing when to leave one exercise and start another. Just because something appears not to work as you expected, it is not necessarily a reason to abandon the exercise. You may be better off keeping your nerve and staying with it, encouraging the group to explore and over-come the difficulty. There will almost certainly come a point in any sustained workshop when the group as a whole feels as if they have hit a wall; they cannot progress with their former heady energy and ease. All you can do in such circumstances is use your own energy to reinvigorate them; remind them that almost anything worth making will, at times, become difficult, the progress slow and the end not always in sight. This is a time when the emphasis in the workshop is on *work*.

Focus and Planning

The workshop should have a clear, pre-arranged focus. What are you going to work on? The initial request for a workshop may be generalized, but if you are the facilitator, you must be specific about what the work will cover, then thoroughly prepare a structure to accomplish it. Whatever the time allocated, think carefully about the objective of the work and the steps you will take to achieve it. Every workshop, irrespective of whether it is a one-off or part of a series, will need an introductory warm-up, which should feed into the subject matter you are going to explore. The exercises that follow should build up to some form of outcome. Whatever the time frame, it is good practice to conclude with some element of 'performance' or presentation, which evolves out of the content of the workshop. At the end of the day the feeling of achievement comes from having made something together.

As the facilitator you will be most active at the start of the workshop to reassure and focus the group during the warm-up. They need to feel that you know exactly what you are doing and why you are doing it; if you are hesitant, especially at the start of a session, that hesitancy will communicate itself to the rest of the group. You cannot always expect them to begin the work with obvious energy and enthusiasm; some people will be nervous and you will need to energize them by a mixture of encouragement and cajoling. Once the warm-up is completed you can move on to the body of the material that you are working on, and gradually hand over responsibility to the participants as they prepare some small show of work on which to finish the session.

While it is essential to have clarity and structure in running a workshop, it is equally important to be flexible, to listen to the group and to adapt the work to what happens in the room. Leading a workshop should be creative and developmental; however, that can only happen if you are working to a clear plan that includes the possibility of expansion and contraction. It is not possible to predict accurately how long exercises will take, so it is useful to have standby activities that can be slotted in if needed, and (more likely) a range of possible end points that will provide the necessary punctuation marks.

Getting started is invariably the worst part of any workshop. At the start of any new social experience, let alone one in a situation that initially feels intimidating, people revert to their animal selves. They stand close to a wall or take refuge in a chair so that they can't be attacked, and appear guarded towards strangers. They clutch their bags and cups of coffee as first lines of defence. However experienced the workshop leader is, she or he will be nervous. The workshop will be a process of allowing everyone gradually to let go and make contact.

At the beginning of a workshop people new to the experience will take in very little verbal information, as they are too distracted by the strangeness of the space and the other participants. You should therefore resist the temptation, if you are leading the work, to keep talking at the beginning, however much it may seem preferable to having to persuade people to get on to their feet and start moving. It is important to get on with it! The facilitator's hardest work usually takes place in the first half-hour, and if you get that right, life becomes much easier for everyone. As the facilitator, you have to take initial responsibility for running the room, and for making people feel comfortable with the space, with themselves and with each other.

The Warm-up (approximately 45–60 minutes)

Once everyone has arrived (it is worth waiting for a few minutes for any latecomers, because it is difficult to introduce new people to the work once the group as a whole is under way), take a deep breath and start. The opening exercises should be such as can be done by individuals working alone: for example, walking around the room, looking at the objects within it, or walking in different ways – e.g. on the heels, toes, with knees bent, etc. You might then introduce games that can be played with the group as a whole alternated with work in pairs. When you ask the group to 'find a partner', always ask them to try to select someone they don't know, and briefly introduce themselves. Use one or two pair exercises taken from the list below, before asking them to 'find a different partner'. Try to make sure people are continually mixing up and introducing themselves. What you will note about all of these exercises is that none of them requires any of the participants to speak – apart, that is, from exchanging names. People are sensitive about their bodies, but (in England at least) they can be even more so about their voices, those automatic signals of class and status. Never begin a new session by asking everyone to say their names and a few words about themselves – it is the kiss of death to future progress. You will spend much of the remainder of the session trying to recover the lost confidence of those who agonized before mumbling a few indistinct words, and dispelling the hostility now targeted at others who immediately spoke out clearly and confidently.

As the group gradually becomes more relaxed and physically at ease, you can add another dimension to the work: being looked at. From the moment they came into the room, you can guarantee that everyone was busily trying to size up the rest of the group by rapid but furtive glances from person to person. Everyone wants to look, but most will feel the need for permission to do so. Furthermore, it is one thing to be able to observe, quite another to feel comfortable while someone else looks at you. Therefore, after a short while, perhaps during some of the pair-work exercises, you need to stop the group briefly and get half of them to observe the actions of the other half. During the next pair exercise, stop again and give the other half the chance to observe.

Finally, after the last of the planned pair exercises, ask the participants to stop, stand facing one another and hold eye contact for a minute (count aloud to sixty as they do this). Most people won't be able to hold the contact for this long: some will break away with a laugh; others, although they appear to be concentrating and focused, will in fact be looking not into their partner's eyes but at their forehead or nose. It doesn't in the least matter that people find it difficult – it is exactly what you would expect in an atomized culture like ours – but it does matter that they should begin to negotiate the difficulty. Certainly by the end of the session everyone should be able to hold eye contact for a short time (in the 'Face to face' exercise, for example) without feeling awkward. As the example of the workshop in Brixton prison demonstrated (see pp. xvi–xviii), to speak effectively you need to be able to look at the person(s) to whom you are speaking. Using the voice is therefore the next stage in the warm-up.

Of course, everyone taking part up to this point will have been speaking unselfconsciously to some extent. People will have said their names several times; they will hopefully have laughed a lot, and some of the exercises (particularly the trust games) will have provoked lively exchanges between partners. Unselfconscious use of the voice is obviously an important early goal of a theatre workshop. However, it is also necessary to extend the range of the voice, and to begin to play with its possibilities. The vocal exercises included in the warm-up are designed to form a platform on which to do this.

Once again, begin this final section of the warm-up with exercises that the group can do together, such as the singing game detailed below. You will tend to find that people need a sense of physical freedom before experiencing the equivalent with their voices.

Physical Exercises for Individuals

WALKING AND FREEZING

- Ask people to walk about in the space.
- Ask them to have a good look at it, taking in details they hadn't noticed before.
- Now ask them to touch all four walls in a continuous and random pattern. It should be a fast walk but not a run. When they have touched one wall they should immediately turn, focus and start off to reach another point across the space.
- They should be walking in straight lines and diagonals.
- On a signal from you they should freeze sharply, hold it for a second, and then move.

The first part of this exercise is intended just to get them looking at and familiar with the space, and the second part is to get them to focus their energy. There should be a sharp contrast between the first walk, which will tend to be a circular amble around the space, and the focused, direct movement of the second.

Using wooden claves or a small drum is effective, as it makes for clear instruction, and this first exercise is also simply about you establishing control in a non-threatening way. You have to be able to take the initiative for them to feel confident that you are able to lead; otherwise you will struggle to bring the group with you. Encourage them to claim the space and to look into the room. Keep the walk quite brisk – have them think of a ship moving through water, and the air parting for them as they travel through the space. Ask them to keep their energy and focus up and out into the space, and remind them to keep breathing easily.

The next exercise continues to develop the individual's concentration and focus.

TRAFFIC LIGHTS: STOP/LOOK/GO

They keep the energized walking in the space of the last exercise. You give three hits on the claves:

- 1 is a signal to freeze
- 2 to change focus by turning just the head

- 3 to follow the head and to move off in that direction.

Practise this a few times, spacing the three hits on the claves evenly.

Then you vary the spacing of the three hits. Pre-empting the next move will catch out people, often moving off into the space before you give the instruction. This usually happens because the participants are busy in their heads thinking to themselves, 'Right, I understand now: 1, 2, 3 and move . . .' instead of being present in their bodies and waiting for the signal. The exercise asks people to let go of their busy minds, to be in the moment and to focus inside themselves. It is an important part of the process of getting them available and sufficiently receptive to work.

Physical Exercises in Pairs

An exercise to allow physical contact.

BIG − SMALL − TWISTED

- Get into pairs. Ask each pair to maintain minimal physical contact (e.g. touching fingertips) but at the same time to use their bodies to occupy as much of the space around them as they possibly can.
- Now ask them to shrink their bodies and, together, to take up as little space as they can – they should crush together, become a ball or a cube, with as little as possible disturbing the shape.
- Finally, ask each pair to use their bodies together to make a gnarled and twisted shape.

Still in pairs, the next exercise works on focus and concentration.

ONE, TWO, THREE

The pair stands opposite each other and makes eye contact.

- They count out loud up to three, alternating the numbers, e.g. A=1, B=2, A=3, B=1, A=2, B=3, and so on.
- Now substitute a clap instead of saying 3. So it will go: 1, 2, clap, still alternating between A and B.
- Now substitute a stamp instead of saying 1. So it will go stamp, 2, clap.
- Now substitute a click instead of saying 2.
- End up alternating stamp, click, clap between A and B.

Out of the three options, using speech and physical sounds, the last one should be the easiest. It is because you can let the brain take a rest, and allow the body to follow the rhythm. It is when the logical brain gets in the way that it becomes difficult, which is what happens when you are trying to combine numbers and sounds, so that it usually ends up in some confusion. The problem is the split between mind and body, and this exercise is about asking people to trust to their physical instincts, rather than filter each process through their over-active brains. This will help with the creative work that lies ahead.

The participants should now be at ease and confident enough to move on to some slightly more risk-taking work. People should by now be beginning to feel more at ease in the space, with the other members of the group, and with you. The trust games that follow are designed to help individuals gradually hand over some of the responsibility for themselves, which they have carried into the workshop, to a relative stranger – the games involve a small but significant amount of physical risk. Once people learn to play them confidently, they really do experience a sense of having lightened a burden, and pleasure in handing over responsibility for themselves to another.

BLIND CARS
- A stands behind B. A is the driver and B is the car. A is going to drive B around the space, with four simple instructions:
- Both hands on the shoulders is STOP.
- One hand on the middle of the back is GO.
- Right hand on right shoulder is turn RIGHT.
- Left hand on left shoulder is turn LEFT.
- There is no reverse.
- B must keep their eyes closed (or wear a blindfold).
- There must be no talking.
- Move slowly around the space. Encourage people to speed up as the trust grows between the driver and the car.

TRUST FALL
- To take this trust work into the whole group, now have everyone moving in the space, eyes open, walking lightly and easily.
- At any point any person (A) puts their hand on another person's (B's) shoulder. B falls slowly backwards, and A breaks their fall, catching them by running their arms under their partner's, stepping back lightly and quickly so as to support the weight and lay them gently on to the floor. B gets up and carries on.

This is a group exercise and each person takes responsibility for any individual they tap on the shoulder. Obviously participants need to use their brains as well as their bodies: someone with a relatively small stature should not seek to break the fall of someone who is considerably bigger and/or heavier.

The final pair exercise included in this warm-up section involves an exploration of the limits of personal space and a concentrated focus on the partner.

FACE TO FACE

- Stand facing your partner.
- Take one step forward on to your right foot so that the instep is parallel to and touching that of your partner.
- Raise your right hand in front of your face.
- Touch the hand of your partner – lightly – back of the hand to back of the hand.
- Hold eye contact.
- Gently let the touching hands explore the space that separates you from your partner.
- Don't let your hands reach above head height, and try not to think about what your hands are doing, or where they are, but keep your focus on the eyes.

The trust work will increase the concentration and cooperation between members of the group, and they should be enjoying the feeling of actively working together – the literal as well as the metaphorical mutual support it develops.

Group Exercises
These exercises take the focused energy established by the individual exercises and connect it to the rest of the group.

BALANCE THE SPACE

- Tell them to keep the energized walk in the space (they will no longer need to be touching the four walls as before).
- Ask them to balance the space by having an even spread of people around the room.
- They must constantly look to fill space as it appears, as everyone is on the move the whole time. Remind them to keep their focus off the floor and out into the room.

- Freeze, and check that people are keeping an even distance between each other.

One of the objectives of this series of individual and group exercises is to get people 'on their energy'. People often make the claim in daily life to be exhausted, seeing their energy as a bank account that has gone into overdraft. Energy is a stream, and in most life situations we have as much as we want to give. The trick is to be 'on our energy', not off it, where we might spend a lot of time as a convenient defence against having to commit ourselves to the present activity.

Having got people physically warmed up, moving confidently in the space, and working cooperatively and freely, ask them to form a circle looking into the centre. Have them stand still, and then begin to conduct some simple physical exercises to loosen them up and make them feel centred.

PHYSICAL LIMBER

Although this is not a group exercise as such, have the group doing it simultaneously. This is a basic short limber through the body that can be adapted and extended as needed:

- Make sure your weight is balanced evenly on two feet, which should be parallel or at 'five to one', shoulder-width apart.
- Adopt relaxed focus at eye level ahead of you.
- Shake out your wrists.
- Stretch your arms up, and let them fall in a straight line with the fingers brushing your shoulders on the way down while sighing out.
- Bring your shoulders up to your ears and let them go with a sigh.
- Swing your arms freely in both directions in large circles with the inside arm brushing the ear. Remember to keep breathing!
- Let your chin rest on your chest and slowly bring your head up, feeling your neck gently lengthen. Allow your head to float up. It should feel like a ping-pong ball balanced on a fountain of water.
- Rotate your hips in both directions.
- Bring your feet together. Hands on knees and bounce your knees over your toes. Rotate your knees and ankles in both directions.
- Starting with your chin resting on your chest, roll gently down through your spine, until flopped over. The knees are 'easy' rather than locked tight; make sure your neck is free and your head is let go.
- Slowly roll up through your spine to a standing position. Let your shoulders fall into place; and the head is the last part to float up.

These exercises warm the muscles and drain tension from the body. You can finish them off by adding a couple of games that require mild physical exertion:

- Ask people to imagine a shelf, full of cans, positioned above their heads, almost out of reach. When you say 'go' they must take down the cans one at a time from the shelf and place them on the floor by their feet. They have sixty seconds to remove as many as possible.
- Tell everyone that their entire body is covered in lint or sticky fluff. They have sixty seconds in which to get rid of as much of it as they can.

Now that people feel more accustomed to the space, calmer and more focused, the next stage is to start building group awareness and team spirit. Nothing will be achieved in a workshop without an active sense of group support; it is that sense of collective endeavour that will allow individuals to take risks and push back the boundaries of creative work.

SEND THE CLAP

The group stands in a circle.

- Start by sending a look around the circle, by passing eye contact around from one person to the next.
- Add in turning the whole body as you pass on the eye contact.
- Keep the eye contact and the body turning, and add sending a clap with it.
- Make it go more and more quickly.
- Then allow it to change direction, i.e. someone in the circle can decide that, instead of passing the clap to the next person, they will send it back the way it came, or indeed send it to someone on the opposite side of the circle.

This exercise, especially when it gets to the stage when participants can't anticipate when they will have to clap, generates terrific energy and focus. It cannot be done successfully (i.e. at speed) unless all the players are totally focused. The game is like a metaphor for performance in which good players are always alert and ready to respond in an instant.

CLAP X 3

- Everybody faces the centre and claps their hands three times all together.

- Each person then turns to their right, and taps their neighbour three times in three different places.
- Turn back to the centre and clap three times.
- Each person then turns to their left, and taps their neighbour three times, once more in three different places.
- Slowly increase the speed and remind everyone always to touch (lightly) in three *different* places.

The group will have to work hard to keep their rhythm and shape together. Encourage them to do this and not to let the shape of the circle fall apart with the increase in speed.

At this stage in the warm-up the space should feel much less intimidating – individuals will be more comfortable with themselves and with being part of the group – so people are ready next for a game in which they exchange names. This will also be the first time they are required to speak out in an actual exercise, and the easiest thing to say is their name.

NAME GAME

People have a need to know each other's name, and it is effective if you as a leader can commit the names of the group to your short-term memory, as it will make people feel included and contacted.

- In a circle: 'Dig for David'.
- Take the first letter of your name and find an action that starts with it. Say and do the action plus your name.
- Everyone repeats it. Carry on around the circle: 'Jump for Jane', and so on.

EXCHANGING NAMES

- Meet everyone in the group, by shaking hands, making eye contact and saying your own name.
- Now do the same again, only this time say the other person's name *and* don't let go of one hand until you have grabbed another, so that everyone ends up entwined. You always have to be connected to someone, while looking for the next person.

The last section of the warm-up focuses on the voice. Just as the body needs to be focused and relaxed, so too the voice needs preparation. Voice work is a complete subject in itself; the objective here is simply to release the voice so that it will not be strained and will have some flexibility for the work that lies ahead. The important first stage should already have been achieved, which is to warm up the body, to get the breath going and to release unhelpful tensions. Most voice work is not about learning skills, but about eradicating blocks. We all had open, free voices as children, and the pressures of growing up serve to constrict and inhibit the sounds we make.

Voice Limber

- Stretch up, and let your arms fall straight down with a sigh out. Connect the out breath of the sigh to the action. Repeat.
- Massage your face and head, and then stroke your jaw down and yawn several times.
- Stretch your whole body and yawn.
- Chew a huge piece of imaginary gum.
- Add a humming sound to the chewing.
- Stop chewing and keep humming; place your hands in front of your mouth and *hum* into your hands, hearing and feeling the vibrations around your face.
- Focus the hum like a laser beam diagonally away from you to a point on the wall or the ceiling. Use your arm and finger to help you pinpoint the sound.
- Keep breathing whenever you need to.
- Still focusing on the point, change the sound out to an OOOH by opening the lips to make an 'O' shape.
- Spread both arms wide and open the sound out to an AAAH, which will cover the walls and ceiling in an arc away from you.
- Repeat the 'hum – oooh – aaah' progression several times, breathing whenever you need to.
- Jog on the spot and put an 'aaah' sound through your feet into the floor. Make sure to keep your body, and especially your shoulders, loose.
- Swoop through your voice. Using your arm to help you, raise it above your head and swirl it down towards the floor, with your voice travelling easily from your upper voice to your lower. Make the reverse journey. Repeat.
- Count to ten on the edge of a yawn, opening your mouth wide and relaxing the back of your throat.
- Count to ten with a lazy, loose face.
- Count to ten with a happy, bright face.

- Count to ten as if you were trying to get the interest and attention of a small child, articulating the words and making the sound alive.
- Ask the group to echo back some sounds, such as: HEY! HEY YOU! HO! YEAH YOU! YOU OVER THERE! to open out the sound.

Singing
Bring the whole of the warm-up section to a conclusion with the following simple group exercise using both the body and the voice:
- Everyone stands in a circle as large as the space will allow, facing the centre.
- Teach the group to hum a simple tune.
- Give them one word (with at least two syllables, e.g. Shakespeare).
- Practise fitting the word to the tune.
- Explain that they are to start to sing together as quietly as possible, and when they have completed a verse, take a step forward towards the centre and begin singing again with increased volume.
- Go on with this, getting louder and louder as the group approaches the centre of the room. The circle will begin to break up as people crush together. Encourage them to keep singing, and to dance and clap too until the whole thing is a crazy Bacchanalian frenzy.
- Repeat the sequence in reverse until the group is back at the edge of the room and singing very quietly.

Another singing exercise can be done by splitting the group into three or four and teaching them a 'round' like 'London's Burning'. You can conduct the round, bringing in one group, then adding another and also signalling for the volume to be raised or lowered.

A warm-up based on the above series of exercises can take a brisk forty minutes, or can easily be taken more thoroughly and last for over an hour. At the end of it the individuals should feel more at ease with themselves in the space and with each other as a group. The next stage will probably be to go into exercises specifically designed to focus on the subject of the workshop. However, provided you have time and facilities to do so, you could take a ten-minute coffee break at this point: the opportunity it presents for further group interaction is valuable. If you can't get coffee/tea or whatever without having to leave the space, it is better not to stop at all.

There will always be a degree of initial resistance from the participants in the exercises; they are being asked to move out of their usual boundaries, which is potentially exposing and embarrassing. An important element of the work is that it is all simple and straightforward to begin with. It is actually far easier to play the first game, and to walk in the space, than it would be to make a point of opting out. Occasionally, when I am working in a school with students I don't know, one or two of them decide to be uncooperative and indeed try to sabotage the workshop. My strategy in dealing with them is to take them quietly aside, split them up, and ask them to watch from the sidelines. After a few minutes the rest of the group ignores them, and they rapidly become bored with having nothing to do. When eventually I invite them back in, they are usually grateful to be included! For everyone, cooperative and keen or sullen and uncooperative, once they have taken part in the first exercise the momentum of the group quickly moves them on to the next, until they end up involved in activities they never imagined they would be doing at the start of the workshop.

As the facilitator you have to have the energy to drive the event forward, as well as the ability to read the group and adapt your delivery of the material to suit their dynamic. As a participant you just have to try to be open, willing to go along with what is happening, and to suspend your judgement for the time being. Interestingly, the basic warm-up material may not change a great deal between a workshop for schoolchildren and one for professional actors; what is all-important is the framing and connecting of the work to suit the people who are doing it. Choosing the right exercises is part of the task, and what is significant is finding the narrative that leads the participants through the exercises to the place where they discover something for themselves.

The plan below is intended only as a rough guide to a possible hour-long warm-up for a theatre workshop. This is not a book of workshop recipes, and we have included it only because of the special difficulty of starting a workshop. It can be adapted and changed to suit the needs of the participants and the experience of the workshop leader. What should probably not be changed is the sequence of activities. Whatever exercises are chosen for the warm-up, whether they are from the brief selection included in this chapter or taken from one of the numerous books containing drama games, a workshop leader should remember to choose those that will achieve the following objectives:
- acclimatize people to an unfamiliar space and help them feel comfortable with themselves

- encourage physical interaction with others
- develop the free use of the voice.

Suggested outline plan for a one-hour warm-up

PART 1: INDIVIDUAL EXERCISES

1	Walking and Freezing	4 mins
2	Traffic Lights	5 mins

PART 2: PAIR EXERCISES

3	Big, Small, Twisted	3 mins
4	One, Two, Three	5 mins
5	Blind Cars	5 mins

PART 3: GROUP EXERCISES

6	Balance the Space	3 mins
7	Physical Limber	7 mins
8	Send the Clap	3 mins
9	Name Games	4 mins
10	Exchanging Names	4 mins
11	Voice Limber	10 mins

N.B. All timings are approximate

2 Improvisation

An improvisation workshop can last anything from ninety minutes to a week, or it can form part of an ongoing rehearsal process. The skills that will be developed by an individual working as a member of a group will include creativity, cooperation, communication and concentration, as well as the ability to listen, compromise, contribute and take initiative. As such, an improvisation workshop is a terrific learning tool for anyone making theatre at whatever level, and anyone who works or lives as part of a team, which includes most of us.

The word 'improvisation' conjures up many associations, some of them springing directly from Keith Johnstone's pioneering work at the Royal Court Theatre in the 1950s and 1960s and his inspirational book *Impro* (1979). The explorations of Johnstone and his colleagues have led to the creation of countless improvisation groups, 'theatresports' (improvised comedy contests) and television programmes such as *Whose Line Is It Anyway?* Improvisation is boundless creativity, free, funny, hectic, anarchic and magical. It has had a hugely liberating effect on both performers and theatre production. When it works, it is great fun; when it doesn't, it can be deeply disappointing.

'Improvisation' also describes any material which is created collaboratively by a working group, as opposed to a play written in seclusion by one or two people. Improvising and devising a piece of theatre is a challenge that starts with a space, a group of people and a deadline, and develops into an intense period of negotiation, problem-solving and making choices. It can also be a nightmare of dead ends, frustration and short tempers. To succeed in improvising, a strategy is required and parameters need to be set. Creativity has to be stimulated, released and pulled together, because using improvisation in the making of theatre will always be as much about what to exclude as what to include.

The exercises that follow in this chapter focus on the issues of selection and definition, using limitation as a means to stimulate creative freedom. They look at the heightened language and structure of theatre, the building-blocks of images and the piecing together of text. The final section considers how to work on the texture of perform-ance material.

Dramatic Language

To make theatre, all that is required is someone to do and someone to watch. It can happen in a theatre in London's West End, in someone's garage or at a chosen moment in a workshop. The blockbuster musical and the primary school nativity play, the student group's devised piece and the latest new drama – all share the language of theatre.

People in all sorts of educational settings are often set the task of improvising a piece of theatre before they have any firm understanding of what it is that makes material dramatic. What is it that makes theatre distinct from everyday life? The 'Triangle Improvisation' that follows attempts to demonstrate some of the key elements in the language of making theatre.

Triangle Improvisation

PART 1: INITIAL IMPROVISATION

Divide participants into groups of three and ask them to plan an improvisation which will use words. It can be any situation, and there has to be a moment of tension (i.e. A and B are to set up a situation, they are joined by C, and the result is a moment of tension).

For example: Andrew is chatting up Barbara in a bar; Caroline enters, who is Andrew's partner. Tension.

Allow a few minutes for preparation and then see the work, one group after another, without comment.

This is a straightforward set-up for an improvisation, like many given out in drama classes every day. However, it is a flawed exercise. It is too vague and the participants are likely to fall into predictable patterns and traps. Let us consider what might result from such an open invitation to improvise a scene.

In my experience, professional actors and school students all fall into the same trap with initial improvisations such as this, by overusing words, words, words. The result is generalized, meandering and vague. People will tend to place the exercise in a realistic setting, for instance in an office. There will probably be lots of chat establishing office life, the sort of conversation they think would actually happen across the desks, which will also be littered with signposts designed to give the audience information, such as that they are fed up, working late when most people have gone home. After a while the meat of the scenario might come out, for example: that Adam has got hold of some documents that have been 'borrowed', which Becky is also interested in, as they relate to a potentially exciting future project. The required tension arises from the entry of the third character, Cathy, the boss, who is surprised to find them working late and suspects they are up to something. This causes more talk and the elaborate weaving of excuses and half-hearted questioning.

There is nothing necessarily wrong with the choice of scenario; effective theatre can be made from almost any starting point. However, the likelihood is that the storytelling will be overelaborate. For the audience, something is going on but it is obscured by a fog of extraneous information. The moment of tension requested will turn into a generalized semi-tension, which will last for much of the scene, and will rumble on, unable to reach a conclusion.

The improvisation is most likely to resemble a television soap opera, with its 'real life' feel, static positioning and overuse of verbal explanation. In the improvisation people will tend to sit around and chat, explaining what they have been doing and what they are going to do: too little action and too much talk!

Improvising is not easy and it is potentially exposing. There is a dread of silence, bringing with it the fear of having nothing to say and running out of ideas. There is a fear that if you stop talking, you will become more aware of people looking at you, and it might seem to them as if you have given up! Therefore, words are the great refuge. If you are talking, you believe you are contributing. Words also act as a cover where you can neatly avoid interaction. As you talk, you don't have to listen, and you don't have to respond; so you can hijack the scene off down the road where you want it to go, and attempt to drag your fellow performers with you. Also, as the mouth keeps working, it is the perfect excuse for the body to go to sleep. People's preferred position for an improvisation is often slumped in a chair, immovable and unresponsive. As the body shuts down, so can the brain, and thought patterns become as fixed as the physical position. The stream of chat will allow so little stimulus to get through the defensive wall that the performer will be thrown back on to familiar territory, and will end up recreating standard material borrowed from previous occasions.

One of the excuses we create to justify an excess of words is that we do it in order to *spell things out*, because when improvising people tend to regard their audience as especially dim:

ADAM I've been working really hard, yeah . . . lot of work to get
    through, lot of data to process, got to keep my concentration,
    never seems to let up . . .

When tapping on an imaginary keyboard, looking intently at a screen, and a puff of the cheeks might communicate much the same information. It is like the improvisation that starts with someone buying a seemingly endless round of drinks, the only purpose of which is to indicate we are in a bar, when the simple raising of an imaginary glass could tell us all we need to know.

As people get into their stride and keep talking to keep the improvisation going, this creates many dead ends:

ADAM I saw Monica from work on the bus today.

The audience think: What is the significance of Monica? The bus? Today? They hold on to the information as it may prove vital later. She is never mentioned again and turns out to be irrelevant. After several such misleading clues the audience grow tired and lose interest.

It is often an easier option to keep the words coming out than to engage with the present. Far from being creative or imaginative, people fill the space with words to put off the moment of truly having to improvise. It is an avoidance of what is really challenging and risk-taking, which is to trust to the moment, and to be open to the other performers. Productive improvisations should be about contacting each other, and working together to let the content evolve, while playing off what happens and allowing the space between you to be alive and expressive.

In setting up this initial improvisation, parameters were set and yet were still intentionally loose. Now, in order to establish a common understanding about what can make effective theatre, tighten the parameters to create a barrier to work against, which will take away the easy option of keeping talking.

Give the groups a second chance to work on the scene.

PART 2: THE FIVE-LINE VERSION

This time there is a limit of a total of five lines of dialogue. Allow five to ten minutes for the groups to plan and rehearse the same scene with the same characters. The outcome should be a maximum of five exchanges spread across A, B and C. For example:

ADAM Here are the papers for the new project.

BECKY Fantastic! How did you get hold of them?

ADAM This place is like the secret police . . .

Cathy enters

CATHY You two are working late . . .

ADAM Cathy! We were just thinking of going for a drink . . .

See all the groups perform their five-line version of the scene.

The contrast between the five-line version and the first improvisation is likely to be sharp. The scene as it is now, with its deliberate restriction on language, will be pointed, precise and probably far more effective dramatically. In having to cut down the words, the actors must compensate by making more effective use of space and body language. The dynamic choices of staging will take on meaning, replacing the deadening effect of generalized chat. Bodies and the space between them can communicate more information, and often with more subtlety, than words. People are forced out of their chairs to release their bodies to do the work of communication. A nervous glance, for example, can say more than repetitious talk about the need for secrecy. A transaction where two people touch, or pass something between them – such as an inclusive 'We're in this together' touch on the shoulder – can become a defining moment. When making television drama the actors must constantly get near to each other so as not to let the screen be dominated by background space. Dialogue often takes place nose to nose, with the camera in close-up. The opposite is often true in theatre, where if the space between actors is crowded relationships lose definition.

Within the framework of this exercise the selected verbal language that remains will be heightened, carefully chosen and packed with subtext. It will suggest far more than is actually stated. It is important for the participants to recognize that what they *don't* say is just as significant as what they do. There will now be a defined moment of tension, which will provide the focus for the scene and change the dramatic action. The scene will be a series of actions, rather than simply comprising talk about action, past or future.

This is *dramatic* language: space, movement and essential words. The content has been boiled down to the essence of what needs to be said, and treats the audience as intelligent, capable of filling in the missing information. Soap opera works on the assumption that you can go and make a cup of tea, come back and still follow the story. In the theatre every moment should be important, with the audience actively engaged, wanting to unfold the narrative.

The playing of the restricted five-line version will be alive. Although the work is pre-planned, it is now a real improvisation because the performers have to work together and listen in order to make the space between them communicate. Their senses are ablaze and they work responsively off each other in order to achieve what they want to say.

When I was working with a group of young actors in Belfast, they improvised a drawn-out scene about three people who shared a flat. At first it was high on fury, expletives and joky references to energetic sex, mixed in with generalized conversation about the undertaking of domestic tasks. When I imposed a reduction to the allowed dialogue it caused the scene to become a tense and terse exchange. Layers of alliance, betrayal and hurt were revealed, as the actors played off each other, and the action was made from moment to moment. The language was heightened and the audience enjoyed the active work of filling in the space around the words. The scene became specific and focused, and while it was not a recreation of 'real life', the relationships in it had a recognizable resonance.

The five-line exercise demonstrates the value of well-chosen words, testing the actors' ability to inhabit the text and make it theatre. Interestingly, the pared-down version of the scene was helped by the actors' experience of playing the first, longer improvisation, which gave them useful background information.

The five-line scene, which each group will now have worked on and shown, can provide a platform for further development that continues to explore the language of theatre.

PART 3: DIRECT ADDRRESS

Continue with the five-line scenes that each group of three has created above. Allow one character to make a direct address (or an 'aside') at any time. It can be of any length (bearing in mind that we have probably discovered that less is more in the exercise so far), and is in addition to the five-line dialogue already established.

Allow about five minutes for preparation and rehearsal.

See the work.

For example, to continue with our earlier scene, we might add in the following after the last line of dialogue, spoken as direct address:

CATHY The new project. How do I let them know none of us are working on it any more?

The direct address works best when it gives the audience new information that shifts their perspective on the situation. There is no point in it telling us something we already know, such as that Adam is worried about the consequences if they are discovered. The aside allows us to see events from one character's point of view, so that we might feel a certain empathy with Cathy's dilemma in catching her colleagues red-handed, knowing she has to disappoint them. It also has the power to make the audience feel intelligent, as they are given knowledge over the characters; so that if the scene were to continue, they would watch Adam and Becky struggle in the light of what they (and Cathy) thought to be the truth of the situation.

To make this convention effective theatre, a direct address is best delivered with the rest of the action frozen. If there was a clock on the office wall, it would stand still while Cathy moved out of the frame to talk directly to the audience. It needs to be clear that it is a different mode of address, which stands out from the dialogue of the scene.

Asides and direct address are used in *commedia dell'arte*, Shakespeare, Restoration comedy and Brecht, through to modern playwrights such as Steven Berkoff and John Godber. They are powerful devices when used selectively, which actively acknowledge the presence of the audience at the theatre event, where the actors stand apart from the action and speak their thoughts directly.

Continue with the scene, keeping with the five-line dialogue and the direct address.

PART 4: THEATRICAL DEVICE

Now ask each group to add in a specific device that adds to the theatrical effect of the storytelling; for example, slow motion, choreographed physical movement, repeated words or phrases, self-generated sound effects (e.g. the exaggerated creak of a door opening).

In our example, Adam and Becky could choreograph their entry into the space from opposite sides with an exaggerated stealth. Cathy could have a long entrance with the sounds of her footsteps echoing, slowed down to increase the dramatic tension. These add in extra layers of dramatic texture that take the scene forward. They give us more information and we enjoy the layers of storytelling. It is not the overexplicit naturalism of TV drama; it is live theatre, which celebrates its ability to tell stories through simple devices that speak to our senses and imaginations. The audience creates the world surrounding the actors and fleshes out the narrative around the essential elements presented to it.

Making theatre is not recreating everyday life. It is not a photograph; it is a deconstruction. It has to achieve a style that lifts it out of the ordinary and predictable into something that is crafted and demands attention. It is a layered event that has to be built up in detail. Improvisation is about shaping, editing and re-evaluating. It is not simply a matter of keeping going.

The worked-on scene of Adam, Becky and Cathy should now have a dynamic shape, should look and sound very different from the first telling of the story. With a group of fifteen to eighteen people, the triangle improvisation, conducted through all four stages, will take around ninety minutes. It is still effective to use just the first two stages, for which you should allow fifty or sixty minutes.

Scene in Johannesburg

With the fieldworkers at the Market Theatre Laboratory in Johannesburg we conducted a triangle improvisation in the four stages detailed above. One of the improvisations turned from a sprawling, rambling domestic drama into a simple, effective piece of work. It was the story of a family torn apart by child abuse and parental denial. Its first presentation was full of shouting, poorly staged violence and confusion. As the work progressed, it was gradually put back together with care and concentration, and the final presentation was a painful exposition of an emotive issue. Gaping silences filled the charged space around the domineering presence of the father, the cowed figure of the daughter and the agonized mother. The three figures were isolated in the space while relating to each other with a choreographed precision. The father stepped out of the frame to address the audience in an attempt to justify his actions, which further disturbed and jolted the assumptions of those of us watching.

The piece affected those performing it and all of us watching. It involved the taking of a real-life situation that I supposed people in the room had direct experience of and using it as a starting point. The exercise pared it down to its raw centre, before putting it back together to make a performance that used effective dramatic language to create a powerful impact.

Had I just offered them British restraint on the whirlwind of their passion? Perhaps, and I could only offer them what I knew. They all saw that the exercise had made a difference, and they liked the clarity of it. What worked in this situation was that, although I was leading the work, I imposed nothing upon them besides the mechanics of the exercise. They still owned the work, and I made no inroads on their content, choices or performances. I provided a framework for them to shape their own material to a point where they could acknowledge that it was more dramatic. As a facilitator, it is important to lead the work rather than to prescribe, to know when to draw back, while encouraging the participants to examine further what they have started to create.

I was pleased subsequently to be invited back, and on a return trip to Johannesburg I saw why this exercise had been so eagerly consumed by the fieldworkers. I attended the Market Theatre Laboratory annual community theatre festival. Over three days some thirty groups from all over South Africa and beyond perform their work for each other. The fieldworkers had only managed to work in any depth with a small number of the groups, and much of the work to be seen featured drawn-out domestic scenes based on improvisation that lacked focus or dramatic tension, which were then interspersed with sensational traditional singing and dancing used to cover the shifting of a couple of bits of token furniture. The work was long, imbalanced and deadly slow to my eyes, although watched by this audience with a notable concentration and respect.

With the fieldworkers confident about using a dramatic language, they felt they had something tangible to work with when seeking to establish further contact with these groups. One group, which had benefited from fieldworker input and had managed to make the transition in their merging of theatre forms, was The Squint Artists, from Alexandra township. They were a collective of young people, orphaned or forced to leave home, who had taken refuge in each other's company and in making theatre. Their piece, 'The Virus', was about sexual abuse within the school system. It comprised sharp scenes employing heightened dramatic language and tension, given a striking frame by the integrated use of song and dance. The overall effect was politically powerful, articulate and moving – experience fed into improvisation and skilfully shaped to make compelling theatre.

Dramatic Staging

In the triangle improvisation above, what becomes essential to its success are the restrictions placed upon the material. This next exercise continues with the idea of restriction from the outset. It is an effective exercise that explores issues of play-writing, dramatic structure, staging and acting.

The Ten-line Scene

PART 1: WRITERS AND ACTORS
Divide into groups of three. Ask them to elect to be a writer, and two actors.

i) Give the writer a pencil and a piece of paper. On the piece of paper, as the facilitator, you have already written the first line of dialogue; for example: 'It was an extraordinary thing to happen.' The writers' job is then to go off on their own and write the next nine lines of dialogue for two characters, to make a ten-line dialogue that starts with the line you have given. You might have up to six or seven groups of three in a workshop, and all the writers can start with the same line of dialogue. It is important that you put the writers under pressure, that they have to write instantly off the top of their heads, so that very quickly they end up with a completed ten-line dialogue for two actors. It should take them no more than five to seven minutes.

ii) Meanwhile, give out pencils and paper to the two actors, who have to invent between them two locations, one exterior and one interior, e.g. a boat on a lake and a café. They write each location on a separate piece of paper, which you collect.

PART 2: FIRST STAGING

i) Reunite the writers with their actors. Ask the writer to cast the two actors as characters A and B in the ten-line dialogue, and get them to read it through once.

ii) As the facilitator, you now shuffle up the bits of paper containing the locations, and give one location to each group, making sure it is not one that they themselves wrote down. The task is now to stage their ten-line dialogue quickly in the given location. So the actors will be faced with ten lines of which the meaning may not be completely clear, and suddenly have to deliver it in a 'motorway service station' or while 'windsurfing'. At no time can any of the ten-line dialogue be altered; it has to remain as it was first written on the page.

Speed is of the essence, and it is surprising what creative choices can be made by the juxtaposition of the dialogue with a random location.

iii) Encourage the groups to present their work, even though they will not feel they have had enough time to rehearse. See all the work and ask the audience where they think each scene is located? Draw out comments as to how the location affected the content and delivery of the dialogue.

PART 3: SECOND STAGING

i) Give each group a piece of paper with a second location on it. They will now stage the ten-line dialogue again in the new, completely different location.

The first staging was intentionally quick in order to see what creative choices were made under the pressure to produce something. Draw out from the group which elements of the process could be given more consideration with time allowing.

Space: Decide how to use the space and where to stage the performance in the room. Consider perhaps using some feature of the room to help suggest the location, such as a pillar for a 'medieval dungeon', or the edge of the stage (if there is one) for 'the riverbank'. Where will the audience watch from, and what is their spatial relationship with the actors? Set: They can use a limited amount of whatever is immediately available to help suggest location, e.g. chairs put together and a broom handle to hang on to to suggest a 'ride at a fun-fair'.

Props: They can have a maximum of three props to help them, e.g. two bags and a magazine to suggest the 'airport departure lounge'.
Costume: One piece of costume each from whatever is immediately available, e.g. a T-shirt thrown over the head to suggest 'a sauna'.
Subtext: They can use the time to explore with their writer what the relationship is between the characters, and how that is affected by the specific location. They can also learn the lines.
Sound: The writer can provide off-stage sound effects, if they are wanted, e.g. the announcements for 'the railway station'.

ii) Allow ten to fifteen minutes for the groups to rehearse these scenes. This will give them time to break the scene down in detail and put it back together.

iii) See all the work, moving the audience around the space as required by the different scenes. Again ask the audience where they think the scene is located and how it affected the choices made.

I was working with some students, and a ten-line dialogue was acted by two teenage boys, the content being about one character's mother and her drunken behaviour at a party. The first staging was located in 'a boxing ring', and the scene was played out with tremendous attack as the boys sparred, while the dialogue was virtually spat across from one to the other. Certain words were hit with an explosive energy; the dialogue was full of aggression, frustration and furious resentment.

The second staging was located at 'a garden party', suggested by a small block covered with a cloth, a couple of chairs, two paper cups and the writer off-stage clinking a spoon against a metal pipe. The two boys did up the top buttons of their shirts, turned up their collars, crossed their legs, looked into the middle distance and conjured up a frightfully posh party in the gardens of a large country house. The audience were spread around the space to suggest the other guests, so that the dialogue had to be delivered with extreme discretion and understatement, so as not to draw the attention of fellow guests to the scandal being discussed. The scene was riveting, and a complete contrast to the previous staging.

As well as being an enjoyable exercise to do and a way of producing instant theatre, there are some clear learning points to be developed. The exercise was originally conceived for a play-writing workshop, to explore the useful benefits of being restricted to ten lines and having to produce instant dialogue, which the actors will then take on and make into a living scene. The exercise also considers dramatic structure, and how often good playwrights will take dialogue and place it in an unexpected location to effect a dramatic tension. The opening scene of David Mamet's *Glengarry Glen Ross*, between two men who work in a real-estate office, takes place not in their office but in a Chinese restaurant. In the opening scene of David Hare's *The Secret Rapture* a family discussion takes place in the bedroom, over the body of the dead father. In Patrick Marber's *Closer* two characters meet for the first time in the Aquarium at London Zoo.

Making effective theatre is often about distillation and dislocation; it is not about the recreation of the expected. Choices have to be made that cause the audience to take notice and look at the familiar in a fresh way. Students using this exercise will start to explore the rudiments of stage design and the use of space. They have to think how to use the limited resources available to create a representation of a particular location, and how the use of the spatial dynamic and the placing of the audience in relation to the actors affect the presentation of the scene.

The exercise also tells us a great deal about the work of the actor, who has to work hard to make the dialogue fit into the given location, in doing which each word has to be justified and based in some experience. In the first staging this process happens very quickly and participants will be working on instinct, with probably varying degrees of success. In the second staging, when there is more time to go through the text, they will work consciously to substantiate everything they have to say. This is exactly the process that actors go through working on any play, looking at the text in great detail and making sure everything they say or do makes sense to them and can be justified in terms of the character.

The acting of the short scenes also demonstrates how much more creative an actor can be when he or she has more than one thing to think about. The attempt to deliver the dialogue with clarity, while also playing the reality of the location, causes all sorts of interesting choices to be made. Telling your boyfriend that you are about to leave him while 'climbing a mountain' throws up all sorts of acting possibilities, as does contemplating suicide 'in the back row of the cinema'.

To run this ten-line scene in all three parts of the exercise, with a group of fifteen to eighteen, will probably take between ninety minutes and two hours, depending on how much discussion and rerunning of the scenes you want to do.

This exercise, together with the five-line improvisation above it, provides a good exploration of dramatic language and structure. They both encourage the participants to examine the content and staging of a scene. The two exercises combine together well as an introduction for students to working on a scene from a chosen play text. By working in detail with these exercises you build up a dramatic vocabulary, which will hopefully deflect what often happens when inexperienced actors pick up an unfamiliar scene, when they tend to rush over the language and ignore the dramatic possibilities that the playwright has indicated within the text. (See Chapter 6 for detailed examples of work on text.)

Dramatic Images

Among the simplest and strongest building-blocks for making theatre are images – also referred to as tableaux, freeze-frames and snapshots. Images are effective tools for consolidating information and constructing narrative, and are used by drama workers to make people stop generalizing and encapsulate a specific moment.

Performance is a series of images. When we think of British drama we think of Shakespeare, Wycherley, Wilde, Shaw, Pinter – collected works all lined up on the library shelf, books full of words – but the text is also a blueprint for a physical realization shaped as moving images on the stage. Brecht wrote that a deaf person at the back of the auditorium ought to be able to understand his plays. If I recall a play I have enjoyed, I don't remember lines of the text, I remember certain images.

To express an idea through a physical shape can be a more instinctive and immediate process than to put it into words. When we express ideas through speech, it can quickly be diverted into a dry, cerebral process, in which we are all too aware of the effect we are having, or think we are having, on others. Starting work with images might seem restrictive – a frozen position, no movement, no words and no sound – but the restriction should be a liberation. A precise image opens out into many shades of meaning, which can be altered by an adjustment of the slightest detail. In a workshop, asking people to be aware of the construction of images, as well as how they can be refined and altered, is an important skill.

To start this work on images, allow people to become comfortable with touching and looking at each other, and with working in detail.

SCULPTING

In pairs.

i) A stands neutrally in the space and is a lump of clay. B physically sculpts A into an instant statue. There is no talking. Allow ten seconds only. Swap over roles.

ii) The same exercise, only this time the sculptor has about a minute: encourage them now to work in detail, noticing how the inclination of the head or the adjustment of a finger changes what the image says; to make something that is crafted into shape. Leave all the statues in the space and allow the sculptors to move around to look at them.

iii) Ask one person to put two of the statues together. They might see some connection, in which case they can 'pick up' one statue and place it carefully next to another to make an image of two figures.

Ask the rest of the group what they see. What information does the image give in the way of qualities? Does it convey sadness, love, worship, humour, violence? What narrative information does the image communicate? Someone might say, 'Greek gods on Mount Olympus'; someone else might say, 'Two people dancing at a nightclub'!

Two statues made in isolation, when randomly put together, create an image that gives us information without words: it is an instant creation of story. If out of nowhere you ask someone to make up a story standing on the spot, their mind will either go blank or start to sort out and reject a legion of ideas. By placing two statues together, material is immediately created. This simple image could be the starting point for an improvisation.

The instant interest of two figures placed together will be: What is their relationship? The next exercise asks people to consider the visual definition of a specific relationship.

RELATIONSHIPS

In pairs.

i) Ask each pair to make an image of a family relationship. They can talk about it for about half a minute, and then form an image of these two people, e.g. father and daughter/two sisters/husband and wife.

ii) Look at the images. What do we see? What qualities come across from the relationship? Love, rivalry, caring? Can we tell who they are? Does the image communicate what is intended? The intention of the pair presenting their image might have been older and younger brother; yet the onlookers may be confused and think it is more like father and son . . .

iii) Anyone may then step forward and intervene to sculpt the image into how they believe it can best communicate two brothers. What has been presented is the raw material, and each sculptor can now adjust details to give a different slant to how the figures communicate their relationship. It is important that people do not articulate in advance what it is they want to do; they just 'mould the clay' of the two figures. It is for those people watching to say what they see and how the relationship has been changed by the intervention.

This way there is no pressure to articulate intellectual opinions. It is less daunting to mould the figures than it might be to pass comment on how you view the relationship. Once the image has been changed, it is up to the rest of the group to justify what has been done. This is empowering for everyone in the group and encourages the less confident people to express themselves.

Working in this way, everyone can see images are powerful: people look strong holding them. Working with a group, it can be good to pick out an image made by participants who appear to be lacking in confidence. They have the chance to become the focus of the group while having to do very little, and the work they present will be positively justified by the rest of the group. A workshop must constantly strive to be inclusive, bringing in those people who instinctively want to drift to the edges. In schools, inevitably some pairs of students will not stay concentrated while everyone else is working. The exercise is, however, basically simple, and if, as the workshop leader, you pull out a seemingly reluctant pair to show their work, instantly their image of 'two good friends' or 'Macbeth and Banquo' achieves a public exposure that gives credit to their effort. They might then go on to work in a group of five and develop an image of 'Macbeth and Banquo meeting the witches'. Teachers have often commented on how individuals who are thought to be reticent or disruptive can, through a process like this, achieve previously unexpected concentration and commitment.

The next exercise is a simple step to creating larger images and building narrative.

CONSTRUCTING IMAGES

i) An empty space.

First person goes into the space and takes up a position. A second person looks and adds in, to build up an image. And so on, with people taking time to look before adding to the image, one at a time, to create a picture. This is rather like developing a photograph in a tray of chemicals, where the image gradually reveals itself.

Ask the spectators: Is the picture clear? Where is the focus? Is it interesting to look at? What title would you give the picture?

We are saturated by images. We are constantly fed visual information by television, newspapers and advertising, all carefully selected to communicate the required message. A picture editor on a newspaper has a large choice of photographs available before choosing the one with the microphones, pedestal and American eagle, which instantly signals to the reader: this is the President of the United States. Pictures of footballers feature the moment the ball is struck for the winning goal, or the ecstatic celebration, rather than some inconsequential moment of play. Images for the theatre have to be as carefully constructed, with every moment on stage communicating more information visually than verbally.

ii) Ask people to continue with building up an image by joining in one at a time, but now suggest titles before the image starts; for example: rush hour on the underground train; in the hospital; the first day of the sales; the arrest; the escape. When the group has made the image, again ask questions about its clarity and how it communicates. Consider the actor–audience relationship: where is the image seen from? Ask people to move about and examine the image from different points of view. Do they get a different story depending on where they view it from?

Touring Shakespeare's *Henry V* from the National Theatre to schools and colleges, as part of the accompanying workshop we asked students to construct images of life in an army: from the send-off at the port to the long march, the first siege, carrying the wounded and sick, making camp, the night before battle, victory in the midst of casualties. The students had to work together and make choices of representation. The images they made were powerful. The moment they started to move, add dialogue and 'act', the whole thing weakened: we were back in the school hall with self-conscious performers groping their way through a demanding improvisation. There is a quality in stillness that has an effect on an audience and on the performers.

The journey of the images is the same as the one Henry's soldiers make from Southampton to Agincourt. Enacting these frozen positions of exhaustion, battle and the wounded gives the performers physical information that triggers an emotional response. Making your body into the shape of a soldier carrying a wounded friend tells you about that experience physically and emotionally in a way that describing it often cannot match. Later, during the actual performance, the students saw the actors as soldiers make the journey they had earlier enacted through the images. A connection was made, and the students opened themselves to feelings about war and comradeship which are at the heart of the play.

Shaping Material

A starting point for an improvisation could be taken from a variety of sources, such as an extract from a novel, a poem, a diary or a newspaper. Faced with some non-theatrical written material, where do you start? If the extract is read out and the groups are told they have thirty minutes to come up with something, they are likely to spend 90 per cent of their time discussing what to do and the remaining 10 per cent hastily patching together a generalized, poorly constructed presentation. Constructing images is a way of starting to make theatre; it forces you to condense material and give shape to narrative and relationships.

The next exercise takes place with the facilitator drip-feeding instructions over seven stages, eventually to build up to a short presentation of devised material. As the facilitator, you will be responsible for driving the exercise forward by dropping in the instructions and exerting time pressure in order to foreshorten the groups' inclination to overdiscuss; other than that, the groups own their work and will be entirely responsible for its development.

NARRATIVE IMAGES

  i) Split a group into smaller groups of five or so people. Read the chosen text out to everyone together; for example, this extract from the Manchester *Guardian*, 3 April, 1945, by Edward Connolly:

The Princess and the Colonel

A German princess who claims to be the great grand-daughter of
Queen Victoria and a distant cousin of King George VI caused a
tiny spot of bother on the front today. The fuss arose when she
and her husband were ordered by an American colonel to get out
of their sumptuous apartments in their 300-roomed palace so that
tired and dusty American troops with no other place to go should
have shelter.

The royal couple are Valerie Marie, the princess of Arenberg,
daughter of the Duke and Duchess of Schleswig-Holstein, and
Prince Inglebert Charles Arenberg. Their lavish Louis XIV residence, a vast U-shaped collection of something like a dozen
buildings set inside a 16,000-acre estate with farms and shooting-
boxes, was reached this morning by armoured columns from the
Second Armoured Division, rushing across Germany to join with
the United States First Army.

The princess objected because she and her husband were told
to leave their private suite and instead occupy two buildings with
over fourteen well-appointed rooms. I was present on the terrace
of the residence when the colonel told the prince and princess
that they would have to leave their suite. He had already told them
earlier and his voice was wearied.

The princess was upset. She was clearly of the opinion that she
could be allowed to remain in her rooms with her husband. There
was ample room in the estate, she thought, to meet the Army's
wishes. The colonel courteously but bluntly told her in effect that
the American Army was 'Boss' and that she would have to do
what she was told. The prince stood by faintly embarrassed as he
explained the princess's wishes.

Afterwards the colonel told me: 'The princess wanted us to
move into a dirty building which German soldiers had occupied.'
He added that the prince and princess had been lucky: 'If we
complied strictly with orders, they would have to be cleared out
of the residence altogether.'

Allow people to listen to it just once rather than handing out
copies. The text is to serve as a jumping-off point from which to
get a strong impression; the exercise is not going to be about
accurate reconstruction.

ii) Ask each group to make an image based on the extract. They will have to confer over what they remember from the reading and select what they believe to be important and interesting. As a facilitator, you will exert the pressure of limited time to prevent too much talk and prompt the groups to take action. When they get to their feet is when the work will start to happen. It is as they commit to physical shape their ideas of the characters, and their attitudes to each other and to the situation, that clear choices will have to be made in order to meet the imposed deadline.

The image should be a composite of selected information, boiled down to present a strong piece of storytelling. You should see all the groups' images and then choose one group at a time to show their image while the other groups watch. Ask for feedback from the observers to check that the visual storytelling is clear. Who is who and what is going on? Notice how different these images will be, although each was based on hearing the same story. Every voice should count, and the particular mix of each group will lead to different interpretations.

iii) Ask each group to clear an empty space in the part of the room they are working in. They will fill that space with the image they have made, entering to a count of six. They will move into the image and freeze on the final count. Notice how the image is made more dynamic by the movement into it. Repeat it a couple of times. The performers will discover more information about their characters in the way they choose to enter the image. Do the soldiers rush in as if straight from the battlefield? Or do they trudge in, weary and desperate? Does the princess glide into a seat? Is she leading the prince, and is he wanting to hang back? All these choices have to be made, and they will enrich the scene.

iv) Now ask each group to make the image *before* the one they have just shown. This could be five seconds before, five minutes, five weeks, five months, five years, or fifteen years before: anything counts from the moments before the soldiers entered the palace to the princess's debutante ball years ago, as long as it has a relation to the main image. Individuals can play the same or completely new characters.

Allow five to ten minutes for negotiation, and check the groups are up on their feet working. Create a deadline for these new images to be made. Ask the groups to make the images dynamic by providing an entrance into the frozen image.

v) Ask each group to find a way of connecting this new image to the original one: start with an empty space. Enter into the *before* image, and find a way to move out of that into the *original* image. Creating the link between the two images should give more information for the characters and the narrative.

vi) Make a third image which is *after* the original image. It can be five seconds or fifteen years after, as long as there is a connection; for example: The soldiers resident in the palace playing cards over the antique dining-table with their feet up on the furniture.

vii) Now you have a sequence: beginning, middle and end. Get the groups to practise connecting them, allowing movement between the images so that one flows into the other. Next add that they can use a maximum of five lines of dialogue or storytelling to make the narrative of their sequence clear. (This connects back to the earlier Triangle Improvisation, see above.) Allow enough time (about ten minutes) for the groups to make their work confident and precise. Present the work one group at a time while the rest form the audience.

Because of the structure of the exercise, the presentations are likely to be interesting to watch. Different choices will have been made about the history of the prince and princess and what their future holds. How do the soldiers react to the royal couple? Does the reporter feature in the story.

The images make a narrative structure based on and developing out of the original text, linked together by movement and the use of space. As a facilitator, you have only been responsible for providing the original extract and for giving out the instructions. The groups have control over their selection of material and artistic choices. They can decide what they think works and what needs to be cut. They own the work, and the opportunity of a final presentation should make for a satisfying outcome.

Working with a total group of about twenty people, the preparatory image work in this section would take about forty-five minutes. Then you could run the last Narrative Images exercise in four groups of five people, for which you should allow a further forty-five to sixty minutes to complete and see the work.

The 'playground' of this exercise is precise and prescriptive. The best work will be achieved by those groups who stretch the creative potential right up against the ropes without falling out of the ring. It is the tension of working within a tight framework that makes for dynamic and imaginative work. The structured approach to generating the material should mean that the work is clear, simple and effective, as a productive first step in generating material that could be further developed by creating extended dialogue and filling in extra scenes. It is also a framework for the creative process and the sharing of ideas. As a team, each group is under pressure to listen, communicate, negotiate, compromise and come up with something to show. They have to get up on their feet and try out ideas rather than give in to the temptation to sit and speculate.

Dramatic Writing

The work of the three sections above looks at minimal dialogue, strong images and communicating what is essential. The following exercise keeps that discipline of selection while giving an opportunity to create extended dialogue.

WRITING EXERCISE

i) As in the Narrative Images exercise above, start by making an image or a series of images, in groups of two to six The starting point could be a piece of writing, a theme, a photograph or an idea.

Choose to work with one image. Ask the group to walk into the image so they can get more information about their characters and the situation; for example: a group have developed a sequence that takes five characters through a day in Paris. The images have been built up and developed by the group based on a photograph by Edith Gerin: 'Le Passant de la première heure' ('Early stroll'), which features a single man crossing a Parisian bridge against a dark early morning sky. The middle image of the sequence features their five characters gathered together on the left bank of the River Seine. Two lovers are entwined and a man is sketching, while a woman reads a letter and another man hurries past. They move in and out of the image to build up a sense of their individual physicality and gain a stronger sense of identity.

ii) Set it up so that pen and paper are close at hand. On a signal from the facilitator people have to leave the image and go directly to write down a stream of consciousness. It has to be written in the first person of their character, and concerns their feelings and thoughts based on the image and situation they have just left. The words should flow out freely and uncensored. The pen should not stop moving across the page, even if it is repeating the same word over and over while waiting for the next thought to arrive. Let people write for at least five minutes, which will feel like a long time. Everyone stops together.

iii) Ask everyone to count up the number of words they have written. Then ask them to halve their number exactly by crossing out. They should be ruthless, deleting entire sentences or individual words and leaving only what they like best. None of it has to make grammatical sense.

iv) When that is done, ask them to halve it exactly again. They will end up with 25 per cent of their original writing.

v) Now, taking the words that remain, go back to their groups. Together they layer in their written words to form a dialogue between their characters. Every word of each person's contribution must be used by their character; nothing can be left out and nothing can be added. The words can be intercut and arranged in any order. It is a painstaking process of collaboration, piecing it carefully together; and you will end up with a finished dialogue.

vi) Going back to the starting image, the scene can now be animated to include the use of the dialogue.

This exercise creates a non-naturalistic text with a heightened and poetic quality.

The original stream of consciousness that each character wrote down is based on a physical sensation of being in the image and the movement in and out of it. It should carry the directness of those feelings of being in the image straight on to the piece of paper. As it would be in acting a scene, information will also come from the other people in the image: 'Why are you looking at me like that? Your eyes bore into me. I love you, but I never trusted you. Trust – you don't know what that means. Ever since that time . . . etc.'

So the Parisian scene features dialogue between the lovers, and an exchange they have with the man sketching. The woman reads extracts of her letter, mixed in with memories, which seem to connect with the man hurrying past. He is on his way to the funeral of a friend.

Once more it is the restriction on the process that provides the edge. The deletion of 75 per cent of the material rids the writing of padding and the predictable. That is why the time allowed to write should go beyond the comfortable, so that people dredge up feelings and thoughts from within themselves. In any improvisation the first material generated is probably the obvious, followed by a period where the energy and ideas fall away, until another layer of ideas is uncovered that is more connected to the creative subconscious.

What should remain after the editing is the essence of people's imaginative and personal work. When it is put together to form a dialogue, it will sound connected, having sprung from a single source. It is a distillation of ideas and words reduced to make an effective and taut piece of writing.

The exercise will take two hours plus to end up with a scene that can be performed. For a group with good concentration it is engaging and fulfilling. Most importantly it teaches about the selectivity and unpredictability of good writing.

Dramatic Texture

Previously in this chapter the work has primarily been about words and the creation of a heightened theatrical language, including the construction of images. They are the strong foundations for making theatre, and now we will look at other layers involved in creating a performance event. Communication is not confined to words and visual information, there being a vast reservoir of sensory experience all around us. In daily life we filter out much of this sensory information in order to concentrate on what we view as essential to our immediate needs.

A piece of theatre works on a rich variety of wavelengths, which workshops can explore and develop. Sound and music create layers of atmosphere and information that communicate on conscious and subconscious levels to an audience. As in the earlier sections of the chapter, this workshop will lead to a short piece of performance. First introduce the group to the idea that the making of music is simple and can be done by anyone:

MAKING MUSIC

Ask a group what the elements are that, put together, make music. (They are: Pulse – Rhythm – Melody.)

Split people into groups of between five and ten, sitting in a circle on the floor, and ask them to make a piece of music. The pulse can be set up by a steady beat on the floor. A rhythm can be put over the top by clapping hands. A melody can be simply sung on a few notes to the sound of 'la-la-la'.

They have now made a piece of music. Listen to all the groups.

The term 'music' can be used to describe all sorts of soundscapes, which can create atmosphere and location, as in the next exercise.

SOUNDSCAPES

Still in their groups and sitting on the floor: ask people to create the atmosphere of: an underground station late at night; a storm at sea; a country garden in summer.

The basic elements of pulse, rhythm and melody must still somehow feature. The melody, for instance, may become a wailing voice, or a repeated command. Listen with the eyes closed to the work of the different groups.

Music and sound are not confined to providing atmosphere. They can also communicate narrative information: take the same atmospheres as above and now request that the soundscape make a clear narrative journey; for example: by using a mixture of percussive and vocal sounds to create the atmosphere of an underground station late at night, a whole story can be told of the waiting, the train arriving, passengers getting on and off, and the train leaving.

This takes us further into the use of sound and how it communicates. Each of us stores a huge bank of sound memories, which enables us, for example, to recognize the voices of family and friends instantly on the telephone. A certain piece of music will evoke a string of recollections; the sound of the sea might take us back to childhood holidays. The Argentinian writer Jorge Luis Borges, even after becoming blind in later life, said that his favourite pastime was to travel; to hear, smell, touch and taste a different world. Our senses communicate to us all the time and stimulate our memories, feelings and imaginations.

In the making of theatre the feelings and sensations of the performers and audience need to be stirred, as well as the intellect. This next exercise is designed to stimulate the imaginative, vocal and aural resources of the participants.

BLINDFOLD IMAGES

Ask two people to participate, and the rest of the group to observe.

  i) Person A sits down blindfolded. Person B has in front of them a big colour picture of a work of art. Nineteenth- and twentieth-century figurative painting works well; for example, 'The Scream' by Edvard Munch, 'Jane Avril Leaving the Moulin Rouge' by Henri Toulouse-Lautrec, 'The Nighthawks' by Edward Hopper. B has to communicate the picture to A using only vocal and percussive sounds – no words. At the end, A removes their blindfold (with the picture out of their sight) and tells what they 'saw'.

The first time I saw this exercise done, like most people in the room I thought that the task was probably impossible. I expected the blindfolded person to say they were confused, or at best to give a generalized impression that would bear little relation to the picture. Instead the person gave some definite information, which included saying that the colours were dark, a person was running away, and could it be 'The Scream' by Edvard Munch? Yes, it was, and we were all amazed! We had seen the picture at the start of the exercise, and had therefore listened to the sounds made by our colleague with our rational brain while focusing on the difficulty of the objective. Meanwhile the person under the blindfold had managed to open themselves up to the experience and had gathered the necessary information.

I have repeated the exercise since and am always intrigued by its success. For example, using Vincent van Gogh's 'Wood Gatherers in the Snow', the subject of the exercise got all the relevant information about the activity, the walking, the extreme cold and even the 'ray of warmth', which is represented by a red, wintry sun in the far background of the picture. It is a great exercise to open people up to the power of non-visual and non-verbal communication. The exercise can be continued to involve everyone actively:

  ii) Work in groups of four, one of whom is blindfolded. The three others have to communicate to them a picture of a work of art. This time they can use *no* vocal sounds, only percussive sounds. This time they can also touch the blindfolded person, and take them on a physical journey to help them experience the picture, e.g. they can overdress her, position her in the room, make her feel different textures, move her about in a particular way. They *cannot* speak either to each other or to the blindfolded player; they can use whatever they can find in the room to help create the experience. Allow five to ten minutes for this work, giving enough time for the three to come up with different ideas of how to communicate the picture. As each group finishes, make sure that they sit down quietly, keeping the blindfold on the person, until everyone has finished their work. Then ask for all the blindfolds to be removed, making sure that the pictures are now out of sight. Each person who has worn the blindfold tells what she 'saw' to the rest of the group. At the end of each description allow that person and the rest of the group to see the original picture.

It is exciting when the unsighted person describes what they saw, and how close it can be to the actual picture. Often they can be astonishingly accurate about small details, the atmosphere of the picture and the specific colours used. As in many exercises, the exclusion of one dominant sense stimulates the others into activity. Because those people looking at the picture cannot speak, their imaginations are stimulated as to how best to communicate the information it contains, and they find inventive ways of 'describing' the image. Those people trying to 'see' the picture without eyes will find their other senses working harder to process the information and to feed their imaginative mind's eye. The exercise takes people out of their usual realm of experience and demonstrates the range of communication available to us.

Interestingly, the only time the exercise has not really worked was when I attempted it in a rehearsal room that happened to be full of costumes, props and musical instruments. The participants had too much to choose from and the subjects of the exercise became overloaded with sensory information. The exercise works best, as is usually the case, when the participants really have to use their imaginations and make the most out of minimal resources.

This exercise can be used as part of the process of making theatre, because a theatre event should be an experience for the performers and for the audience. The performers need to taste the sensory world of the characters and the situation, to give depth and life to their creative work. The audience need to experience the performance on different levels, where the words and the visual images combine with sounds to form a range of communication, making a complete sensory event.

*

Finally, an exercise to bring together elements of all the work considered in this chapter.

IMPROVISED PIECE

In groups of about five people. Give each group a new picture to work from. Using it as a starting point, give them forty to sixty minutes to make a short piece of performance.

When considering the task of making a piece of theatre starting from a given picture, hopefully all the disciplines we have looked at above will now inform the process: the detailed selection of the triangle exercise; the use of location and design choices, and of images to establish narrative clarity; the creation of a heightened language through the writing exercise; and an awareness of the possibilities of a textured performance that uses sound and imagery to speak to all the senses. It is a structured approach to process which will make for a stimulating journey and a worthwhile product.

At the conclusion of a workshop I gave one group 'L'Absinthe' by Edgar Degas. It is a gloomy picture of a man and a woman in a bar, sitting next to each other but making no contact. They look lonely, pensive and probably drunk. The group of five opened it out to feature the various characters who frequented the bar. It started in the morning, with the cleaner who mopped up after the night before. The dragging rhythm of her bucket across the floor was later joined and taken over by the first customers, who combined snippets of dialogue with the sounds of bottles, glasses and pouring drinks. A short and sharply written scene then took place between the café owner and an important customer. A drunken man shuddered across the floor, knocking into the furniture and fellow drinkers. An argument ensued, conveyed by repeated phrases and choreographed movement. An edgy calm was restored and two excitable young women entered, chatting about their day and the evening ahead . . .

What is satisfying about watching this kind of work is the attention to detail and the imaginative choices that go into telling a story and making a piece of theatre. It is true improvised ensemble work, with the performers listening and working together with discipline and skill. It is a long way from the first triangle improvisations at the beginning of this chapter, with their 'naturalistic' assumptions, lazy, overused dialogue and sluggish physicality.

Theatre as Community

A workshop process is an opportunity to explore and develop. A performance of any description offers the chance to show the work and to provide a punctuation mark along the way. Theatre presentations can offer an affirmation of who we are as performers, and as audience, and the community we share. Improvisation can create material or enhance the skills needed to realize an existing text. Only when the work is shown to an audience can its impact be gauged.

As part of a youth theatre scheme run by the National Theatre I have seen many shows by young people all over Britain, in a range of venues including the school hall, village hall, scout hut, theatre and classroom. I have enjoyed each for its commitment and sense of occasion. What makes every one a dramatic event is the audience's knowing the actors, and the shared will to make it succeed as a celebration of the work that has taken place. I remember a dimly lit, tiny village hall in Dorset on a winter's night, and the young actors enacting a story of local history watched by three generations of their families. The event was specially made for that location and that community, and the value of the work would have been diminished on another stage.

A very different theatre event was a performance of *The Tempest* in Maidstone prison put on by inmates with the assistance of a professional director and two actors. The performance I saw was for the families and friends of the cast. It was a highly charged event with over a hundred people packed into a small room; and I remember the actor playing Stephano delivering his whole performance to his father and teenage son and daughter seated in the front row. The cast used the performance as a justification of their identity beyond being prisoners.

I was at the Market Theatre in Johannesburg when they revived Athol Fugard's *The Island* with the two original actors (John Kani and Winston Ntshona) who had created it with the author twenty years earlier. Set on Robben Island, it had originally played to acclaim in New York and London and focused attention on the plight of political prisoners in South Africa. This particular performance in 1995 was attended by President Nelson Mandela and members of the government, who had been in prison when the play was first presented. The evening was a moving testimony to the bravery of all those who suffered and made sacrifices, and a celebration of a world turned around.

Making theatre makes a difference. The task is to make something that will entertain and possibly educate an audience. It is a creative process that requires rigour and clear boundaries if it is to be successful.

3 Making Shakespeare

Brixton prison, April 1994. The Education Department of the Royal National Theatre had chosen to stage *Hamlet* with a group of inmates. Hamlet comes from a broken home; his uncle is a murderer; he regards himself as a prisoner in his own country; he is watched wherever he goes; his letters are intercepted; he is at one stage deported; he is abusive to women, indulges in verbal bullying, macho posturing and casual acts of violence. However, the most important reason for choosing *Hamlet*, rather than a contemporary play, was that it was a hugely demanding and difficult text for any group of actors in any situation to tackle. To get that play to work in performance in Brixton required lengthy periods of intense concentration from people who had begun to believe themselves incapable of concentrating for more than a few minutes. It demanded their commitment, cooperation, punctuality and responsibility. Ultimately the challenge of the text was rewarded by raising the self-esteem of those who had very little to start with, and made notorious underachievers justifiably proud of what they had succeeded in achieving.

It would be unwise to underestimate the extent of the challenge playing Shakespeare represents to most people, whatever their role in life. To most of us, Shakespeare is *the* pinnacle of high culture, admired from a distance but never scaled, at least by us.

In some respects, young people who may know the least about Shakespeare experience fewer problems than those who are older, and who may well feel overshadowed by, and in awe of, the magnitude of Shakespeare's cultural status. Large companies spend thousands of pounds sending their executives on outward-bound courses designed to build team spirit, engender greater cooperation and promote imaginative approaches to problem solving. Often they take the form of adventurous and sometimes even hazardous expeditions, where people accustomed to the soft furnishings of the executive suite are suddenly cast into the hard reality of climbing mountains, fording rivers and staying out all night in atrocious conditions. This strategy is also used with delinquents; it's only a short remove from the notorious 'short, sharp shock'. And yet, if these same executives had been assigned the task of speaking one of Hamlet's soliloquies to their colleagues, and given only an hour or two to prepare, the scale of the challenge and the benefits that would be forthcoming from successfully negotiating the text would quite equal those that allegedly follow from more physically strenuous forms of management training. Getting to grips with Shakespeare not only brings with it confidence that enables individuals to make more effective use of public language, it gives them the ability to listen, respond, think quickly and share the information and insights contained in highly subtle and complex texts. Like so much else in good workshop practice, experiencing making Shakespeare in the company of other people, all of whom are starting from the same point and under identical circumstances, creates group solidarity and a collective spirit as well as an individual sense of achievement and satisfaction.

That sense of satisfaction is enhanced not only because we have learnt to do something that is difficult, but because, once we begin to make Shakespeare work for us, to serve our needs, we also start to shed some of the weighty cultural baggage we have probably carried around for years. For like it or not, we all carry around a lot of Shakespearean luggage, the weight of which can sometimes inhibit our freedom to act spontaneously and creatively when faced with those famous and often intimidating texts. When I was a schoolboy in the 1950s, I watched on our recently acquired television set a children's drama serial about a group of British prisoners of war held in Germany. I can't remember much about the action other than that they had a plan to escape, and that it came to nothing because they were betrayed to their captors by one of their own men. The focus of the drama was the subsequent attempt to find the traitor in their midst. One of the main characters was a British officer, a man who spoke with a public-school accent and who had an encyclopedic knowledge of Shakespeare. He was continually quoting him, and for almost every situation he had an appropriate quotation ready: 'Much ado about nothing, old boy,' he'd say; or, 'Take but degree away and hark what discord follows' – that sort of thing. I was really impressed – he was able to make Shakespeare work for him because he always had an apposite phrase to hand. Of course it turned out in the last episode that he was the one who had actually betrayed his country and his colleagues, but his familiarity and ease in using that special language made him, for me – and I suspect for many thousands of other young viewers – an object of admiration, and the least likely suspect.

My youthful, armchair, arm's-length encounter with Shakespeare remains vivid. If you happened to be at school in Britain in the 1990s, thanks to the National Curriculum, it was impossible to avoid a much closer and usually far more problematic encounter with Shakespeare. Sometimes I'm not sure who dreads that meeting most: teachers or their students. What I do know is that there has been a revolution over the past decade in the way Shakespeare has been taught in many schools, and that where teachers are confident enough to use a workshop approach, the energy and vitality of the work they produce with students can be extraordinary. Young people who at best are often tongue-tied (and mute when it comes to Shakespeare) can be encouraged to use language expressively. Once they begin to do that, to stake their claim to knowing Shakespeare, they can begin to mark the text as their own territory, not simply that of people unlike themselves. It is not, however, simply about young people obtaining ease and familiarity in using what is an archaic language. That language is not transparent, and carefully designed workshops can also open up debates about meaning, reveal issues and demonstrate in a graphic way that all of us – teachers, students, actors, readers – consciously or unconsciously make choices about what Shakespeare means.

A Shakespeare workshop, by looking, for example, not only at different kinds of language – legal, romantic, introspective, didactic, formal and informal – but at how they can be used to maximize dramatic effect, makes available a range of valuable, transferable skills. These connect directly with problem solving in relation to language, something most professionals have to do every day of their working lives, whether they are decoding (scholars), encoding (writers, etc., including scientists) or performing (as in court or school). However, not everyone feels confident enough to use a language-based practical workshop approach to Shakespeare, and not every workshop works.

At an early rehearsal of Shakespeare's *Pericles* at the Royal National Theatre in 1995, the actors were all sitting in a circle with their director Phyllida Lloyd, when she suddenly stopped the read-through of the play. She then asked the actors to continue, but instead of using Shakespeare's words they had to substitute their own. Almost without hesitation they began to give a fluent, accurate and witty word-for-word translation. I was astonished at the ability of some of the cast to do this, to put Shakespeare's words into colloquial English without any apparent loss of pace or energy. It was *very* impressive, but I couldn't help noticing that not all the actors volunteered; quite a few of them avoided the exercise altogether. Not surprisingly, it tended to be the most experienced actors who had the least trouble in doing what their director wanted. They seemed to have the necessary confidence as well as the seemingly complete familiarity with Shakespeare's language required to effect this form of simultaneous translation. Those participating in the exercise displayed considerable skill and sensitivity to language, but for our purposes, more significant were those who, for whatever reason, chose not to speak, and whom the exercise excluded.

It is easy to assume that actors, because of their training and their job, will automatically feel immediately at home with Shakespeare. They don't. Many experienced professional actors feel that knowledge of Shakespeare signals (as it does to young people still at school) membership of an elite, your ability to play a part in the drama of high, and not just popular, culture. Failure successfully to negotiate Shakespeare appears to threaten the precarious social status of actors. All of them, like all of us, therefore have an understandable fear of being caught out, of not knowing how to pronounce a particular word, or of not understanding immediately what a line actually means. This isn't simply a social fear of appearing uneducated or ignorant in the face of your peers; it is also a professional concern. Anyone can become professionally paralysed in such a situation, so learning to break through this kind of barrier in a workshop can pay a wide range of dividends. So how were those silenced by the director's task brought to full and confident inclusion in the final performance? To understand this process, it is useful to think about the nature of rehearsals and the role of workshops.

Not so long ago, when actors attended rehearsals, they would be dressed formally, men in suits with collar and tie, women in colour-coordinated, tailored clothes. On their way to the rehearsal they could look forward to sitting in a circle for the whole day, perhaps round a table, drinking cups of coffee, reading the play, and subsequently discussing it at great length and in considerable detail. Days if not weeks would elapse *before* even thinking about getting on their feet to 'block' the moves. Today actors coming to rehearsals look more like athletes than actors, in their unisex tracksuits, jeans and T-shirts. They anticipate having to think on their feet from day one. But despite these superficial changes, British actor-training and a great deal of theatre practice still encourage an analytical approach to Shakespeare, where actors mine the language for clues that will reveal the motivation that drives their character, and makes their actions real. If the text sometimes makes this process difficult, or appears to resist character analysis altogether, then the actors, in their anxiety to please, begin to generalize, and when they generalize they start to sound (to themselves) unreal. If, however, they insist on waiting until they think they know exactly what a line or a series of lines from a Shakespeare play really means before attempting to speak it, theirs will be a lengthy and unnecessarily arduous journey of discovery. Another way of approaching Shakespeare is through a physical process, literally a practical and not an academic exercise. It encourages flexibility of interpretation, prevents actors from getting bogged down in language, and instead lets them manipulate and engage with language in all its forms. The process starts with a willingness to play around with words.

Words, Words, Words

The objective of this work is to prise language lose from the constraints of what it might literally be taken to mean, and instead to encourage people to play with the texture, sound, shape and form of words.

- Ask everyone to think of a line or phrase from *any* Shakespeare play. Often people claim not be able to think of a line, so you will need to be prepared to offer some that are well known or at least easily remembered. I suspect that everyone, absolutely everyone, could think of at least one line by Shakespeare, but at this opening stage in a workshop people are terrified of getting it wrong and therefore won't chance saying it in public.
- Encourage people to 'hear' their line being said in their mind.
- Get them to speak the line aloud – everyone speaking at the same time. If you have a group who are particularly self-conscious, play some recorded music loudly, or use a sound-effect record of a thunderstorm, and ask people to try to get their voice heard above it. By controlling and varying the volume of the amplification, you can get people using their voices at different levels and with different amounts of energy without becoming too self-conscious.

- Ask individuals to volunteer to read their line to the whole group, stressing any verbs. When the first verb is spoken, the rest of the group shouts, 'What?' The speaker then repeats the line, putting even greater emphasis on the verb. If there is a second verb, the group interrupts again, making the speaker go back and start the line again. This can go on until the group is satisfied that the speaker has given it sufficient emphasis.

Physicalization

Encourage people not to start from the literal meanings of the phrase, but to try as far as possible to distance the words from their dramatic context; they should play around with what sounds the words make. Get them to try, for example, elongating the vowel sounds, or stressing the consonants. They need to relish the taste and texture of the language, and be aware of what their mouths and tongues have to do in order to say them in sequence. Continually prompt people to find out for themselves how a particular word sounds: Is it harsh or smooth? Is it polysyllabic? Get people thinking of the words themselves as if they formed a physical structure. What is that structure like? What are its properties? Does it have volume and density? Is it solid or fluid? Does it move or is it static? Is it elegant or ugly? If they had to represent the word in a drawing, what would it look like?

When the whole line is spoken aloud, try getting them to make a physical shape for it by using the body. Get people to say their lines aloud, and, as they do, use their body to form the structure and activate any movement the line suggests to them.

Follow this section of the workshop by giving everyone a piece of paper and something to write with.
- Write down the whole of the line or phrase.
- Rearrange the words in a different order, not caring about literal meaning, but choosing for whatever reason which word should sit next to another.
- Rearrange the words in the original line in three or four different ways, and, having chosen the one you prefer (not the original), speak it aloud.
- Invite everyone in the workshop to speak their new line to one another two or three times, and ask the others to listen carefully to see if they can guess what is the original.

In working through this opening part of the session, and subsequently until you sense there is a feeling of confidence and trust among the group as a whole, avoid focusing on individuals. Treat the group as a whole, and if you need to speak to someone to encourage or discourage him or her in any aspect of the work, try to do it when the rest are occupied with an exercise. It is important at the start of the work that people who are insecure (and that is *most* people) feel that, whenever necessary, they can hide behind the anonymity of the group. Inevitably many of those taking part will assume that, sooner or later, they will have to begin to 'act' Shakespeare, and that, when they do, they will be judged not only by you, but by their peers. For this work to succeed the workshop must avoid being judgemental or competitive. Obviously this is not easy, but you can only expect people to take personal risks – dare to make a mistake – if they feel that the environment created in the workshop is safe.

Suiting the Action to the Word

Building on the previous individual work on very short pieces of text, now have the group work in pairs.

- Each person takes a different line, either of their own choosing or one they have been given.
- Repeat the previous exercise by looking to find a movement that goes with the language as it is spoken.
- As the pairs explore and finally decide upon the movement, ask them to break it down into three distinct parts. They will need to do this to be able to teach their partner the movement and the line of text on which it is based.
- Once both have learnt movement and text and rehearsed them together, show the result to the rest of the group.

The point of this exercise is to achieve a level of cooperation between two people in which responsibility is shared, helping them to engage with the plasticity of Shakespeare's language. The performance of the resulting product also opens out the possibility of sharing an interpretative process with their peers that is neither judgemental nor threatening. When, for example, the energy and shape of a particular movement results in an expressive use of the accompanying language, those who have created it, as well as those who observe it, experience surprise and satisfaction. You will find that through creating a focus on meeting the physical demands of the exercise, the self-policing that holds individuals back from vocally experimenting and playing with language is minimized.

Speaking very short extracts, however expressively, is of limited use if what you need to achieve ultimately is a positive engagement with the text as a whole, and an ability and confidence to see Shakespeare's language as an opportunity rather than as a threat. Therefore, once people in the group have grown accustomed to hearing themselves, to hearing and seeing other people speak the text, and to being favourably surprised that doing it is both enjoyable and revealing, it is time to tackle a longer extract with a different set of challenges.

Exploring Language

Below is a lengthy and complicated piece of text from *A Midsummer Night's Dream*, Act 2 Scene i. It is precisely the kind of material that individuals need to be able to negotiate with confidence if they are to work effectively with Shakespeare. If they can learn to do that, other texts in other contexts, such as the world of work, which are perhaps less complex but to the speaker and listeners no less important, become more manageable in prospect. What follow are some suggestions on how to approach this text (or any other) in a workshop, concentrating on an exploration of dramatic language. At first the text is worked on by the whole group, then in smaller units and finally as individuals.

TITANIA These are the forgeries of jealousy:
 And never since the middle summer's spring
 Met we on hill, in dale, forest, or mead,
 By paved fountain or by rushy brook,
 Or in the beached margent of the sea
 To dance our ringlets to the whistling wind,
 But with thy brawls thou hast disturbed our sport.
 Therefore the winds, piping to us in vain,
 As in revenge, have suck'd up from the sea
 Contagious fogs; which, falling in the land,
 Hath every pelting river made so proud
 That they have overborne their continents.
 The ox hath therefore stretched his yoke in vain,
 The ploughman lost his sweat, and the green corn
 Hath rotted ere his youth attained a beard.

The fold stands empty in the drowned field,
And the crows are fatted with the murrion flock;
The nine-men's-morris is filled up with mud,
And the quaint mazes in the wanton green
For lack of tread are undistinguishable.
The human mortals want their winter cheer;
No night is now with hymn or carol blest.
Therefore the moon, the governess of floods,
Pale in her anger, washes all the air,
That rheumatic diseases do abound;
And through this distemperature we see
The seasons alter; hoary-headed frosts
Fall in the fresh lap of the crimson rose,
And on old Hiems' thin and icy crown
An odorous chaplet of sweet summer buds
Is, as in mockery, set. The spring, the summer,
The childing autumn, angry winter, change
Their wonted liveries, and the mazed world
By their increase, now knows not which is which.
And this same progeny of evils comes
From our debate, from our dissension.
We are their parents and original.

   A Midsummer Night's Dream, Act 2 Scene i

Many rehearsals in the theatre are run like university seminars, and a speech like this would be carefully dissected word by word, line by line. Such an approach privileges actors who are self-confident and articulate, and who share the same critical vocabulary as the director. However, it fails those who are more modest and reluctant to express their opinions, perhaps because they have not been taught to value what they think. In a workshop whose aim is to stimulate sensitivity to the myriad possibilities of language, there is no need to begin with an analytical debate about possible meanings in this, or any other, speech.

Move into a circle and explain that the group will now speak the entire speech, but one word at a time.
- The leader speaks the first word, then the person on their right, and so on, round the circle until the speech is finished.
- Repeat this, but ask the group to do one of two things: when it is the turn of an individual to speak, if they find the word interesting

(for any reason at all), they should emphasize it, saying the word to the circle as a whole; on the other hand, if they do not find the word interesting, then they should simply say it without emphasis to the next person on their right.

- Ask everyone to look again at the speech, and select two separate but complete lines from it. They should not say what they are. Explain that the group is going to find out who has chosen what in the following way: they are to attempt to 'hear' the speech in their heads, and when – and only when – they think it is time to say their line(s), speak it aloud.

- The leader decides when the exercise starts, and everyone tries to concentrate and 'hear' the progression of the text. Of course, no one knows who has chosen which lines, and there may be no one at all to speak the first, or indeed the first few lines, before one or more persons begin. If this is the case, and no one has chosen any lines from the first four or five, the exercise is made even more tricky, and the leader might, when repeating the work, decide to make it a little easier by personally deciding to speak the first line.

- Remember to remind everyone that when someone does speak, the rest of the group should adjust the pace of the voice in their head, slow down or speed up.

People often find that they have selected the same line, and the exercise affords an opportunity subsequently to discuss who chose what and why and whether it appears to say anything about Titania's speech. Is there, for example, a hitherto unspoken agreement now revealed by this exercise that some words or lines are apparently more significant to the group than others?

Follow this with an exercise that will help to focus attention on the structure of the language and in particular on Shakespeare's choice of the first and last words in every line. Often those first and last words carry an additional weight of meaning. Sometimes the gist of a whole speech is contained in those first and last words.

- Divide the group into two roughly equal halves, standing or seated facing one another.

- The first group speaks the first word of the first line: 'These', and the others then respond together by saying the last word of that line: 'jealousy'.

- Keep alternating the first and last words of every line until the end of the speech, trying to keep a rhythm going throughout.

The next exercise will help individuals approach language through its structure and form.

THE JOURNEY OF THE SPEECH

- Ask people to read the speech aloud (but to themselves) while moving round the room.
- At each punctuation mark they should change direction. The stronger the punctuation the greater the change: thus a comma might signal a slight veering to the left or right, a semi-colon could suggest a diagonal turn, a colon a complete reversal of direction. A full stop should mean just that.
- When the group have worked on this, ask them how many changes they had to make. Why do they think there is so much (or so little) punctuation, and what does it suggest about the thoughts being expressed?
- Repeat this exercise, but this time ignoring the punctuation and changing direction each time they think the thought changes.
- Look again at Titania's speech as if it were a kind of map designed to help the actor negotiate a complicated and lengthy journey in the mind of the character. The objective is physically to retrace this journey in the actual space of the workshop. Before setting off, individuals need to reread the 'map' once again, and then attempt carefully to recreate Titania's journey stage by stage.

To help this exercise, remind the group that we often talk about our thoughts being 'all over the place' or of 'going round and round in circles' and so need to consider the direction of Titania's thoughts. Does she always/sometimes/never appear to know where she is heading? What is her state of mind and how can it be expressed in movement: is she at times agitated, at others calm and focused? Is the journey of the speech linear, and if so where does it begin and end? Does it progress in a straightforward, uncomplicated manner, or is the route tortuous and circuitous? Where are the clues in the language that indicate a change in the speed of thought or its direction?

Getting into the language in physical ways such as this helps to avoid the paralysis that can result if actors believe they can never say a line *until* they know what it means. It also stops the temptation to take a short cut with the speech, and instead of exploring its complexity and detail generalize it to mean simply that Titania is angry with Oberon. The physical freedom of movement that the exercise develops leads in turn to a greater freedom of thought in the actor.

- When individuals feel ready to attempt it, ask them to show to the others their physical journey.
- Ask the spectators at the end what adjectives they would use to describe what they have seen. Is the journey seamless, smooth, or jagged and halting. It is only the movements that need to be demonstrated.
- Next ask that they speak the speech while remaining physically still, but recalling the physical journey in their mind.

Baz Luhrmann's stunning film version of *Romeo and Juliet* (1997) was successful in holding the attention and winning the admiration of cinemagoers throughout the world. The film's winning combination of hot colours, spectacle and blistering sound all projected and intercut at breakneck speed seemed very far removed from the altogether cooler, more restrained and measured Shakespeare that is available on stage. But however wonderful and festive Luhrmann's film is, it largely avoids a close encounter with the language of the play. All the soliloquies are edited, most of them radically, and much of the dialogue is restricted to brief exchanges. This is not in itself a surprise or a problem: film works primarily through images, and images can carry a narrative just as effectively as words spoken by actors. However, the success of this new and popular Shakespeare seems based on an assumption that contemporary cinema audiences are not able (or do not wish) to listen to spoken language for more than a few minutes at a time. This may well be the case, and certainly the dramatic output of most cinema and television makes few demands on the spectator as listener. How do we encourage people to re-engage not only with speaking Shakespeare, but with listening to him?

Verse: Patterns of Sound and Sense
In what follows I suggest ways of 'refreshing' the speaking of Shakespeare's language, something that will help actors and non-actors alike, as both speakers and listeners. If you ask most actors about verse speaking, they will immediately acknowledge its importance; but go further, by asking them how they speak verse as opposed to prose, and you will often draw a blank. Most actors, certainly those trained in the

last twenty-five years, have no idea how to speak verse. Drama schools do not spend the time needed to teach verse speaking; after all, most of the work their graduates get will be on television, or in small studio spaces, neither of which requires rhetorical skills, and certainly not the speaking of verse. Verse and verisimilitude don't seem to go together: the former sounds false and 'actorly', not like the spontaneous, natural sounds of the street. However, if we try speaking Shakespeare's verse as verse and not as prose, it can make individual words resonate, can catch the detail of a line, and with it hold the attention of the listener. The discipline imposed by the form resists the free-flowing narrative drive that is so common in our experience of contemporary drama and popular Shakespeare. Initially it may appear to be a reactionary step because, at least for some actors, verse speaking is associated with the antiquated and unfashionable 'voice beautiful', which, although it may at first sound rich and resonant, is dramatically hollow because it sounds false. However, Shakespeare's language when spoken as verse and not as prose is a key that will unlock some of the more neglected possibilities of this dramatic language.

Verse can be used to advantage in challenging the current orthodoxy in how Shakespeare is spoken. It is ironic that verse, considered by some young actors (and directors) to be an archaic form of little interest or relevance to contemporary conventions of playing Shakespeare, should be talked of as an innovative tool for textual exploration – paradoxically, one of the most vigorous uses of verse, rap, comes from the urban streets – because a re-investigation of verse speaking can offer a great deal to a workshop focusing on alternative ways into Shakespeare. It is certainly not *the* way to speak Shakespeare's language, maybe not even the most appropriate; but it is a useful and interesting method to introduce it. It can often create surprises in what it reveals about language and meaning; especially when material is relatively well known, it defamiliarizes it, and makes the actors look at it afresh.

The familiar rhythm of Elizabethan/Jacobean playwrights, including Shakespeare, was based on a verse form that used the iambic pentameter. It was used because it most closely resembled ordinary speech patterns. An iamb is a verse foot with the first syllable unstressed and the second one stressed, as in con*fuse*. Pentameter means that there are five feet per line: ten syllables in all, five of them stressed.

The following exercises are designed to explore language further, firstly by looking at the importance of rhythm in Shakespeare, and at his use of verse.

SEND THE CLAP

- Have everyone standing in a circle, spread out as far as the space allows, and facing into the centre.
- One person starts the exercise by clapping both hands together as if to 'throw' the clap to the person on his or her immediate left.
- That person responds by clapping once and passing it on to the next person, and so on round the circle several times, getting progressively faster.
- This clapping version of the 'Mexican wave' needs to speed up as it goes until it sounds almost as if it is the sound of one giant clap.

Now vary the exercise. Start by having everyone facing into the centre of the circle.

- Ask one person to turn bodily ninety degrees towards the person on his or her immediate right.
- Simultaneously that person turns to their left, leaving the two of them facing one another.
- When they come together, both clap hands at the same time, and then both turn back to face the centre.
- The initiator of the exercise stops moving here, but the other person continues the movement by turning 180 degrees to the person on his or her right (who anticipates the move) and both clap. This continues round the circle several times, aiming all the time for speed and accuracy.

After a time, stop the exercise, and ask what people thought of it. What did they feel when someone failed to anticipate the necessary movement, and mistimed the clap? What did it sound and feel like when everyone did the exercise correctly and sustained the rhythm and energy?

What the exercise produces, of course, are rhythmic movement and accompanying rhythmic sound. When people play it, they inevitably do so with smiles on their faces. Rhythm is important in Shakespeare. There is in his text an underlying rhythm that acts as a motor, driving the language forward and energizing it as it does so. If that rhythm is ignored or fractured, the pace drops and the energy seeps out of the text, leaving the speaker with more and more to do in order to try to recover it. This also tends to shift the focus of the listener away from the specific nature of what is being said, to a wider (and unnecessary) consideration of who is saying it.

IAMBIC FUNDAMENTALISM?

- Have the group, still standing in the circle, clap out the rhythm of an iambic line of verse.
- Give them an example of one to speak while marking the rhythm with a clap: 'In *sooth* I *know* not *why* I *am* so *sad*' (*The Merchant of Venice*, Act 1 Scene i).
- Ask the people what the most famous line in all Shakespeare is. The majority will probably reply with Hamlet's line, 'To be or not to be, that is the question.'
- Try clapping out the rhythm of this line: 'To *be* or *not* to *be* that *is* the *question*.'

Of course, the line does not fit – it has one too many syllables. If participants get used to tapping out the underlying rhythm of the language, and above all if they succeed through practice in internalizing it, they will notice when, for example, a line of verse does not fit the pattern of iambic pentameter. For an actor, disruption of the regular metre can signal a disturbance or obstacle in the thought process of the character; for example, in the first line of Hamlet's soliloquy an excess of syllables leaves the last word 'question' hanging off the end of the line, inviting you to dwell momentarily on a word that, in this context, is very important, suggesting as it does the uncertainty and indecision in Hamlet's mind.

Rhythm is important, but there is much more to verse than rhythm. Are there any rules about how to speak it, and if so what are they? Peter Hall suggests at least three (he learnt his verse speaking from the actor Edith Evans, who always urged that verse should be spoken as Hamlet urges the players to speak it: 'trippingly on the tongue'). The rules themselves are straightforward but, especially for those used to speaking (and hearing) verse as prose, initially difficult to carry out. Following Hall, I have included workshop exercises that will enliven both speaking and listening.

Rules of the Game

- Always observe the linear form of the verse, acknowledging each line as separate from the others, and consequently never run on from one line into the next.
- At the end of each line there should be a very slight pause (unless there is a full stop, in which case it is permissible to halt).
- Always avoid taking a breath in the middle of a line, and indeed avoid pausing anywhere in the line, irrespective of what the editor's punctuation indicates. Although this advice appears to ignore the existence of what is called a caesura (a pause within a line, usually after the second or third stressed syllable, sometimes marked by editors with a full stop or colon), it certainly moves the verse along at a brisk rate, and can also reveal subtle shades of meaning that are obscured when the verse is treated as prose in the cause of naturalistic acting.

For an example of how these rules can open up possible meanings in the text, look at the first few lines of Juliet's soliloquy in Act 3 Scene ii of *Romeo and Juliet*, spoken as she anticipates the imminent arrival of her husband and struggles to control her mounting frustration and desire:

JULIET Gallop apace you fiery-footed steeds
Towards Phoebus' lodging; such a waggoner
As Phaeton would whip you to the west,
And bring in cloudy night immediately.
Spread thy close curtain, love-performing night,
That runaways' eyes may wink, and Romeo
Leap to these arms, untalk'd of and unseen!

Romeo and Juliet, Act 3 Scene ii

The words reflect the level of sexual excitement and anticipation Juliet experiences as she waits for Romeo: Gallop apace . . . whip you . . . immediately . . . spread . . . love-performing . . . arms. The temptation for the actor is to generalize by focusing on playing the energy and excitement, and in doing so rush over the surface of the words. This results in a display of emotion, but one that lacks detail and depth. The energy and spirit of the language as well as its multi-layered meaning can be magnified and highlighted if the form of the verse is observed by the actor, so that due weight is given to each significant word. In this case, the discipline verse imposes actually heightens the tension in the language. It is as if you are passing a powerful current down a long cable. If the cable is straight the current will flow quickly from one end to the other; but if the cable is coiled, the current meets resistance, and as it struggles to pass through, the cable heats up and glows with energy. For example, the two lines

That runaways' eyes may wink, and Romeo
Leap to these arms untalk'd of and unseen!

are invariably run on to make one line by the actor in performance, who speaks the text as prose not verse. But if a slight pause is made after 'Romeo', and the line does not run on, the resistance energizes 'Leap'. It also draws attention to the possible sexual meaning of the word 'Leap' – i.e. become rapidly erect. Similarly the second and third lines

Towards Phoebus' lodging; such a waggoner
As Phaeton would whip you to the west

when run on as prose lose the sense that Juliet's mind is in turmoil, and she has to reach for the appropriate words to express her feelings. Here, the missing beat after 'waggoner' lifts the emphasis on 'Phaeton', reminding the listener of that other doomed youth, who rode his father's chariot too fast and was killed.

If the whole of this speech (and others like it) is spoken as verse, it is, initially at least, a somewhat unsettling experience for the speaker. Inevitably some will react by saying that it feels false, and that by observing the form they fracture the sense. However, once the speaker observes the form, what she is able to do is, in an almost Brechtian sense, make the language strange, and distance listeners from what casual familiarity leads them to expect, thus making the language sound new. The process is analogous to cleaning the varnish from an old oil painting: once it has been cleaned you can see the images literally in a new light. After all, Juliet's famous speech is usually summed up in retrospect as a familiar picture: the young girl, full of a flammable mixture of excitement and fear at the approach of her husband, antici-pates the act that will effectively end her childhood. It is all of this, but also a great deal more: the detail – the often uncomfortable detail – of a young woman's sexual fantasies is masked by actors who concentrate on playing Juliet's emotional state, and forget in the process that the language, like the character who speaks it, is constrained by rules that shape its meaning.

Stripping Away the Layers
- Have someone read Juliet's soliloquy (as verse not as prose) while the others literally surround her.
- Whenever she says a word that sounds to the listeners sexual – however remotely – they should repeat that word in a whisper.

There are many subtextual resonances in the speech, and this exercise draws them out. Now add to it another simple exercise designed to explore the energy and urgency driving the thoughts within the form that make them comprehensible. The physical effort the exercise requires will release the language.
- Draw a line on the floor, and have the rest of the group stand along it. 'Juliet' should stand about three feet away from the line, facing towards it.
- Her objective is now to attempt to pass through the line while continuing to read the soliloquy as verse.
- The rest of the group have to try to prevent her from crossing the line.

Another interesting exercise designed further to sensitize actors to the potential of using verse as dramatic language is to play a kind of striptease with words. It makes the speakers more conscious of the power they can exercise over their listeners if they fully exploit the possibilities of language. I have chosen Sonnet 91, and numbered each line to help the speakers remember to treat them separately.

1 Some glory in their birth, some in their skill,
2 Some in their wealth, some in their body's force;
3 Some in their garments, though new-fangled ill;
4 Some in their hawks and hounds, some in their horse;
5 And every humour hath his adjunct pleasure,
6 Wherein it finds a joy above the rest;
7 But these particulars are not my measure,
8 All these I better in one general best.
9 Thy love is better than high birth to me,
10 Richer than wealth, prouder than garments' cost,
11 Of more delight than hawks and horses be;

12 And having thee of all men's pride I boast
13 Wretched in this alone, that thou mayst take
14 All this away, and me most wretched make.

You will need some simple props and a few pieces of costume in order to ensure that, at the start of the exercise, everyone is wearing at least thirteen pieces of clothing or personal effects that they can easily and quickly remove, e.g. a hat, two gloves, scarf, glasses, bangle, jacket, shoes, socks, shirt, trousers/skirt. Start by getting them to work individually on their sonnet, observing the form of the verse and, at the end of each line, removing one of the thirteen articles until, by the time they reach the last line of the sonnet, they have shed them all. What this game achieves is a heightening of the process of revelation that the verse form delightfully and artfully facilitates. As the sonnet progresses, layers are peeled away to leave the speaker metaphorically naked at the final line; everything has been said, there are no more secrets. If individuals practise this a few times, trying not to let it slow down the pace of the verse too much, they will begin to enjoy that sense of holding back momentarily the next revelation, giving the speaker a powerful sense of being in control. The art of this is in being able to sense just how long you can hold out before the next revelation. Sometimes it is only a heartbeat; sometimes it can feel like an eternity. Try getting individuals to perform the sonnet (with the accompanying actions) to the rest of the group, experimenting all the time with what will and what will not work for the listeners. Finally, each person should say the sonnet to the whole group while simultaneously imagining the striptease.

Improvising

Another useful way of working on Shakespeare is to encourage people to do something that, in everyday life if not always in rehearsals, they are very good at – improvising. If the workshop leader uses the text to provide an initial stimulus, then the imagination of the group let loose on it may well throw up interesting perspectives on the play's meaning. The problem is how to set up an improvisation. A theatre director who makes good use of improvisation in her rehearsals is Phyllida Lloyd. Working on *Pericles* in 1995 at the Royal National Theatre, she used a great deal of improvisation in the early days of rehearsals in order to explore the very different worlds visited by Pericles in his odyssey: Antioch, Tyre, Tarsus, Pentapolis, Ephesus and Mytilene. Lloyd always gave her actors ideas to build on, but never told them what the building itself was supposed to look like. One improvisation focused on the arrival of Pericles in Tarsus, an arrival that, like that of Oedipus in Thebes, signals the end of the suffering plaguing that city. Pericles redeems the citizens from their fate. Lloyd began by giving the following brief but concise ideas for the actors to build on: Tarsus was a 'broken-down world', and in their forthcoming improvisation the actors were to remember what Tarsus once had been (a rich and prosperous city). They should bear in mind 'that Tarsus was a city now struck by famine; that its leader's attempt to intercede with the gods on behalf of the people had failed; that the arrival of Pericles is, at first, terrifying. Then comes a sense of gradual but profound relief, and finally a desire to respond positively and thankfully to the person who has delivered them.' This scenario is a good example of how to give actors a useful outline of a situation, but without giving them so much detail that their creative role is limited. There is a frame to the picture, and a narrative, but the colour and detail to bring it alive are left to the performers.

The improvisation began with a focus on constructing an icon-ography of the starving, with actors scattered round the space like victims of some horrific catastrophe: bodies lay at awkward angles, some cried out in pain, others sobbed, most were silent. Gradually some of them began to move slowly, as if in great pain, from the extremities of the rehearsal room towards its centre, to confront the one person able to stand upright: the newly arrived figure of Pericles. As the improvisation progressed, with the actors now presenting a scene of total destruction and intense despair, Douglas Hodge, as Pericles, shifted the focus and direction of the work from death and despair towards life and hope. He created a series of gestures, which, as he moved among the stricken actors, sprinkling them with water from a bowl, echoed Christ's feeding of the five thousand, not with loaves and fishes, but with, as if it were, the water of life. His actions triggered a revival of the supine bodies of the citizens and, having restored their bodies with water, Pericles began to restore their souls too by taking a trumpet from a box, and with it, slowly, one by one, making the citizens of Tarsus literally begin to dance for joy. As the actors danced and began to make their own music by clapping, singing and stamping their feet, they took Pericles and placed him on a low trolley, drawing him around the stage and following in his wake. One actor picked up a paper umbrella found lying around in the rehearsal room, unfurled it, and used it to shade the head of the redeemer of Tarsus, creating, consciously or unconsciously, a classic image of colonialism. It was a powerful image thrown up by the improvisation, and one that survived into the final production.

The other example from this same production comes from an improvisation begun by an exercise led by the actor Kathryn Hunter. (It worked well in the case of *Pericles*, but it would also provide a very interesting way to begin an exploration of the opening of *The Tempest*.) Here the action begins with the crew onboard a storm-tossed ship attempting to manage the vessel in the face of huge and finally overwhelming natural forces. The cries of the boatswain and the crew as they struggled for control were integrated into the movements and energies explored in Hunter's seascape improvisation. This lasted for about fifteen minutes, centring on the world of Ephesus and the iscovery, then recovery, of Pericles' wife, Thaisa. She has been buried at sea by her husband, who presumed her dead, and her coffin washed ashore at Ephesus. In this scene the audience witnesses the priest Cerimon's extraordinary act of bringing Thaisa back to life, and then ushering her to the seclusion and safety of the temple of Diana. Once again, before work began Phyllida Lloyd gave the company a direction: the scene was to have 'the energy of the storm (when Thaisa is put into the cask and placed in the sea) carried on into it'.

The first challenge was to discover that energy for themselves. Hunter asked everyone to come on to the rehearsal floor, find a place on his or her own, and remember a real place that they knew, where the sea could be seen. She asked people to shut their eyes and remember what the place looked like, the beach and the coastline. When that image was firmly established, she encouraged the actors to make an adjustment by responding with their bodies to the idea that they were actually themselves outside, in the open air, seeing the sea from that place. Next they were to imagine themselves as having walked slowly *into* the sea, first up to their ankles, then to their knees and finally to their thighs. As they stood there, she asked them to begin to move, and slowly add the sounds the sea makes as they did so. Hunter asked people to try to feel the stronger movement *under* the sea, trying all the time to breathe into the motion, feeling the volume of water, which is heavy and very powerful, and gradually growing stronger under a darkening sky. The actors stayed on the same spot on the floor although their bodies were moving, feeling the sea coming up through their toes, into their legs, swirling into their backs, and finally into the cavities of their heads. The actors also had to concentrate on the wind that began to move greater and greater volumes of water and, when the weight and pressure of that water became too much, then and only then could they move off the spot, but always they must try to stay on it. The strength of the imaginary waves was tangible but invisible. Actors began to hold on to imaginary objects in order to help them maintain their position and resist being swept away. They searched for something to help them on to dry land, some of them clinging to one another as the storm increased in ferocity.

Eventually, and spontaneously, they formed a human chain to lead them to shelter from the storm that gradually abated. All this was achieved without any mechanical aid or amplification. It did create a surge of energy in the company, which, as Phyllida Lloyd had wished, carried on into the scene. Having the actors establish, with the aid of a few properties, a kind of clinic where Ceremon, with the aid of some helpers, was assisting the night's casualties, began this. Two actors then took the improvisation into its final stage by discovering the coffin in which the 'dead' queen is concealed. Hunter (who was to play Ceremon in the final performance) orchestrated the gradual revival of Thaisa, binding her arms gently in scented cloths, giving orders for a fire to be lit, for 'rough' music to be played. Then, as some actors began drumming, everyone in the room gathered round and made a deep humming sound, hands outstretched over the body as if in benediction, seemingly willing Thaisa back to life. Ceremon's voice grew stronger in an incomprehensible shaman-like chant, while everyone else was by now blowing or banging something, creating a terrific, climactic sound that would raise the dead. Suddenly Thaisa leapt from the coffin in terror, frightening everyone, including the actors, and screaming, 'Save my baby, save my baby!' None of this had been pre-planned, and it was a wonderful theatrical moment in which energy was released. The improvised work from this session survived virtually intact in the final production. Although the director and Kathryn Hunter had set it up, the improvisation worked because it succeeded in tapping the imagination of the whole company. Moreover, it succeeded in involving everyone in the making of the scene, all at the same time.

I have given a lot of space to these examples of the way in which improvisation was used in one particular production of Shakespeare, because the director's skilful use of improvisation enriched the actors' individual understanding of many of the issues in *Pericles*, and would have done likewise for any other group of people working on the play. From the perspective of how to integrate improvisation into a workshop, the exercises are noteworthy because they did not rely on one or two individuals, but succeeded in involving and engaging the whole company of twenty-three performers.

A very high level of participation and creative energy was forthcoming through this workshop method. Unlike some more traditional rehearsals, the one conducted by Phyllida Lloyd encouraged shared, collaborative participation. As her choreographer Jonathan Lunn said, 'the way we have been working has been wonderful (and also crucial) to build a company within a short space of time. We don't start off from day one with a hierarchy that has already been established. Everyone and anyone has an opportunity to create images and sounds and to share in the making of meanings, irrespective of how many (or how few) actual lines of text they have been cast to speak in the play itself.' That is exactly what a good Shakespeare workshop, whether it lasts for half a day or a week, should strive to achieve. The method of working eschews the traditional theatre, educational and business hierarchies in which the director, teacher or manager is at the top of a pyramid of responsibility, with the leading actors, brighter students, self-confident employees just below them, and the majority – especially those who are less confident and experienced – very much at the bottom.

The rehearsals of *Pericles* succeeded in devising genuinely useful improvisations because the director herself did *not* rely on improvisation, but planned appropriately and in advance. She thought carefully about what to say to the actors, as well as what not to say. She offered them enough material to get started, but never said what she wanted them to achieve by way of an end product. The actual playing choices were always left open to the actors. In working like this she gave the company not only an opportunity to become collectively and collaboratively engaged in constructing meaning, but a sense of the shared ownership of the production. Workshop leaders should, ideally, always be facilitators of the creativity of others; their objective is not to direct, manipulate or steer the group towards a particular vision, nor is it to focus on any one individual or group at the expense of the whole. Good workshops engage and enthuse those who take part in them by harnessing their energy and using it to stimulate and focus creative activity. At the end of each exercise should come a sense of satisfaction at having succeeded in making something together, not necessarily in having made it 'correctly' but in having completed it. Ideally all workshops should try to conclude with the group presenting something that they have made together.

Planning to Improvise

Another Shakespeare play, but one that uses very different kinds of language, is *A Midsummer Night's Dream*. At the opening of the play the action moves from the world of the Court at Athens to the world of the Mechanicals, and from there to the magical world of the Forest. A workshop leader could set up improvisations designed to explore the different aspects of these worlds.

For the purposes of the improvisation, read the first scene of the play, asking people to think of the world of the Court as an uptight, formal and strictly hierarchical place with lots of petty rules and regulations, where personal freedom is severely restricted. In this world two couples (Theseus and Hippolyta, and Lysander and Hermia), who are desperately in love, are prevented from fulfilling their natural desires by laws requiring obedience or death. When the scene has been read, ask the company to improvise the encounter at the Court between the Duke, the lovers, and Hermia's father, Egeus. Make the restrictions that the laws of Athens impose upon its people into an actual physical restriction of the actors. Deny their freedom of movement by allowing them to use only a very limited range of gestures (nothing flamboyant or extravagant), and bind their legs together loosely with some cloth, giving them only enough room to take very small steps, nothing more. If they wish to speak, they can use their own words or words taken from the scene, but they are only allowed to speak a total of three times for as long as the improvisation lasts. When they do speak, they must *never* say more than three consecutive words at a time. All the group (under exactly the same conditions) should be involved as courtiers, servants, etc., who observe the drama, comment upon it and respond to it.

The world of the Mechanicals is dominated by their overriding desire and need (often frustrated) to make a play. After reading Scene ii, have the actors improvise, in small groups and using their own words, the Pyramus and Thysbe story, not as a comic parody, but as a romantic tragedy. Remind them of Theseus' rebuke to the mocking courtiers who watch the final performance in the last act: 'For never anything can be amiss/When simpleness and duty tender it.'

The fairy world of the Forest is characterized by lost humans and argumentative superhumans, and by a natural world turned upside down by a quarrel. As Peter Brook long ago pointed out (in *The Empty Space*), a major problem for any director coming to this play is how to create the magic world in such a way as to convince a largely sceptical, materialistic twentieth-century audience of its efficacy. A simple but demanding improvisation that would explore ideas of magic would be to ask people to work, at first individually and later together, to create their own version of the magic creatures that people the forest. How are they to be represented? Are they to be superhuman or even non-human? Or do they take recognizable human forms, like the lost boys in *Peter Pan*?

As a starting point, ask participants to begin by recalling their dreams. Can they recall a dream in which things happened to them that could not have happened in reality? Have they any experience of paranormal phenomena, and if so what is it? Move from the sharing of this information among the group to a focus on how the individual might choose to represent one of the supernatural inhabitants of the forest. They might explore the creation of some kind of creature that moves and communicates in an unusual way; but if they do, tell them that only one part of their body (head, a hand, a foot) is superhuman. They may choose to give the supernatural being an external appearance of normality, but every now and then to make the façade split to reveal something unusual, perhaps threatening.

Another exercise that could be undertaken by the whole group would be to explore the power that the magic world has over the mortals. In the Forest some of the inhabitants are visible to one another, and some are not. Try blindfolding those who cannot see the supernatural beings (but can hear one another), and have their movements guided by those who can see and whose sight gives them power to control. The blindfolded mortals' feelings of confusion, of being lost and at the mercy of powers they can feel but cannot see, will give an edge to their language.

Improvising with Objects

Improvisations don't have to involve everyone in the group, or last for a long time. Sometimes you can use a brief improvisation to help an individual actor with a specific acting problem. For example, in a rehearsal of *The Tempest* that I was directing, the actor playing Caliban was finding difficulty with the speech from Act 1 Scene ii that begins:

This island's mine, by Sycorax my mother,
Which thou tak'st from me.

He couldn't find the sense of outrage that he believed the situation required of him because the island was simply, to him, an abstract idea and not a reality. He also found it difficult to feel the huge difference in status and power that exists between Caliban and Prospero. To help with both of these acting problems I asked Caliban to bring to the next rehearsal something that belonged to him, and to which he felt a deep attachment, while Prospero was to bring a pair of boots. The following day Caliban came to the rehearsal carrying a small silver cross, which, with some mild embarrassment, he explained had been given to him as a child, and which he had always kept with him, although he never wore it. Prospero brought wellingtons. In working again on the speech I asked Prospero wear his boots, while Caliban was asked to play the scene in bare feet. The absence of his shoes helped the actor, making him feel literally more undressed than Prospero, and therefore more vulnerable. Prospero was also given the cross, and held it up in front of Caliban, flaunting his possession of what rightfully belonged to Caliban. The actor tried hard to snatch it back, and as the two of them chased and almost fought for possession of the cross, Caliban grew more and more outraged at what was happening to him. That small but significant object had become for the actor the island, *his* island, *and his* identity, which Prospero had stolen.

After a few minutes, Prospero was instructed to allow Caliban to take the cross back, and hold it. When he then spoke those opening lines of the speech, he simultaneously showed the cross, not only to Prospero, but to the rest of the company, who had been watching the improvisation. His language was completely grounded in an emotion that was real for him, and therefore for everyone else who saw and heard him.

Objects have other, less symbolic but equally useful, purposes. Watching and listening to people trying to make their way through a long and difficult speech from Shakespeare can sometimes make the journey look like an ordeal. It is not uncommon for even experienced actors simply to reach a point in the text where they stop, unable to go on. Whatever it is that is blocking their progress, it can be helpful in these circumstances to give them a concrete action to perform while they speak. For example, if you ask an actor, as he speaks one of Hamlet's soliloquies, first to take off his shoes and socks, and then, after carefully examining his feet, put them back on again, the focus the action creates deflects attention away from whatever it was in the language that was causing the block.

Improvising with Language

Improvising with language is also productive when it is shared by, for example, asking two actors to make a monologue into a duologue, or dividing up a lengthy speech into an exchange between three or four people. Useful work comes from improvised situations in which the actors are given an entirely different context from that suggested by the play. For example, try dividing Prospero's 'Ye elves of hills, brooks, standing lakes and groves' speech (*The Tempest*, Act 5 Scene i) into an angry exchange between two people. Give both of them an identity (they could be lovers) and a scenario: they are in bed, it is late, but neither can go to sleep until they have concluded an argument, which has been rumbling on for days. They cannot raise their voices because other people in the house may be disturbed. Relocating the language in this way not only proves how extraordinarily flexible it is, but helps actors as both performers and listeners to revitalize text and discover hidden possibilities within it.

Another exercise in which you play with language by removing it from its given context and placing it in another involves using small groups of actors. Two groups of four or five face each other across the space. Each is given a collective identity, e.g. one tarts, the other vicars; or one football hooligans, the other Members of Parliament. One of the groups (say, the tarts) begins by hurling actual lines or phrases from the play at the vicars, aiming to insult them, or seduce them, or embarrass them. In their turn the vicars now use other extracts that they have chosen in order to preach at the tarts, urging their repentance, or else threatening them with hell and damnation.

I remember a friend of mine who is a teacher telling me once that he knew that his teaching of Shakespeare was finally having some impact on his students when he overheard one of them during break spontaneously insulting another student by calling him a 'shag-hair'd loon'. All of the work in this chapter is intended to increase the confidence of individuals likewise to claim ownership of complex language. It is also an attempt to demythologize speaking Shakespeare by showing how simple but effective exercises can create an active and lively engagement with words. Each of the exercises improves the facility to use language in all its aspects, thus making for a greater understanding not only of how Shakespeare uses it, but of how individuals can use their *own* language with confidence, pleasure and skill in the daily dramas of meetings, debates, public speaking and so on.

4 Mask, Chorus and Text

Alternative Theatre Languages

One of the advantages of choosing to work with ancient plays such as classical Greek tragedies is the relative unfamiliarity and absence of inhibiting preconceptions trailing behind them. Unlike the early modern plays of Shakespeare and his contemporaries, we know very little about how they were performed or who performed them. The names of their dramatists are obscured by history, and their language is not familiar to our ears like household words. There isn't, as far as I know, any enthusiasm to build a replica of the ancient Athenian theatre of Dionysus in London, and to restage the ancient canon there. No one really knows (although some scholars speculate) how these plays worked in performance, and what they might have meant to their original performers and audiences is probably irrecoverable. They are now a theatrical curiosity, occasionally staged in Britain by the two major national companies, and seldom (professionally) by anyone else. Their relative absence from British contemporary theatrical culture, and their marginality within the school curriculum, affords a unique opportunity to rediscover a powerful and, to modern eyes and ears, alternative theatre language.

If people pause to think about the performance of drama in the pre-Christian era, what probably comes to mind is a vague but impressive image of a large number of performers, probably wearing some kind of mask, standing together in a huge stone amphitheatre open to the sky, and chanting in unison an archaic text of operatic intensity and cosmic resonance to an audience of thousands. The scale of the whole event – the size of the cast, the auditorium and the audience – as well as the vast range of human and emotional geography to be traversed, appears unfamiliar and probably daunting. From the spectators' point of view, the performance conventions could not be more different from those of the current forms of popular dramatic representation: cinema and television. Today there is little room – literally *or* metaphorically

– in our performative experiences for such epic occasions and, for a whole variety of reasons (not the least of which are social and economic), we produce and consume dramas preoccupied with domestic issues tailored to a human scale.

The decision to explore a classical text through a series of workshops is not, however, an excuse to engage in a barren process of theatrical archaeology. These plays make demands unlike those of most contemporary dramas, but they also contain opportunities to connect the drama of the past with personal and political issues of the present. They can liberate us from the conventions of psychological naturalism: the mask removes the constraints normally imposed by gender casting, enabling women to portray men, and men to play women; the Chorus requires a high level of narrative skill, physical dexterity and spatial awareness, and the text, especially if translated in verse, requires a disciplined approach and a sensitivity to language over character. The form demands that the individual actor's body become sensitized to those of other actors, if the delicate choreography of choric movement is not to be disrupted. The voice of the actor will still be heard, not just as a solo instrument, but as part of an orchestra of sound.

Ultimately this is why these ancient texts are so productive in the context of a workshop, because in order to realize how such plays can be made to work as performances, the individual must be willing to sacrifice, if only temporarily, his or her personal artistic agenda to the overriding needs of the group's as a whole. The plays cannot be rehearsed and studied in a workshop in such a way as to release their potential unless individuals are prepared to learn collective physical and rhetorical skills, and to recognize their mutual dependence.

The importance the text in performance places upon the group, rather than on any individual, runs contrary to much of contemporary theatre, educational and business practice. The need to learn particular techniques and skills also militates against the carefully constructed mystique of individual creativity. Just as in the National Curriculum, for example in the teaching of English, the private act of reading has been allowed to eclipse the value of collaborative learning afforded by drama, so in the making of much of our current theatre the work of the ensemble has become marginalized in favour of the foregrounding of individual performances. Rehearsing or workshopping Greek tragedy immediately reminds those who take part of the fundamentally cooperative nature of its conventions. The relative novelty of this, added to its unfamiliar technical demands, provides an excellent opportunity to pause and reflect upon our conventional processes of making and reading performance; perhaps even to relearn the potential of ensemble acting and rediscover the pleasures of collaborative action.

In preparing a workshop strategy to explore some of the performance possibilities of Greek tragedies it is best to divide the focus of the work between three established elements of the original conventions: Mask, Chorus and Text. That potent combination can be frustrating and problematic for contemporary performers, but it can also unlock the often latent potential of the human voice and body as vehicles for expression, and can cause some surprises.

Masks

In 1996, after more than a decade's absence, Peter Hall returned to the National to direct Sophocles' *Oedipus the King* and *Oedipus at Colonus* in new translations by Ranjit Bolt. The majority of the cast of twenty-one who rehearsed the Oedipus plays before they opened in the ancient theatre at Epidaurus, Greece, and subsequently in the Olivier Theatre at the National, had no experience at all of either classical Greek tragedy or of acting in masks. For whatever reason – perhaps a fear of theatrical clichés, perhaps a wariness of the sheer emotional scale of the language, perhaps simply not wanting to have to perform in a mask – it had never been part of their professional experience. Of course, all acting involves, in an important sense, the putting on of masks, and even today many actors still persist in the largely technically redundant but still significant ritual exercise of putting on make-up before performing. Modern lighting may have made make-up unnecessary, but the need that actors feel to employ a rite of transition, signalling their transformation from personal to professional role, remains.

Masks in contemporary society carry a range of associations (many of them negative) from disguise and deceit to something to hide behind. They can be worn during celebratory social theatre, often by children, at Hallowe'en and in carnival, and have their uses in therapy and, as protection, at work. Theatre historians may know the masks used in *commedia dell'arte*, and non-Western drama, but (with the notable exception of Trestle Theatre Company) they are not much used in theatre in Britain. However, mask work is fundamental to what acting is about because it allows the wearer to be truthful. The actual mask that is put on in a workshop gives the wearer permission to express feelings that the daily social mask, your everyday face in the mirror, usually chooses to conceal. Once the features that distinguish you as an individual are concealed, another, usually hidden self can be released, and the social mask in which we invest so much significance can temporarily be discarded. It does not, of course, follow that people in masks immediately become anarchic creatures, dangerous to themselves and others; but in a workshop in which masks are used the mask wearers are helped to experiment with how they move, how they relate to others, and to experience how in or out of touch they are with a range of different emotions. Masks afford privacy (they hide the face) while also giving a very public persona with which to begin to negotiate the situations thrown up in the workshop. Masks can help to relax and free their wearers and strengthen the bonds between group members. They can release tension as the face of the masker gradually unlocks beneath the mask.

An Act of Possession?

The tragic mask remains a powerful symbol of dramatic art which, in the case of Greek tragedy, looks at horror without blinking, and with a mouth always open to speak of the unspeakable. As far as actors are concerned, they rapidly discover that masks are certainly not a 'safe' refuge for a lazy actor to hide behind. Not only do they reveal rather than conceal the person wearing it, but they can surprise and unsettle the wearer in unexpected ways. There are plenty of stories, not all of them apocryphal, of actors being unable to cope with masks, and breaking down emotionally while wearing them. Putting on a mask may liberate the wearer, but it can also become the trigger for an act of possession in which the consciousness can be temporarily but radically altered.

At one of the early rehearsals of Peter Hall's Oedipus company in which masks were being worn, an extraordinary event occurred that shocked and perplexed the company. In an improvisation during the workshop involving all twenty-one actors in mask, the suggestive power of the mask temporarily threatened to overcome at least one of them, who became possessed by powerful emotions that he could not fully control. The improvisation centred on the idea of the illness, suffering and plague that ravishes Thebes at the beginning of *Oedipus Rex*. The actors were establishing this when one of them broke down in paroxysms of grief. He wept and wept and couldn't stop. The rest of the

company continued with the improvisation but reacted to the manifes-
tations of distress in different ways. Some moved quickly to help the
stricken figure, attempting unsuccessfully to raise him from the floor
where he had slumped. Others tried to hold him, to comfort him.
Nothing could stop his crying, which seemed to come from deep within
him, and shook his whole body. One actor actually moved to where
he was lying and, instead of offering help, kicked him. It wasn't a hard
kick, but it was still shocking to observe. It was a desperate attempt to
stop this graphic and almost unbearable demonstration of suffering.
The improvisation continued for some time, but the actor's harrowing
tears, although at times muted, were never absent from it. When finally
it ended, there was a palpable sense of relief, not least from the actor
whose mask had prompted this invasion of grief. He had not been
prompted by the director to act in this way, and could not explain why
he had behaved as he did. It may have been that the mask raised the
stakes, and that during the exercise his behaviour changed from actoral
to actual, causing him to pass through a barrier of repressed emotion.
Whatever it was, the mask unblocked it.

Workshop Strategies

Of course, a mask can be anything from a paper bag over your head
to a carefully and skilfully made lifelike representation of a human face,
complete with hair. Certainly when undertaking a mask workshop the
quality of the masks themselves is very important. In choosing them
you have to ask yourself what you want the workshop to achieve.
If you are using masks as a device, for example, physically to liberate
a particularly self-conscious group of adolescents (and masks will
perform that function), then almost anything that covers the face
will do. In this case you will not require a lengthy period of preparation
prior to asking the group members to wear the masks. They are there
simply as a disguise that helps facilitate a heightened physical interaction with others. The kind of plain masks that can be bought cheaply
from any novelty shop will certainly make the body of the wearer freer
than it otherwise would be, and will often succeed in producing a range
of expressive physical movement. Such masks, however, are unlikely to
help their wearers make greater use of their vocal potential or sustain
interesting work. They help physically, because they offer a degree
of anonymity, but that anonymity is immediately punctured by the
undisguised voice of the wearer. Masks that clearly signal their associ-

ation with a well-known fictional character, such as Mickey Mouse, or masks of animals or birds, are really of little use in a workshop, because they immediately tend to dictate to their wearers how they should respond while wearing them, closing down rather than opening up acting choices. Plain and inexpensive masks do have a useful function, but if what you want to achieve is more than simple disguise, you will need something better.

To facilitate a creative and imaginative engagement between the mask and the mask wearer, and to sustain a relationship that will grow and develop over time, you will need high-quality, well-made character masks. If you do not have access to such masks, then you have a choice: either to make them or buy them from a mask-maker. Either way it won't be cheap, in terms of either human or material resources; but it will pay dividends in what a mask workshop can achieve.

If you announce in advance that a workshop will be using character masks, those who turn up on the first day will be eager to get hold of them pretty quickly. In my experience, it is more profitable in the long term to make them wait, and to begin to prepare to wear the masks in the following way.

FACES AND MASKS

- Have people move around the room, and as they are doing this, ask them to look at one another. They need to be encouraged to look carefully, and get used to allowing themselves to be looked at.
- Give them at least five minutes before offering the opportunity to stand still. Choose one person to focus on, and look at her or him carefully, starting with the face. This should not be a casual glance, but a detailed study of the body and body language of another person. Note the length of their hair, the shape of their mouth, colour of their eyes, etc. Look at their body, at what they are wearing and how comfortable (or uncomfortable) they appear to be. What impression does that person make on the observer?
- Now ask everyone to move around the space, and as they do so to look at the whole group. This will take some time. Finally, ask everyone to be still, close their eyes and try to compose a mental snapshot featuring all the group members. Once that image is established, ask people to consider, while retaining the image in their head, how it is organized: Who is at the front, who is at the rear? Has anyone been missed out?
- Now work in twos sitting on the ground facing a partner, within

touching distance. For the next five minutes both need to look at one another's face. Each should try as far as possible to dissociate from any personal knowledge of their partner, and concentrate on their face and head as if what is seen is an actual mask.

- Encourage people to absorb as much detail as they can: texture, colouring of the skin, eyes and hair, the bone structure. The process is helped if, from time to time, both explore the texture of the face and hair by lightly touching them.

- This is almost bound to make people self-conscious, and as a result they often want to giggle and laugh. Don't discourage them: it is a useful way of discharging tension. As both become more familiar and at ease with the exercise, they should try shutting their eyes for a moment to see how clearly they can recall the 'mask' opposite. Ask them to test the accuracy of their memory.

- As the exercise continues, ask people to try to imagine what it would be like if they could, by means of some magic power, literally put on the face/mask that they have been studying. How might it make them feel? How would they move? What voice (if any) would they have?

- When they feel ready to try, ask them to reach out and take something from their partner – a watch, a ring, a jacket, anything – and sit with the object for a time before putting it on, or holding it. Then, reaching out with both hands and touching their partner's face gently on either side of the head, they should imagine, as their hands move back slowly, that they are actually carrying the weight and volume of their partner's mask/head.

- They have magically removed the mask from its owner and claimed it as their own. This stage of the exercise must be done carefully but deliberately, and when the newly acquired mask/face is worn, each pair should turn slowly away from their partner towards another point in the room and remain still.

- From now on they are looking at the room and the people in it through different eyes. Get them to take a long look. Ask them what they are seeing (but do *not* require them to respond orally). Who and what can they see, and how do they now react to seeing it?

- When individuals can, and only if they feel they can, they should try getting up and moving around. Encourage people to concentrate at first on trying to find the right physical language required by the mask/face. They may get no further than this, but if they can, and without forcing it, try getting them to focus on whatever feelings are suggesting themselves; the mask/face should react, if at all, without being consciously manipulated.

- It is important not to force the pace of this exercise, and not to do anything that feels awkward or false. If people feel that, they should stop immediately, be still, shut their eyes and try to recover the lost mask. It is always possible to see a mirror reflection of 'yourself' by finding the original mask/face. If the mask/face can't be sustained, or if at any other time during this exercise anyone feels uncomfortable, they should simply move to one side of the room, sit quietly and watch until the others have finished.

- As people either move or remain still, you need gently to encourage them to engage with other mask/faces. How would they greet someone? How would they wish to be greeted? Is there any physical contact – handshaking, for example, or a kiss on the cheek?

- See how far this exercise will go (you can easily tell who is still focusing and who has lost it) before asking people to find their original partners and sit down facing one another.

- It is important to enact the transference of the mask/face back to the original owner as carefully as it was taken. The hands should be placed gently but firmly by the side of the head and then, feeling the weight and volume, the mask/head moved on to the partner's shoulders, letting it sit there before, in turn, receiving back their own head/mask.

Occasionally exercises like these are disturbing for some of the participants, and it is important to stress at the start that they can drop out whenever they feel like it. I always leave some time after concluding such an exercise as that described above for people to talk about the experience. Some say that they enter a kind of trance-like state, others that they felt as if they were in a dream. Most people lose track of time, and enjoy what is a highly concentrated, intimate and tactile experience; but it is an important exercise because it legitimates natural curiosity about other people, and provides a safe framework for a delicate experiment with personal identity. There is a sense in which the individual self is willingly given or loaned to someone else (a process helped by the giving and receiving of personal objects), and the letting go of that self is just as important as the temporary assumption of another.

Putting on the Mask

When you are satisfied that the individuals in the workshop can concentrate and focus for an extended period, and have begun to experience acts of personal transformation, you can move on to wearing actual masks. There are many different ways of approaching mask work, but basically I think it boils down to two choices: either you take the mask and, without hesitating, put it on, immediately look at yourself in a mirror and respond according to what kind of a charge the mask gives you; or, alternatively, you take a long time to study the mask very carefully before putting it on your head, and once it is on you never look in a mirror. Given the choice, I prefer the latter approach of letting the mask give the actor a charge before putting it on, but there are no rules about this, and having looked long and hard at the mask before wearing it, some people still feel the need to see a reflection of themselves before they can progress further.

You can give people a choice of either selecting their own mask or having the one that you choose for them. I usually have everyone spaced around the room as far apart from one another as possible before I take the masks and place one in front of each member of the group, telling them just to look at it, not touch it. Just as they did in the previous exercise with their partners' faces, they will need to try being open to whatever the mask seems to suggest to them. When they feel ready (and it is important not to rush), they can touch the mask, feel its texture and weight. Finally they can put it on.

Once everyone is masked, prompt them to look around the room at the other masked faces and, when and if they feel inclined, try moving about in the mask. Again you need to stress that when wearing the mask the performer should not try to push things too far too quickly. Participants should try to avoid demonstrating either to themselves or to an audience what they are thinking and feeling. The performer needs to be just as true underneath a mask as he or she is without one. Truthful actions are prompted by how an actor is thinking and feeling, and if those thoughts and feelings aren't connected to appropriate actions, the mask, far from disguising it, will magnify the falsehood. The desire, or sometimes the impatience, to express excitement or energy at the expense of that truth needs to be resisted, because if the temptation is yielded to in performance, an audience will immediately recognize the fiction. What usually happens when people are trying too hard and pushing too early in the process is a series of gestures, usually with the hands, sometimes with the head, that simply clashes horribly with the signals being emitted by the masked head. Soon, if they are not impatient, people will learn what works in the mask and what does not. For example, most people feel that they cannot physically touch their masks with their hands, and that quick naturalistic head movements feel (and look) quite wrong in a full head-mask. Almost invariably the mask requires you to do less rather than more with your body.

Costume

One of the most familiar daily rituals throughout our adult lives occurs in the morning when we look at our faces in the mirror to apply make-up, shave, brush our teeth, or sometimes do all three. Our preparations to 'face the world' also include decisions on what clothes and accessories to wear. Many of us dress to suit our professional roles, because it is expected of us. Putting on those work clothes, or alternatively putting on clothes for a celebratory occasion, is also a form of masking – one that often increases our self-confidence.

To add intensity to a mask workshop, symbolically to connect the mind and body, and to stimulate the imagination, the workshop leader should be prepared to provide appropriate costumes and properties. If you can, it is best to have a generous selection of costumes – what kind depends on what masks you are using and why you are using them, but for those unfamiliar with mask work costumes that envelop the body are particularly useful, as they increase the chances of anonymity. Long scarves are also useful, because they can be worn over the head of the mask and help link it to the body of the wearer. Allow people to choose what to wear and how to wear it, but encourage them, so long as their costume is not contemporary clothes, not to wear anything on their feet. With bare feet you can more easily feel your way in the space, and this is particularly important if, as is likely, the mask restricts peripheral vision. It also doesn't help sustain a lengthy improvisation in costume and mask if you suddenly notice that underneath the costume of one of the other maskers a pair of shining white trainers protrudes! It isn't just the trainers themselves: in this work the participants should be anonymous, and therefore anything that might distinguish one individual from another (such as a watch or a ring) should be removed prior to starting.

Don't do this divesting of distinguishing marks as a casual, unimportant event, but make it central: a starting-off point in which, before they begin, the performers deliberately divest themselves of as many familiar and recognizable objects as they can. Ideally, participants in a mask workshop should undergo a physical rite of passage – perhaps a bath or shower, followed by dressing in unfamiliar and neutral clothes – before beginning work. Realistically, however, use a table on to which people can place all their familiar personal objects: rings, necklaces, earrings, watches, etc.

Improvising in Masks

Once participants begin to feel comfortable in their masks, space opens up for the workshop leader to throw in suggestions as to how, for example, an improvisation can develop. In the Oedipus plays at the National, all the cast (except Alan Howard, who played Oedipus) were also Chorus members, and at the start of rehearsals Peter Hall wanted to play around with the idea of beginning to establish a Chorus of Theban Elders. In one of the first improvisations undertaken by the company, his injection of outside stimuli into the impro was timely, and a good example of how to use extended improvisations to develop the conventions of the drama. The improvisation began with the actors all in mask and costume, moving or sitting still, some acknowledging the presence of others, some ignoring them. After a time Hall said in a loud voice, 'Heat! [pause] Ha! Heat! [pause] Ha!' The actors hadn't anticipated the intervention and had to respond to it spontaneously. After a while he intervened again, this time by saying, 'Jocasta, our noble queen, is dead!' Once again, the actors responded spontaneously to the stimulus.

Interventions of this kind in an improvisation don't have to be spoken. At a later stage in the same exercise a long stick was rolled into the centre of the space, scattering the actors in surprise to the sides of the room. It lay there until finally someone, watched intently by the others, approached it with great caution before picking it up and waving it above his head. The tension and then the release produced a cry from the group, and the assumption of the role of leader for the wielder of the stick. As the improvisation progressed, this power relationship was explored and challenged, leadership fluctuated between individuals and groups, and actors found themselves totally caught up in a continually evolving dramatic event.

This kind of improvisation is there for the benefit of the participants and not for an audience. What these experienced professional actors got out of it could just as easily have benefited non-actors, for to sustain the work requires intense concentration and the willingness to be flexible, responding imaginatively to the events as they unfolded and not blocking them. It requires considerable physical and mental stamina, too, and the length of mask workshops should be carefully judged so as not to demand too much too soon in the learning process. From their experience in such lengthy improvisations, the National actors learnt what was possible in their masks, and what was not. They discovered that, although it was relatively easy to begin to move in a mask and, once you got used to the lack of peripheral vision, to look at other people, it was almost impossible to speak. Finding a way of moving that suited the mask was one thing, but finding a voice for it proved quite another. It was only after a very considerable period that the actors gradually began to experiment with making sounds – often unrecognizable, non-human sounds – and finally to use recognizable language while in mask. Other more technical things that emerged with this particular set of masks, which covered the whole of the actor's head but had an open mouth, was that you couldn't turn your head suddenly: it had to be a gradual movement. If you were turning away from any spectators, your body had to begin to turn first while your mask retained contact with the spectators until the last possible moment. But the work began to condition the actors' bodies and minds, like athletes, improving stamina as well as concentration, and enabling them to focus and direct their energy where and when it was most needed.

Chorus

A fundamental aspect of acting (and living) is how to work cooperatively and successfully with other people. Successful Chorus work in Greek drama demands group cooperation and coordination, and results in a genuinely shared experience and sense of purpose. Unlike most contemporary acting and most living, it does not focus on the identity or quality of any one individual, but on the group as a whole. When the masked Chorus speaks, it is virtually impossible for an audience to tell which of its many members is speaking. Although it imposes responsibility on each individual, it also requires anonymity. How, in a workshop, do you capitalize on this, and devise exercises that draw individuals together – in which they lose their isolation and gain instead a liberating and powerful identity that comes from being part of a group: the Chorus. What is a Chorus? How to you make being part of it a different experience from that of being part of a crowd? You start to address these questions as you would start any workshop, by building up the confidence of the group, and establishing them as a team.

Building the Group

HA!

- Everyone stands in a circle, legs slightly apart, arms by their sides, trying to stay relaxed but alert. The leader explains that, without warning, they are going to make a sudden movement while at the same time shouting 'Ha!'
- Demonstrate the movement (from a standing position take a small jump forward, landing with the knees bent and arms in front, elbows bent and palms facing out) together with the sound.
- The aim of the exercise is for the group to be aware of when the leader is going to do this and do it at exactly the same time. The exercise can be varied by not saying who is to move, but instead leaving it up to anyone in the group to take the initiative.

SPOT THE LEADER

- Again have everyone in a circle before selecting one person and taking him or her outside the room, where they will remain until you collect them.
- In the meantime the rest of the group decides on a leader. He or he then starts a simple movement (say, rubbing their nose with their hand), which the rest of the group copies. That movement is then changed by the leader into another, which is also mirrored by the actions of the rest.
- Once this changing pattern of movement, initiated always by the same person, is established, bring back the person from outside the room and have him or her stand in the middle of the circle. Their task is to attempt to spot the leader.

BLINDFOLD TAG

This is a simple but highly effective tag game in which, as the title suggests, some of the participants are blindfolded. It serves to heighten the senses, and makes the participants extraordinarily aware of their physical movement and the proximity of others, skills that are vital for choric movement.

- Separate the group into two halves; one half is blindfolded, the others not. The sighted players form a protective circle round the rest of the group. The workshop leader then explains that s/he will select a blindfolded 'catcher' by gently squeezing his or her shoulders.
- When the game begins, the catcher attempts to 'tag' everyone. Of course, those who are wearing blindfolds cannot tell who the catcher is, and so to tell them that they have indeed been tagged as opposed to having simply been touched by another person, the catcher will signal the 'tag' by squeezing a person's shoulders. When that happens, the tagged person should let out a loud cry, fall to the ground, then take off the blindfold and join the encircling group of onlookers.
- At first the tagging moves quickly, but as the size of the blindfolded group decreases, making it progressively more difficult for the catcher, the exercise slows down, and the movement becomes almost like slow motion as the remaining players stretch their senses in order to try to locate (and stay away from) other people.
- When, finally, the catcher has caught everyone, change around so that those who were spectators have the chance to try out the game.

THE FISH

The early rehearsals of Peter Hall's company were concerned with building a group identity and, more specifically, with working to find a collective physical language to establish the way in which the Chorus should move and respond. Michael Keegan-Dolan, the movement director, introduced a deceptively simple but significant exercise that was to be used extensively. Known variously as 'The Fish' or 'The Flight of Birds', it is based in Britain on work done by Théâtre de Complicité, a group whose considerable reputation rests on its ability to generate consistently interesting physical theatre. The objective of the exercise is to enable a group of actors to move together spontaneously as one body without recourse to a leader, like a flock of birds, turning and wheeling in the sky.

- Begin the exercise by having people working in pairs, linking arms and walking round the space.

- As they travel, ask them to vary the movement, for example, walking with bent knees, on tiptoe, crawling and so on. Each pair should try not to have one member leading the other, but to sense the time to change and follow their instincts.
- As they become more fluent in their movement, ask them to drop the physical contact but stay side by side, continuing their movement within the space.
- Keep this going for several minutes before asking couples to join with others to make groups of four, all of whom then try to move together, again without an identifiable leader, aiming for fluidity, variety and spontaneity.
- The next stage is to create groups of eight, then sixteen, until finally the whole group is moving together without any obvious leader.

THE FISH SPEAKS

If, by this stage in the work, the participants know at least one of the Chorus speeches, you can then get them to play the same game, this time not moving at all, but using language.

- Begin in pairs, asking each pair to say together an entire Chorus speech. When they have done that, they should speak it again, but this time without any agreement on who will speak the first line, or when the first speaker will stop and allow the second to begin. They should avoid the easy solution of alternating at the end of each line, but try to vary the pattern of speaking while at the same time aiming to give the impression of one voice speaking.
- As with 'The Fish', gradually increase the size of the group from two to four to eight and so on, until everyone is engaged in moving and speaking the text spontaneously. Of course, it may happen that some Chorus members speak the same line together, while others miss out entirely when the whole of the group is doing the exercise. This doesn't matter; simply have the group say the speech through at least three times, never in the same order. They need to aim, just as they have done physically, for fluidity, spontaneity and variety in the sounds they make and in what they do with the language.
- Finally, put both halves of this exercise together by first building up the group movement again in exactly the same way and, once that is established and moving freely, give them a signal to speak the text as they move.

Watching and listening to a big group moving together swiftly, confidently and finally gracefully through a relatively big space as they connect their movements with the language they are speaking produces an impressive, unpredictable and fluid image, like a microscopic organism. The exercise is significant in terms of the future movement vocabulary of the Chorus, not least because vision in the mask is often highly restricted (the National actors' masks had very little peripheral vision, like a pair of blinkers), and so, if many people are to move successfully as one, they have to learn to sense when a colleague is behind or beside them. What 'The Fish' also achieves is the recognition that, although many different voices speak the text, it is, for every individual actor, always *their* text, irrespective of who is speaking.

There are few occasions when individuals can experience being a part of such an almost overwhelmingly intense but positive group experience. Building the Chorus joins people together in mutual self-reliance and celebration. For the most part we have only pop concerts, football matches or religious revivalist meetings where we can become caught up in a crowd and experience a phenomenon that makes us feel powerful, excited and frightened all at the same time. Generally, simply being in a crowd makes us feel negative at the lack of space and the oppressive and imposed intimacy of so many proximate bodies. However, the collective energy that can be released when individuals temporarily and willingly lose themselves in a group, and suspend at least some of their social inhibitions to focus on a form of ecstatic release and celebration, is powerful to experience. In a workshop, exercises that stimulate these experiences are not entirely without the threat that they will run out of control, so that the excitement of the moment temporarily blinds individuals to the consequences of their actions. But acting is about always remaining in control, no matter how extreme the circumstances of the drama, and the workshop leader's job is to lead and not follow.

There is an understandable tendency for both actors and non-actors to distance themselves from any situation in life or in art that might appear to threaten a loss of control. Letting go, surrendering the self, even if only temporarily and partially, feels risky. The mask is one useful tool to counter our timidity, the anxiety that stops us exploring who we are and who we might become. I would not advocate generating a kind of mass hysteria on the lines of some performances by the Living Theatre of the 1960s, but there is room to help individuals unused to the extremes of classical tragedy to explore conditions such as frenzy and possession without being physically or mentally hurt in the process. To play Greek tragedy does require us to be in touch with both tragedy and terror, and if we are, so too will our audience be. The actor has to find a life for those he portrays, and that life, particularly the intensity of it, is very different from our own day-to-day experience. What marks out these particular plays is the degree of heightened tension that surrounds the actions of the characters. It seems that it always involves risk, acting on the edge of reason, the brink of control. Antonin Artaud once said that what he wanted was a theatre in which everyone felt unsafe, as if 'we are not free, and the sky can fall on our heads'. A workshop on Greek tragedy ought, at the very least, to echo that sentiment. It ought to unsettle us, to wring our senses, but it should also remind us of what we have in common, and what in time we can all expect. After all, the Greek god of drama is Dionysus, not Apollo.

Classical Greek drama offers those who play the Chorus an opportunity for the exploration of collective action, of what it might feel like to be truly part of something bigger than yourself. The focus of the audience is not on the individual Chorus member, but on the group, which offers an enticing anonymity, and through it a heightened expressive freedom.

THE WEDGE

Divide the group into two roughly equal parts, and place one half in one corner of the space, the remainder facing them on the diagonal. Keep the participants physically close and get them to form a wedge shape, with one person alone at the point of the wedge, two behind and so on. Give both groups simple but slightly different choreographed movements. For example, one group might start with the weight of the body evenly distributed, and the feet comfortably spaced apart, looking directly in front. On a signal each person takes the weight on to the left foot and steps forward in a strong movement on to the right. As the right foot comes down, the body collapses from the waist, so that the torso and head hang forward at the same time as the right foot hits the ground. Still keeping the body bent, draw the left foot up to be parallel with the right, keeping a comfortable, balanced distance between them. As the weight is transferred to the left foot, bring the right together with it and at the same time draw the body up to its full height. The other group could, for example, start from a position in which the weight is evenly distributed, and the legs are apart. At the start they could take a forward jump, both feet in the air, and on landing thrust both arms high and throw the head back. Both movements, or any variant of them you or the group chooses to make, need to be executed while the groups move towards one another in the space. Once they can do this series of actions coherently and in a disciplined way, suggest that they use some language from the text to add to the movement.

As coordination improves, so the groups can be given longer extracts of text to speak. What may surprise them is just how difficult it is to move and speak at the same time, but this is a skill that is essential in Chorus work. Although they begin with a movement that has been choreographed, it is important to stress that the groups can begin to modify and vary their movements, provided that they stay together.

SOUNDS, MOVEMENTS, SPECTATORS

Working in masks as members of a Chorus for long periods can be very tiring; it also creates a problem in that the participants are never really sure of the effect the mask and the Chorus have on an audience. The following exercise splits the group into three in order to replicate that experience. Each of the groups has to make music, perform in masks and watch and listen to the performance. One section of the group will be acting as musicians, one as masked performers and the others as the spectators.

First, you need to set up the musicians.

- Have the whole group sitting in a circle and, by slapping the floor with their hands, establishing a regular pulse. Then, while the majority continues to make the pulse, have three or four people add a rhythm; finally, as the pulse and rhythm continue together, three or four others should add a simple tune over it until all three – pulse, rhythm, melody – are heard together as 'music'.
- Divide the group into three equal parts. Each of them should begin by using the 'pulse, rhythm, melody' method of establishing sound. They should then elaborate the rhythmic and melodic sections by making sounds with found objects: coat-hangers, shoes, paper bags, doors, bottles – in fact anything available in the space.
- Set each group a specific goal: to use their 'instruments' and/or bodies to create an atmosphere that suggests a specific condition

relevant to the play. In the case of *Oedipus Rex* this might be, for one group, the plague sweeping Thebes at the start of the action. They have to find ways of suggesting that people are begging the gods to bring relief. For another it could be the intense heat and stillness of the land at noon, an atmosphere in which to accomplish the simplest action is difficult. The final group might take the idea of making a sacrifice to propitiate the gods. It might include making an offering – not an elaborate thing, but something tangible and real, like an apple.

Each group rehearses before, in turn, performing the results to the others, who should have their eyes closed in order to heighten their imaginative response. If the listeners don't know the others' objectives, it will be interesting to see whether they can guess what they are signalling. When all three have performed their pieces (each should last no more than five minutes) and everyone has listened and commented on the results, move on to playing, performing and spectating.

The group who will provide the sounds for the performers should place themselves so that they can see the actors clearly. The focus of the masked performers should be on the audience. At a signal from you, the musicians begin to establish the framework – for example, the heat and stillness of Thebes – as the Chorus enters. What then happens should be improvised by both the choric group and the musicians, but within the atmospheric framework supplied by the latter. The Chorus must listen to the sounds and try to respond to them spontaneously.

All three groups should experience making music, performing in masks and costumes, and watching and listening. This division of tasks gives a more rounded perspective on key elements of performance and stresses their mutual dependence. It also affords an important opportunity to experience the relationship between physical representation and music.

Text

The reality of any period of lengthy study, whether it takes the form of rehearsals or a series of workshops, is that the majority of participants will sooner or later experience lengthy periods of intense boredom, accompanied by feelings of disempowerment. These will be enlightened with only occasional flashes of insight and an elusive sense of being in control. However much fun there is to be had in establishing the group, exploring the masks and improvising, sooner or later everyone comes up against a wall that halts their progress. They won't all meet the wall at the same time, but you can be sure it will be there.

The early stages of a workshop will be controlled and directed by the workshop leader; it should feel like a safe and structured experience that introduces the problems and opportunities of the tasks ahead. However, the objective of the workshop leader will ultimately be to hand back responsibility for what happens to the individuals who make up the group. When that finally occurs, they will recognize that if their work is to progress, it won't be easy or straightforward, and certainly it might not feel like fun any more. People have to be prepared to push themselves, to work and to work hard if the wall is to be overcome.

In the case of the Peter Hall company, the wall they hit wasn't built of masks or made of the Chorus; it was the text itself that proved the major obstacle. The actors in Hall's company found the poetic form of Ranjit Bolt's translations of Sophocles' Oedipus plays (rhythmic, alliterative and rhyming) very difficult to master. Although the basic rules of verse speaking had been learnt, it took time before they became second nature to all the actors. The discipline required and the technical demands it made ('like bagpipes, you have to keep your breath constantly topped up' – Peter Hall) were probably more familiar to singers than actors. Some of the cast found the verse awkward; it felt to them like trying to speak a foreign language. Some of the actors complained that strict observance of the metre became an unwelcome imposition, moreover one that threatened to fracture the sense of the text. Instead of freeing them, as it theoretically ought to have done, the form was becoming a prison. Hall required that they should observe the underlying pulse – 'like a dance step, it needs rigorous drilling' – not take a breath in the middle of a line; and that the end of each line should be marked by a slight but distinct upwards inflection that gave energy to the next line and, often, in the case of the Chorus, to the next speaker. Full lines should not be allowed to run on into the next line, but should be marked by a slight pause. Where there was a full stop at the end of a full line it was a signal to the actor indicating that a change of attitude, tone or pace was required. The mid-line caesura should not be allowed to hold up the energy in the line, as it sometimes did, but was there as a reminder to 'stop the brain from running on', as Alan Howard (Oedipus) put it.

Our everyday speech habits are relaxed and highly informal, and although almost all stage acting involves a use of heightened language, the actors using it would be mortified if anyone told them that they sounded unnatural. For both they and we are used to judging the quality of acting by reference to the extent that it remains invisible. All of us, when we speak, and especially when we speak in public, want to sound sincere and to convince our listeners that we believe in what we are saying. A verse text presents a big challenge to the accepted conventions of how to speak dramatic language, not least because its formal nature appears to militate against spontaneity and truthfulness. Most actors, including those of the Oedipus company, have limited experience of speaking a verse play; for the majority Shakespeare is the only model with which they are familiar. Even here, many actors, perhaps even the majority, speak a text originally written as verse as if it were prose, rather than as verse.

Verse, either blank or rhyming, is certainly not the kind of language heard every day on the street or on television, but it is a form of language that holds much promise for those (both actors and non-actors) prepared to explore it (see the section on Shakespeare's verse in Chapter 3). As with masks, the unfamiliarity of the form distances the speaker from most if not all pre-learnt conventions of dramatic discourse. Like masks, it can prise actors away from a contemporary fixation with constructing a character and make redundant that modern actors' mantra: 'Who am I, and what do I want?' In the Oedipus plays (and arguably in Shakespeare too) there is no subtext: everything the speaker needs is in the language. Verse, far from being a limitation, can open a space in which it is legitimate to experiment with the sounds and texture of that language, as well as with the literal meaning of the words. In speaking verse you have to learn to examine every word carefully, to hold it up to the light with tweezers, as it were, seeing how it fits, discovering where it belongs.

One of the most difficult aspects of verse speaking is the requirement that the speaker should not lose the energy in a line by pausing in the middle of it (this means ignoring full stops) or by running one line into the next. For example, this is the opening section of the Second Messenger's speech from *Oedipus the King* (translated by Ranjit Bolt), in which the horrified audience and on-stage Chorus learn what has happened to Jocasta and to her husband/son Oedipus:

She killed herself. You didn't see, and so
You're spared the pain of this – at any rate
The worst of it. However, I'll relate
What I recall of that poor creature's fate.
She was in a frenzy of despair.
She rushed into the hallway, and from there
Made for the marriage bed, tearing out her hair
In fistfuls. In the bedroom, first of all
She slammed the doors shut; then began to call
On Laois, long since dead, remembering
Their coupling, long ago, that was to bring
Death to her husband, she being left behind
To bear more children of a monstrous kind.

If, as a reader or an actor, you approach this speech (or indeed any
other speech written as verse) as if it were prose, you will invariably
try initially to follow the sense at the expense of the form. Thus, the
first three lines will be made into one continuous line: 'She killed
herself. You didn't see, and so you're spared the pain of this – at any
rate the worst of it.' Of course, prose could work in the delivery; it
would carry the sense. But if these lines, or the whole speech, were
treated similarly, it would fail to make the most of the dramatic opportunity afforded by the form in which it is written. This is not only
verse, but rhetorical speech, designed to be spoken aloud. Once you
begin to speak it, the problem of the form is immediately foregrounded.
If you choose to ignore the form and the conventions that define it,
the result will be a loss of tension and precision in the narrative. The
pace will slow, and the speech, instead of projecting a searing image
on to the mind's eye of the listener, will instead almost inevitably
become a speech about the effect that witnessing the events had on the
Messenger.

In this speech, as in the case of Juliet's soliloquy cited in the previous
chapter, the verse acts as a framework that is continually having to
struggle to contain the powerful emotions threatening to overwhelm
the clarity and distance needed if an audience is fully to imagine the
event for itself. If the speaker doesn't run on the lines, and instead
adds a heartbeat's pause after 'so' and 'rate', the listener senses the
weight of 'You're spared' and 'The worst of it'. Or take another example:
it is not simply that Jocasta was 'tearing out her hair' but that she was

'tearing out her hair/In fistfuls'. The listener should sense that the Messenger is fighting to hold on to the details of what he has seen, not allowing either them or himself to be lost in an ocean of generalized horror. If this speech works, the listener will remember what happened and how it happened, will see in his or her imagination the details of those terrible events behind the closed doors of the palace as clearly as if they had been there.

The distancing of the audience by the form in which the events are narrated to them is exactly what, thousands of years later, Bertolt Brecht wanted to achieve in his version of Epic theatre. In an essay called 'The Street Scene' he talks of an imaginary situation in which someone is the sole witness to a terrible car accident. Having witnessed the event, and been harrowed by it, the witness is subsequently asked to explain in detail what happened. He cannot remember the detail because he is too emotionally caught up in the suffering that ensued. He can describe that suffering, even relive it, but however heartfelt and genuine his response is, ultimately it is of no use to anyone because nothing can be learnt from it that might prevent future accidents from happening. The distancing effects of mask and verse make audiences emerging from *Oedipus the King* not just recall the horror of Jocasta's death and Oedipus' self-mutilation, but help them to understand the wider significance and meaning of their actions.

The need to observe the form of the verse is not restricted to the lengthy narratives of the various messengers in Greek tragedy. Look at the following short extract from Bolt's translation of *Oedipus the King* in which I have highlighted the stresses in the line and indicated where one line ends and another begins. Oedipus is confronting the blind prophet Tiresias. The rhythm here is iambic – there are ten beats in each of these lines, five stressed and five unstressed – but some of the lines are broken, the first started by Tiresias and finished by Oedipus, the second started by Tiresias and finished by Oedipus. When spoken, the stresses are not heavily marked, but they are there to ensure that the rhythm is even, and that the rapid-fire pace of the exchange is emphasized. Lines are divided between speakers but the energy is continuous:

OEDIPUS You **mock** the **mind** that **won** – will **win** the **day.**

TIRESIAS That **stroke** of **luck's destroyed** you.

OEDIPUS **Should I care?**

I **saved** this city.
TIRESIAS I must **go**. You **there** –

Boy – **come** with **me** and **guide** me.
OEDIPUS **Let** him, **then**.

And **maybe** I shall **have** some **peace again**.

Take this section, or try working in pairs on the following more metrically complicated but fierce exchange between Oedipus and his brother-in-law Creon. Use the exercise 'Spanish Steps', i.e. where the person speaking stamps the rhythm with his or her feet, as they say the words, in the manner of a flamenco dancer. This will help to identify and then internalize the rhythm.

OEDIPUS No. It's death for you.
CREON From what you say
    It seems you won't believe me or give way.
    I can see that you're not sane.
OEDIPUS Not so.
    I watch my interests.
    CREON And should watch mine.
    OEDIPUS No.
    You're a traitor.
CREON What if you're a fool?
OEDIPUS I must rule.
CREON So you must. But don't misrule.
OEDIPUS The city!
CREON I'm a citizen, like you,

One of the benefits of making the form your friend, as the academic and director John Barton once put it, is that it allows the individual speaker to experience a sense of being in control of the language, of never being in the position where the events threaten to overwhelm and finally sink you in a sea of generalized emotion.

Speaking a long verse narrative, or sustaining a brittle interpersonal exchange while wearing a mask, to a mass audience requires technique. But so too does all rhetorical speech; it is simply that verse makes us more aware of the necessity for it. Using dramatic language effectively is not simply a matter of having the right instincts, the 'right' kind of voice, of looking the part, or of having a charismatic presence. It is not something that comes naturally; it has to be learnt.

There are simple but effective exercises that, for example, help a Chorus pass the lines between them with greater sensitivity to the nuances and texture, and that help resist the particular temptation to skid through polysyllabic words. If in your work you have decided to have all the lines spoken by the Chorus spoken as if by everyone, listening intently to every word becomes crucial in order to pick up and hand on the narrative without losing either energy or subtlety.

PASS THE TEXT

- Divide the text so that everyone has at least two lines to speak, and all know the order in which it will be spoken.
- Have people lying down on their backs, bodies close together, with their heads facing the centre of the circle. In this position ask them to speak the text from one or more of the Choruses quietly, but with emphasis, trying to pick up the line from the previous speaker in such a way as to create, for the listeners, a seamless development.
- Use a football in this next game, which is designed to demonstrate that whoever has the responsibility of speaking needs to take up the language with sufficient energy in order to carry it forward without losing either momentum or clarity.
- The workshop leader tosses the ball into a crowd of actors, one of whom has to catch it, and hold on to it until either someone else takes it off them or they throw it into the air for another actor to take. The ball symbolizes the text, and the person with the ball takes the energy and uses it to speak.

NARRATIVE

Storytelling is the one dramatic form that all of us have experienced directly at some period in our lives. As children (if we are lucky) parents will have read us bedtime stories, and we in our turn pass on this experience to our own children. However, it is a domestic and intimate experience that succeeds usually because there is no particular pressure on the speaker to address a crowd, let alone a crowd of strangers. I use the familiarity of this situation as a starting point for work on more lengthy dramatic narratives.

- Sitting or lying on the floor, ask everyone to recall a familiar place – it can be a room, or a street in a town, or a place in the countryside. It needs to be somewhere they know well and can instantly recall in detail.
- Ask them to be really specific and truthful: from where they are located, what can they see (and what can't they see).
- Give everyone three or four minutes to establish that image clearly. Then, working in pairs, one of whom wears a blindfold, have the sighted one describe to their partner their chosen location.
- Their objective is to help the 'blind' partner see the place as clearly, and in as much detail, as possible. It is also desirable for the speaker to convey more than a simple factual description – to attempt, by colouring the words, to give the listener a sense of the atmosphere of the place and, indirectly, what it means to him or her.
- Give each pair five minutes or so to describe the place and to imagine it, before reversing the roles.
- At the end of this section of the exercise give all of them the opportunity of describing to the rest of the group as much as they can of what they were able to see and feel about the place that was described to them while they were blindfolded.

This is not a memory exercise, but one that gives an opportunity to create a detailed mental picture for someone else, a fundamental requirement of most effective storytelling.

- Go back into the same pairs, and ask both to explain to the other what they still retain of the image that was described for them, and why they think they retained it. What did they notice (if anything) about the way in which their partner painted the image with words?
- Separate the group, and once again ask everyone to close their eyes, but this time to think of a journey they have undertaken. It can be a routine journey, like that to or from work, or it can be a special journey like that from home to church on the day they were married, or a journey to a memorable holiday destination.
- Repeat the storytelling, again working in pairs and having one person blindfolded, but this time the task is more complicated and the image is not static.
- Once more, change roles, so that the listeners become the narrators, and then, finally, have everyone recall to the rest of the group the journey as it was described to them. When this is completed, ask

people what some of the differences are when a personal narrative is being narrated one to one, and when that narrative is retold by someone else to a large group. Which of the narratives does the group as a whole remember most clearly? Why are some memorable and others less so? How much is the difference the responsibility of the story itself, how much that of the storyteller?

- Finally, ask the group to think of two tragic stories. One of them is fictional, the other true, drawing on personal experience and knowledge. Like the other stories, neither should last more than three or four minutes, and both should be told without a pause between them to the listening partner, who is again blindfolded. At the end of the session ask whether partners could guess which of the stories was true and which was false. Discuss too the problems for the speaker in dealing with potentially difficult material with which they may feel a close affinity. What kind of language is used?

The work in this chapter requires a high level of cooperation, concentration and focus. It increases the individual's sensitivity and awareness of the needs of others, both bodily and vocally. Although at times it will undoubtedly tax people's patience, it will also graphically demonstrate to them that what they are capable of achieving together could never be reproduced by anyone working in isolation. Finally it offers a huge sense of satisfaction when people combine together to make theatre.

5 Playing Character

Two actors prepare for the evening performance.

Bob arrives at the theatre two hours early to start his preparation: stretching, breathing, physical loosening, vocal work-out, followed by relaxation exercises and a shower. He goes to his dressing-room to get into costume and make-up as part of a ritual that includes listening to specially chosen music from the era of the play. He looks at the pictures of his character's 'family' on the dressing-room walls and reads some of his character's journal entries. On the way to the stage he improvises in role with one of the other actors in the play. He stands in the wings, gathering his energy and concentration, ready to make his first entrance.

Tony signs in at the stage door exactly at 'the half'. Goes to the bar and has a pint, chats to some of the stage crew and reads the evening paper. He watches the show 'go up' on the TV monitor. The assistant director notices Tony at the bar as she passes on her way out of the stage door, where she picks up a couple of messages. She makes her way to the front of the theatre, up the steps, and enters at the back of the circle just in time to see Tony make his first entrance on stage in full costume and make-up.

Bob and Tony play their big scene together, and they both enjoy it thoroughly. The audience and the assistant director watch two skilled actors doing an excellent job. Their approach and preparation are very different, and beg the questions: 'What is acting? How do you do it, and can you teach it?'

The American writer and director David Mamet, in his book *True and False*, attacks the 'cult' of actor training and asserts that the only place to learn to act is in front of a paying audience. This chapter makes no claims to any definitive answers as to how actors should be trained, but it does recognize the thirst young performers have to explore and experiment with some of the issues surrounding acting. Working with inexperienced actors, where do you start? How do you prepare them for making acting more than just learning the lines, holding their nerve and hoping for the best?

None of the workshop approaches that follow will add up to a recipe for acting successfully. You cannot follow them to the letter in the belief that, at the end, you will have a character that works. They are exercises that demand concentration and stimulate the imagination, and give the individual the opportunity to focus his or her physical, vocal and mental resources on a specific task. What is most important is that you, as the workshop leader, stimulate the participants to consider acting as an absorbing craft about which they can always learn more. Acting is an eclectic art. Actors do not belong to one school or another. Plays demand a mixture of performance styles, and actors have to be highly flexible. There is no dogma: actors have to borrow whatever is useful and stirring to make the work come to life. It is liberating to encounter different ways of working, which can stimulate the individual to forge his/her own approach out of diverse experiences.

The workshop material that follows is primarily aimed at a group of Theatre Studies students starting work on a chosen character. In practice it has also been of interest and benefit to all sorts of people who want to exercise their imaginative resources in meeting a new challenge. With only minor adaptation it will serve a wide range of groups, from primary-school children to amateur and professional actors, or a business team that wants to develop creativity. If you choose to explore the ideas further, there is sufficient material to keep you busy for a week; however, the main body of the material can be adequately covered in one or two days.

Acting

When I first started to lead workshops I was in the acting company of the director Mike Alfreds at the National Theatre. We were rehearsing a trilogy of Carlo Goldoni plays written in Italy in the eighteenth century entitled *Countrymania*. They could have been approached as the last delights of *commedia dell'arte*, with their archetypal characters and comic situations, or the beginnings of psychological drama, with urbane personalities taking their greed, lust and insecurities with them to the country for the holiday season. Mike Alfreds chose the latter, and since he was a rigorous teacher and director, with a well-defined approach to rehearsing plays that comes out of a lineage reaching back to Stanislavsky, I learnt a lot from him about the craft of acting.

There was a great demand from schools and colleges for workshops in response to the Theatre Studies A-level paper on practitioners. Stanislavsky workshops were constantly being requested, and when I was asked to lead them, I simply combined some of our rehearsal methods with exercises taken from college and elsewhere. It made a workshop that I hoped would be appropriate for Theatre Studies students. I subsequently went on developing and adapting this workshop with students and teachers, the product of which process forms the main body of this chapter.

There was a similar demand for work on Brecht, and for the opportunity to compare his approach to performance with that of Stanislavsky. I remain wary of going too far down this route, as the danger in the course of a one-off workshop is that the work of these two colossi of Western theatre might be reduced to the opposition, as it were, of two teams in a football match. Their practice converges as well as divides, and what they importantly share is the asking of fundamental questions about what theatre is and a conviction of the need for exacting detail in the making of performance.

What I do believe is useful at the start of a workshop that is going to look at playing character is to conduct two exercises that highlight some of the issues around acting and making theatre. Most people's experience of watching acting will happen largely via television and film, where the distinction between the actor and the character is often blurred. The convention is geared to making the viewers forget they are watching something artificial. In making quick-turnover television, the only reason a scene will be reshot is not that the actor wants to do it again to make it better, but that the sound boom came into shot, which would remind the viewers that the whole thing is a fabrication.

The distinction between actor and character is further confused by numerous stories of screen stars, from James Dean to Daniel Day Lewis, who allegedly take their research into playing a role to the limits of dedication, by obsessive need to know the background of their character and to experience the detail of their life. Actors lock themselves away to experience solitary confinement, put on weight to become the ageing boxer, infiltrate some dark underworld – all to get 'inside' the character.

In contrast David Mamet says that asking about the history of the character is as pointless as asking of the subject of a portrait: 'I wonder what underwear he has on?' The character only exists as a few lines on a page; there is no life elsewhere. Therefore, this first exercise raises a question about being on the inside or outside of a character.

CHANGING IMAGE

- Split the participants into three groups (A, B and C) of about five people each.
- Out of sight from the others, each group is to decide upon, and make, a frozen image or tableau of an event, e.g. a wedding, a fight, a rock concert.
- Bring everyone back together again.
- Group B close their eyes. They are now 'lumps of clay'.
- Group A mould group B into group A's image of, for example, a tennis match.
- When group A are satisfied that the tennis match has been recreated, they clear the space, leaving group B in the space in the frozen positions.
- Group B can now open their eyes while being sure not to change position.
- Group C watch.
- Can group C tell that the image is a tennis match?
- Repeat, swapping around the groups.

Almost always the watching group can tell what the image is meant to be, even though the actors are manoeuvred into position with their eyes closed and have no conscious understanding of the situation. The actors know nothing about the characters they are portraying, yet still the physical image communicates the story to the audience.

Do actors need to understand their characters from the inside? Is it not sufficient to get the external image right? After all, the audience want to be told a story effectively; they don't want to watch actors indulging themselves in character. Acting is action. Certainly the epic tradition of theatre is rooted in storytelling, where performers play clearly defined roles rather than characters. The story of Little Red Riding Hood needs the introduction of the Big Bad Wolf to move the story forward: what is important is his function in the narrative, not the detail of his psychological character, which is an archetype. Greek drama, mystery plays, melodrama, Shakespeare, Brecht, street theatre – all use archetypes. What is important is the actors' ability to convey their role in the narrative directly to the audience.

When considering playing character, it is important to understand the actor–audience relationship and the effect it can have on how theatre communicates. In the convention of naturalism the audience are voyeurs, unacknowledged by the actors: they are drawn into a world of make-believe, encouraged to believe they are watching 'real' characters up on the stage, until the illusion is broken at the final curtain call. In reality every piece of theatre responds to its audience in some way, and in other conventions, such as the Greek, Shakespeare, Brecht and the 'epic' theatre, the actors communicate directly with the audience and include them openly in the making of the event.

The second exercise illustrates the alternative actor–audience relationship and how it affects the communication of information.

TELLING STORIES

Divide the group into pairs. The first part is simply to get people to tell their stories.

  i) Allow two minutes for one person in each pair to tell their partner a true story that happened to them. The partner just listens to the story. Swap over.

 ii) Ask for two volunteers who were not previously paired together. Sit the two opposite each other on chairs, and ask Amy to tell Ben her true story. The rest of the group is the audience, who watch and listen.

iii) Ask Amy and Ben to sit facing the audience. Ask Ben to retell Amy's story to the audience, indicating that it is about Amy.

When Amy tells her story to Ben, the audience are passive observers who eavesdrop on the exchange without being directly acknowledged, as in the naturalistic convention. Amy's story tells of how she was on holiday in New York, and that she and a girlfriend met some people who recommended they all meet up at a new night club. Amy and her friend went there by subway, and when they started looking for the club they realized it was in a rundown part of town. They found the club, but their friends were nowhere to be seen, and they got persuaded to go upstairs to look for them at what turned out to be a private party, where they felt out of their depth and scared. They managed to leave the club but couldn't find their way back to the subway station; people were stopping and staring at them, and they were feeling increasingly panicked. By luck they managed to hail a yellow cab and got back to where they were staying.

   Listening to this story, the temptation is for the audience to be drawn in and to identify with Amy and her fears. We run the film in our head as the story unfolds, with ourselves in the leading role, experiencing the vicarious feelings of alarm, panic and relief at the final overcoming of adversity. However, in the retelling of the story by Ben, he is talking directly to the audience, describing what happened to Amy on her holidays in New York. The audience are now once removed from the narrative by the role of the storyteller, as in the epic convention, and they can take a more objective, distanced point of view of the information given. The danger that Amy spoke of previously as the onrushing hand of fate, as now related by Ben will be a set of circumstances that can be appraised rationally, and the narrative told is the outcome of a series of choices. The feelings of panic are seen as subjective reactions rather than inevitable fact, and we the audience are invited to assess Amy's actions and responses. Amy's telling of the story will probably contain more personal and emotional information, whereas Ben will tend to communicate the main narrative points.

Acting has different functions within different pieces of theatre. What is constant is the need for preparation and the ability to know how to start constructive work.

The above two exercises together will take thirty to forty minutes.

Acting Up

Acting as a term can cover what happens on television, on film, in pantomime, the community drama, the West End or Broadway play, Shakespeare and street theatre. They are all aspects of performance, and while most people are happy to consume what actors offer, actors and acting can still have all sorts of negative associations. These find expression through everyday phrases such as 'putting on an act', 'play acting', 'acting up', all of which imply superficiality and deceit, suggesting that acting is about putting something on and showing off – in fact just the sort of things adults say about 'naughty' children. Perhaps because acting can only take place in public, actors are sometimes assumed to be immature extroverts searching for an opportunity to grab attention.

Actors might also be viewed with suspicion because of their chameleon-like ability to assume the appearance and nature of someone else. Acting can seem like a cheap disguise using costume, make-up and a shuffling walk. Some trickery happens on the surface and the real person is hidden from view; actors efface themselves behind the characters they are playing. In reality the opposite is more likely to be the case. Far from acting being about an outer shell of disguise, it is rather more about a journey inwards. Good acting is about an openness and a willingness to reveal the character you are playing through the prism of yourself, using the resources of your body, voice and imagination. Acting is essentially a projection of yourself. Playing character is a journey towards being someone else, and that new creation has to be connected and interwoven with you. It can be a demanding task where you confront your own limitations and stretch your imaginative and emotional resources to embrace the life you are taking on. Since plays usually deal with people in crisis and conflict, that makes the challenge of truthful connection with that character all the greater. Far from acting being about having the nerve to stand up in front of others and be extrovert, it is a challenging craft that demands you put yourself at the centre of the work.

Because so much can be personally at stake with acting, individuals become important and a subject of interest. The positive association of actors is that they can be much admired for what they do, and there is an appetite to know about who they are and how they do it. Although inevitably there is always the desire to revere individuals and to discover the latest 'star', acting is rarely a solo process and is without doubt best facilitated by collaborative work.

Most actors want to work in companies where there are shared opportunities to learn and progress. Company workshops are a vital part of building a spirit of collective work. My spirits sink at those rehearsal call sheets in theatres detailing only separate call times for certain actors in specified scenes, meaning that some actors are not needed for days on end. While this might seem enviable, in fact it often leaves actors feeling isolated and disconnected from the ongoing rehearsal work. Without that sense of group exploration and endeavour, it is easier and less risky to fall into old habits, which may result in stock, uninspired performances.

The workshop plan below will provide an opportunity for the participants to experiment, share and test themselves in a safe environment. As with all the work in this book, it cannot be done alone: it needs the company and energy of others to enable us to explore and develop. A workshop approach is used to try out the building-blocks of constructing character, which inevitably brings with it the opportunity to delve into the well of personal material that will feed the work.

Character work is not there to block you in; it is there to make you feel simultaneously secure and inventive in the moment of performance. If you know who you are, you are free to play. Rather than 'putting on an act' you can channel your creative energy through the focus of the character. Performance is a high-energy activity in which the actor should be at the height of his or her powers, concentrating physical and imaginative resources to fulfil the task. Workshops serve to prepare the material and train the creative faculties.

Playing a Role

Playing a role is a challenge, and it is not only actors who have roles to play. We all play different roles throughout life: as a son or daughter, as a student, as a partner, as a parent, as a work colleague. These various roles inevitably bring with them important challenges. We can often feel underprepared and unsupported as we are thrust into a situation before we are ready. What are we meant to be doing and what is expected of us? Do we 'play our role' with conviction, or can people see through us? Do we have the 'character' to see through the difficult times?

Challenges are said to be 'character-building'. They might be if you succeed, whereas failure can leave confidence shattered. Each of us tends to have a habitual way of dealing with new challenges. Whatever the issue that confronts us, from new responsibilities at work to the birth of a child, to redecorating the hall, to acting in a play, we probably react to it in a way that follows an inbuilt pattern that mixes panic, bluster, ignorance, evasion and hard work.

A workshop that investigates the challenge of playing a character will give an insight into an actor's process, and will inevitably also become a forum for people to learn about themselves, irrespective of whether they aim to play that role or act at all. A new challenge will raise fears of the unknown and of possible failure. Confronting those fears and approaching the task in a constructive and ordered way can be a journey of self-discovery. You begin with yourself, accepting what you are, and having faith in your ability to expand. The experience leads to an increase in confidence and sheds light on strategies to approach other daunting tasks. Transformation of a given situation need not be disguise or trickery, but can be a fulfilment of your potential brought about by the opportunity to develop. The workshop leader's task is to provide a clear framework within which people can travel. It has to be secure as well as challenging, so that people are able to take risks. A workshop is like childhood play: a safe place where you can test out who you are in the world, where you can experiment with situations and possibilities without the consequences of them being real.

One of the very best performers I have seen is not an actor at all; he is a Danish-born businessman and teacher. When presenting seminars he is totally engaged and truthful, speaks his text with freshness and gives a performance that holds his audience captivated. He is engaged with life using the resources of his body, voice, imagination and intellect to powerful effect. It is remarkable to meet people who are full of life and vigour; how often we interact with people who are slightly tired and dejected. We meet many people and remember the ones who enlighten us. A candle is unremarkable, until it is lit and has a flame, when it is transformed into a source of light and a thing of beauty.

As a student I heard the playwright Edward Bond give a talk, and he said that somebody should write a book that guides us on how to live our lives, the only trouble being that it would take someone their whole life to write and the rest of us our whole lives to read. Art condenses those lessons. Theatre workshops offer a framework for us to explore who we are and how we live and communicate.

Preparing the Resources

There are many different warm-up games and activities that could usefully feed into the challenge of playing a specific role. I want to outline two connected exercises that draw on personal memory and experience, which are the raw material to stimulate the imagination.

A free and creative imagination is part of a healthy psychological state, and who are the most imaginative people we know? Children, with their natural gifts of fantasy and play. Childhood is a time full of rich impressions that shape our view of the world and is fertile reference material. This next exercise will stimulate memories from childhood.

CHILDHOOD MAPS

i) Give each participant a big sheet of paper (e.g. flip-chart size) and a felt-tip pen. Ask them to draw a map of the home they most associate with their childhood, detailing the layout of the rooms, the garden and so on. As they conclude the rough drawing, ask them to put an X to mark the spot associated with a particular incident from childhood, which will probably have occurred to them as they went through the house.

ii) Ask an individual to hold up his/her sheet in front of them and to show the whole group their drawing. Get them to describe their home while taking people on a journey through the rooms. Ask them to conclude with the story of their recollected incident.

As people draw the map their minds will be flooded with childhood experiences, smells and feelings that give a powerful sense memory. When they go on to describe their homes, it is revealing to see people who may be awkward in a workshop lose their self-consciousness.

During a workshop I noticed that a teacher had been consistently moving to the edge of the group. She literally hid from view during the physical warm-up, and she was always the last person to find a partner when asked to get into pairs; I was therefore surprised when she volunteered to describe her childhood home. She started very quietly, taking us on a journey around the veranda of what turned out to be a colonial home in Kenya. As the story unfolded, it was full of rich detail and vivid recreations of childhood experiences and the people in her world. As she told her story she became bright, alive and emotionally connected to everything she said.

As a speaker she was riveting to listen to, achieved not by a commanding voice, theatrical emphasis or a clever use of pace, but by a simple veracity. It is this identification with the words you speak that holds the listener. Turn on the radio and you can tell within a split second whether it is an actor speaking someone else's words or someone talking from real-life experience.

A vivid example of this occurred during the funeral of Diana, Princess of Wales, in 1997. Compare the tribute of Earl Spencer to his sister with Prime Minister Tony Blair's reading from 'Corinthians': the tribute was a deeply personal statement sharpened by passion and anger and delivered to stunning effect, while the schooled politician's reading of an established text was unable to transcend conventional ritual.

Actors have to work hard on the detailed justification of the text they speak in the attempt to blur that easy distinction between a received text and personal knowledge. We all carry with us a fund of information and experience. Often only a narrow seam of our life experience is required for the day-to-day demands of living, and all that rich material lies dormant. For creative work the raw material of life experience is the storehouse of the imagination, to be constantly called upon to flesh out and justify the role a person is playing. Rather than closing in and shutting down, all life is there to be taken in. Nothing is wasted and everything, especially the personal events we might see as difficult, provides an opportunity to learn about the world and ourselves.

This next exercise allows us to practise using our imaginations, in order to blend our real-life experience with another person's.

SUBSTITUTION

i) Divide into groups of three. Each person tells a true story that happened to him/her to the other two members of their group. The group then decides to select one of those three stories.

ii) Choose one group of three. Ask everyone else to form an audience. One after the other each member of the group of three retells the chosen story in the first person as if it happened to them. The audience listen to each one, and at the end have to decide whose story it really is.

The key to making it difficult for the audience to decide who the story actually belongs to is the substitution of personal detail while keeping to the main events of the original narrative.

For example, Carole's true story is from her childhood and tells of going to stay with her aunt and uncle in Weston-super-Mare, where she was cold and homesick. Once, because they knew she liked acting and being in plays, they entered her for a local talent competition. She found this excruciatingly embarrassing, but she never summoned up the courage to tell them she didn't want to do it. Carole's telling of her story is full of detailed recollections, such as her uncle's cough, the smell of the linoleum in her bedroom and the pink frilly dress her aunt made her wear.

David's retelling of Carole's story needs to dovetail her narrative with his own real-life experience. He tells the story based on his experience of staying with his grandparents in Eastbourne, including details of the breakfast cereal they always had, the sense of boredom and feeling homesick. He makes the story of the talent competition sound convincing by imaginatively placing himself into that situation and using his memory of his own embarrassment when he was made to go on stage with other children at a pantomime.

What usually denotes the true storyteller is an attention to detail and a convincing sense of place. In attempting to sound plausible, David substitutes his own experience to fill in the detail of the given situation. This is a key skill in building character: using your imagination and memory to substantiate the given circumstances of the play. It is a skill useful elsewhere in our lives, to get inside somebody else's experience and relate it to our own, however far distant it might initially seem.

A vivid, fertile and rich imagination, fed by ready access to memory and experience, is a vital resource for an actor to use and develop the world of the character and the play. Fiona Shaw was playing the lead part in *Machinal* by Sophie Treadwell at the National Theatre and agreed to lead a workshop on the play for some teachers. Written in 1928, it features a character who is adrift in New York, takes a lover, murders her stifling husband and ends up going to the electric chair. Some psychological journey for an actor, and plenty of material from which to explore the character's state of mind and desires. Instead Shaw chose to set up an exercise to stimulate the visual imagination of the actor, where participants used sounds and physical sensations to communicate a picture to someone who was blindfolded (see Chapter 2, 'Blindfold Images'). The exercise, while fascinating, seemingly had nothing directly to do with the content of the play.

When questioned as to why she had chosen it, Fiona Shaw said that this sensory and imaginative exercise was, for her, the most important aspect of playing the part. Indeed it is this facility to engage creatively in an imaginative world that radiates out from the reality on-stage that can sustain a performance with freshness and life time after time. At the workshop a teacher asked her how she managed to come out of role after the final shocking and disturbing sequence, where the audience watch her preparation for and execution on the electric chair. She said, 'Ah, it takes two seconds,' confounding the idea that acting is about tortuous psychological struggle and suggesting that it is more about finding a successful way to engage imaginatively and richly moment by moment.

The length of time for these two exercises will depend on how many examples you want to hear. You should allow a minimum of sixty minutes. Taken with the two exercises in the 'Acting' section, and allowing for a warm-up to start the day, this could provide the material for the first two hours' work.

Preparing the Ground

Playing character is about having faith, believing in the process and not constantly looking to the end result. Acting is full of insecurities. Professionally it is desperately hard to find work, and your livelihood depends on your being successful enough in one role to secure the next. Whatever the context of the production your vague groping in the dark towards playing the role is watched with close attention by your colleagues before being examined by a paying audience, and often then critically analysed in print. This pressure leads to fear, which is the enemy of creativity. Always there is the voice in your head ready to tell you, 'You can't do it, you're no good!' which causes actors to cut and run, pulling on the cloak of a performance as soon as possible in rehearsal in order to convince themselves and their colleagues that they will be all right: they will not let the production down.

Starting a workshop at the National Theatre with drama teachers on Ibsen's *A Doll's House*, after a few warm-up games I asked a participant to get up and 'act the part of Nora' on her own in the room. She duly rose to her feet and started flouncing about and looking agitated. I thanked her, asked her to sit down and enquired as to how it felt? 'Awful,' she replied. Of course it did. Here was someone who had a knowledge of the play but no experience of working on the character, who was willing to get up and play the part in front of twenty other people! It was the equivalent of jumping into a freezing-cold swimming-pool with her clothes on just because someone suggested she might. And this is what happens in rehearsal rooms everywhere: people jump into character without the faintest idea of who they are or what they are supposed to be doing, in a forlorn attempt to make it feel manageable.

Stanislavsky, as actor, director and teacher, developed and wrote down an approach to acting. He formed the Moscow Art Theatre at the end of the nineteenth century with Nemirovich-Danchenko, and with playwright Anton Chekhov transformed the way Western theatre thinks about acting. However, if you were to sit in on a rehearsal at the National Theatre in London today, and during a break you approached one of the actors to ask her view of the teachings of Stanislavsky, she would probably look insecure before making her excuses and heading for the tea urn. A vague memory of college and some books she never managed to finish. Yet when the rehearsal resumes you'll see the actors asking the routine questions: 'What do I want here?' 'Where have I just come from?' and 'What is my relationship with you?' – the basic questions that Stanislavsky formulated and that are a central part of our performance culture.

Stanislavsky is sometimes dismissively thought of as only being about a 'naturalistic' approach to acting. He was an avid explorer of the theatre, always asking questions and looking for new ways of working. It is this spirit of enquiry, and the detailed investigation that leads to the building up of performance layer by layer, that is the legacy he passes on to us today. Whatever the part in whatever play, and also in devised work, there are questions to be asked that help the actors find the truth of what they are doing and to connect it to themselves. In practice every rehearsal period is as individual as the mix of director and actors that makes up a company. Sometimes it might be assumed that character work is a process that goes on discreetly around the day-to-day work on the text; at other times extensive improvisations are set up to explore the backstory of the play. What is important is that the actors adopt a clear approach to working on their parts, and it can take place (preferably) in the collective work of rehearsal, as well as in the actors' homework.

Setting Out

Teachers of the Alexander technique of body alignment, which is integral to most actor training, always remind students to beware of 'end-gaining' – not to look for the results of better body posture but simply to concentrate on the process. Being cast to play a part, the temptation is to race ahead and focus on the end result, imagining yourself in the glow of success and praise. Following that flight of fancy, reality steps in and you are faced with the question of where you start and what you do. Preparation is essential. It is a myth that good actors can somehow just 'do it'. Good actors work hard finding out information that will feed their creative process.

In the format of a workshop we will go through a process of commencing work on a character. It could be a well-known character from a famous play, and that makes it even more necessary to ask the participants to start with a blank page and rid themselves of any preconceptions. Often our first creative impulses are stunted by some half-remembered impression of what a play or character ought to be like, taking us back to school and the search for the 'right' answer.

In preparation for the workshop participants should therefore try to read the play with their minds open for first impressions, and to make a note of any immediate responses. Then they should read it over again, mining it for every possible piece of information that will feed into the life of the chosen character. It is one thing to read a play casually and another to extract the information needed to form the basis of playing a character. The words the playwright has written will be the ones the audience hear, and they are the ones that should form the foundations for constructing character. The engaging of the imagination is a vital part of the process, but it has to be firmly rooted in information from the text, or the actor will have a hard time justifying what he or she chooses to play in the overall shape of a production.

Certainly for a production, and possibly in preparation for a workshop, 'homework', consisting of the following exercise, can be set that will make sure the participants comprehensively gather and begin to assess all the available information from the play for their character.

THE FOUR LISTS

Choose the character to work on. Using the following check-list, work through the play, copying verbatim anything that will fit into one (or more) of the lists. This will be time-consuming and in effect will be like writing the play out more than once, but in the process each person will get to know the play and start sorting out the information it provides for the work ahead.

1 All the facts about the character: reliable biographical information as opposed to characters' opinions: for example, age, relationships, job, where they live, where they grew up, etc.
2 Everything I (the character) say about myself.
3 Everything I say about other characters.
4 Everything other characters say about me.

This is a worthwhile exercise in preparation for any character in any play. For the example of this workshop I have chosen to work on the character of Madame Ranyevskaya from Chekhov's The Cherry Orchard, because it is well known and provides rich material with which to work. The process we will go through on the character can hold up, with some adaptation, for any character in any play.

During rehearsals the whole company may sit down and listen to the four lists each actor has prepared about their character. This, of course, takes up a great deal of time. It is useful because it enables everyone to hear the information from the play in different ways, and to gain knowledge beyond their own preoccupations with what they are personally playing. Each character will hear how they feature in the life of other characters, which is important for building up the world of the play and the interrelationships within it.

In this workshop every person (male and female) will collectively work on the one character of Ranyevskaya.

You will probably only have time to listen to the first list of character facts. As the facilitator, you can have prepared them in advance in order to hand them out to all the participants, as they will provide a solid platform from which to start the work.

Ranyevskaya: List of Facts

Lived abroad for five years.

When a young, slim girl looked after Lopakhin when he'd been hit, and took him to the washstand in the nursery.

Mistress of house and estate.

Her rooms – the white one and the mauve one – have stayed just as they were.

Slept in the nursery when a little girl, with her brother.

Born in this house, loves this house.

Journeyed for four days.

The train was two hours late.

Has a daughter Anya, aged 17.

Adopted daughter Varya, aged 24.

Brother Gayev, aged 51.

Governess Charlotta.

Chambermaid Dunyasha.

Clerk Yepikhodov.

Footman Firs, aged 87.

Footman Yasha, who was in Paris and brought back with them. Had to be fed.

Developed a habit of drinking coffee.

Lived in Paris on 5th floor. Had visitors: Frenchmen and ladies, an ancient Catholic priest.

Anya arrived; she kept hugging her and crying.

Has no money left. She would sit in the station restaurant and order the most expensive item on the menu. Tips all the waiters a ruble each.

Has debts, with interest owed.

The cherry orchard is to be sold on 22 August.

Bought Anya a bumble-bee brooch.

Husband died six years ago. Month later Grisha, her son aged 7, drowned in the river. She fled abroad.

Loves her country. She wept on the journey.

Dresses in Paris fashions.

She makes an impression on men.

Her father, grandfather estate owners and owners of serfs; lived in this house.

Nanna died while she was away.

Estate thirteen miles from town, railway has now come through right next to it. Has a river. Consists of house, old buildings, large remarkable cherry orchard.

She has 100-year-old bookcase.

Telegrams come from Paris.

Takes pills.

Has rich aunt, a countess, in Yaroslavl.

She married a lawyer, a commoner. He made debts, was a drinker; died of champagne.

She spends money; she throws it away.

Fell in love with someone else, at the time her son drowned. He followed when she fled abroad. Bought a villa outside Menton, he fell sick there, she looked after him as an invalid for three years.

Last year villa sold to pay debts, went to Paris. He robbed her and took up with another woman, she tried to poison herself.

Returned to Russia.

Loves man in Paris.

They used to give a ball in the old days with generals, barons and admirals.

Ask the group to read out loud the list of facts. Once everyone has heard this basic information, they can start to move on and make suppositions about the character of Ranyevskaya based on them.

For example, it is a fact that she dresses in Paris fashions and bought her daughter Anya a bumble-bee brooch. We could then suppose that she likes beautiful things, has an appreciation of style and is aware of her self-image. This could be developed into a character trait that expands from the detail of her appearance to how she relates to her immediate environment. Possibly she likes to touch furniture and objects, to feel their texture and shape; perhaps she surrounds herself with, and is comforted by, beautiful things.

It is a fact that she has debts with interest owed, and that she tips all the waiters in the station restaurant a ruble each. We can therefore suppose that she is a generous person, or that she wants other people to believe that she is not in financial trouble. We can also surmise that she prefers to react to the immediate situation rather than face up to the larger picture, that she responds to her impulses rather than taking a rational, long-term view. These suppositions are rooted in the specific references Chekhov makes, and are broadened to create a fuller picture of the character.

You can now prompt further consideration of the character by asking the three following questions:
1 Which animal is most like the character?
2 Where is the character's centre of energy?
3 What is the character's super-objective?

WHAT ANIMAL?
For instance, if you were playing a politician you might choose an owl or a weasel. For the corrupt landowner, a large fierce hound, or a greedy rat. Make a choice: often it is instinctive and it can always be changed. For the character of Ranyevskaya, possibly a pedigree cat? Or a colourful bird?

Working with young people, if I was simply to say, 'What do think of the character of Ranyevskaya?' I would be met with either complete silence or the recycling of a textbook answer. If I ask, 'What animal do you think she is like?' all sorts of interesting answers and ideas start to emerge, as immediately the imagination and instinct are engaged. Someone will say a cat for Ranyevskaya without fully knowing why, and then will go on to talk about her desire to be in a comfortable home, her need for care and attention and her love of fine things. These are physical sensations and will feed into the process of developing the character.

CENTRE OF ENERGY?

Where is the centre of the character's energy and how does it drive her? As you sit reading these words, imagine your energy being active and centred in your guts. Now imagine it centred in your upper chest. It is a very different feeling, isn't it? The guts seem to be related to churning emotions, such as shame and guilt; the upper chest with excitement and volatility. If someone was scheming and crafty, the energy might possibly be centred in their eyes. For Ranyevskaya, is it possibly in her heart? Or perhaps her hands?

As with the animal above, at present we are just asking the questions to stimulate a response: the heart, perhaps, because she is impulsive and generous; the hands, perhaps, because she is sensuous and tactile. Soon we will structure an exercise that allows the participants to explore practically the possibilities of the centre of energy and the animal.

FINDING THE SUPER-OBJECTIVE?

This is a Stanislavsky term for discovering what the characters want overall during the course of the play, what drives them forward. It is important to find a super-objective that is strong and inclusive without being generalized, as you could say most people want, for example, 'to be happy'.

For Ranyevskaya, perhaps it is: 'I want to keep the cherry orchard,' meaning that she wants life to stay preserved as it is on the estate, with the cherry orchard intact, while she is free to be in Paris or doing whatever she wants.

Consideration of the list of facts and the initial questions are designed to stimulate discussion and thoughts, and you should allow a minimum of thirty minutes. Many of the initial ideas may change as practical work on the character begins. It is now time to lead the group to start work on their feet.

The First Steps

Establishing information about the character in a way that is digestible is important. Translating that information into a tangible, physical reality starts the process of enacting the character. Having set out and considered the necessary information – the 'given circumstances' – you are ready to 'have a go' at being Ranyevskaya.

In this workshop it is valuable if everyone works on the same character all together, taking the role of Ranyevskaya in the exercises that follow. This provides focus and allows the participants to feed off each other's work. It can also be a useful way of working for a company rehearsing a play – to take each character in turn through the Four Lists above, and for everyone to work practically on each character in this initial 'Trying Out' exercise. While it will end up an individual task to play the character, it is also a shared responsibility, and everyone can taste the experience of being each character. This places every character in everyone's knowledge, and also gives more information to the individual actors, who get to try out their roles during the exercise, as well as being able to observe their colleagues working.

It is important that the work that follows should function on a basic, instinctive, physical level. Rather than looking down on the character and the text from a literary-critical point of view and talking about Chekhovian this or that, the actors should be burrowing up through the character and the given circumstances of the play, discovering simple real things such as how they should turn their heads if something attracts their attention. It is simple, like learning to crawl, and part of the process to create something that is rooted and organic.

Trying Out

Ask people to close their eyes for twenty seconds and let any thoughts about Ranyevskaya float into their minds. Ask everyone to move in the space, 'having a go' at being Ranyevskaya. They should not interact and should be working in isolation, while also being aware of each other. How does the character walk? sit down? drink a glass of water? look out of the window? It is good to keep the character alive and active, discovering the basic experience of how she exists in her world.

Are they now 'in character'? Well, no. It is more like going to a shop and trying on a coat. You try it on, take a look in the mirror, and then try again with a different size and colour. You, the actor, are motivating the action, conscious of trying things out and assessing what feels right and what doesn't. How does the character get out of a chair? Try it, and if it doesn't seem right, go back and try it again in a different way. You are not lost inside the character; you are simply trying it on for size.

*

During the course of this exploration participants can physically try out the Animal work and the Centre of Energy, experimenting to see what happens and what it tells them about the character.

TRY OUT THE ANIMAL

Have people become the animal they have chosen for Ranyevskaya. For instance, someone might choose a deer. Ask them to find a corner of the room, settle down and imagine they are a deer asleep in its lair. Encourage them to sense the world around them in detail: the grass, the leaves and the landscape. Then they wake up and start to explore the environment, going on to look for food and moving through the animal's world. Prompt them to be 100 per cent that animal. How does it move? What is its rhythm? How does it look for food? How does it look at the world? How does it breathe? What are its particular characteristics? Then ask them to become 75 per cent animal and 25 per cent human; then fifty–fifty; finally ending up 25 per cent animal and 75 per cent human, back in Ranyevskaya's environment.

This process, which requires concentration and commitment, can produce a recognizably human character, with rooted movement and gestures that arise out of the physical reality of playing the animal. Working with a group, great energy can be released by this exercise; the room becomes full of people moving in different ways, stretching and testing their physicality. Once, in a workshop, a teenager did unnerve me by spending the entire time hanging upside down from the ceiling bars. He later claimed to have been a particular South American bat, and that during his vertiginous sojourn he had discovered important things about his character!

TRY OUT THE CENTRE OF ENERGY

Ask each person to focus on their choice for the centre of energy. So, for instance, someone might have chosen Ranyevskaya's heart. Ask them to exaggerate the pull of it to see what physical sense of being it gives them. How does it lead the movement? What does it do to the breath and the rhythm of movement? Get them to allow the pull of it to become more discreet while still providing a strong impulse. It may not now be obvious to the outside eye, but the centre of energy is still giving the character a strong inward propulsion.

These Trying Out exercises are good at establishing a physical sense of the character, at breaking the actors out of their habitual rhythms to take on a different tempo. A roomful of Ranyevskayas working in various ways will find a connection in their physical movement and energy. Then, if you had done the preparation and were to change to the character of Lopakhin, you would notice how the rhythm changed and the room took on a different vibration.

Allow this exploratory work to take its time before discussing what people discovered. In most areas of work the acquiring of knowledge is a private business, and then that information can be given out selectively by the person who holds the power over it. It is a basic assumption of this work that discovery is to be shared, and that the constructive cooperation of twenty heads is better than one at finding the creative possibilities. What you, as the workshop leader, want to hear is simple, instinctive discoveries that come out of physical activity and prompt the imagination, rather than brain-led ideas about what the character is. Better to hear 'I found that Ranyevskaya is restless, always touching things, and listening out to hear if anyone is coming' than 'I think she is the spirit of old Russia.' It is very hard to play the spirit of old Russia. What you want is a specific person living in a real world.

Having allowed about thirty minutes for 'Trying Out', the participants should feel that the foundations of the character have been established and tried out. Now they are launched upon a journey where the character will continue to be built up layer by layer.

Imaginative Leap

Commit and Discover
Right at the start of a workshop when people first get to their feet, I might ask them to take a stretch. Out go the arms, waving about in a vague fashion as people reluctantly do what they have been told, thinking they have given up their time to learn something new, not to do stretches! Well, this is where it starts, Stanislavsky, acting. There is little point in 'going through the motion' of this or any other exercise: it has to be connected. The stretch has to start in the centre and radiate out, so that it is full and committed and the individual gains something from it. Participants have to put themselves into the process and commit to each exercise along the way, even if it has been done many times before. Only by connecting everything they do to themselves will they provide the chance for their creativity to engage. As Arthur Miller says

about acting, 'You have to put yourself into the dilemma of the character.' You and your passion have to be in there with the character. If on a spectrum the character starts at one end and the actor at the other, they have to arrange to meet in the middle. The two merge to create something unique. There is not one perfect Ranyevskaya; everyone's version should and will be different, and the work helps them to engage themselves with the character.

At the beginning of the workshop the resources of memory and experience were prepared by the 'Childhood Map' exercise. This has a good connection for Ranyevskaya, as at the beginning of the play she returns to the house and specifically the nursery where she grew up, to which she has a strong attachment. Now you will ask each person to step into the magic 'if' of his/her imagination. *The Cherry Orchard* takes place on a Russian estate in the early 1900s; 'if' I was there, what would it look and feel like?

Visualizing it may not be easy. The best help would be to travel to the area where the play is supposed to take place. Meanwhile it is more affordable to look at paintings, photographs and films, as well as reading books and taking in the information the playwright has given us. Conjuring up memories of visits to large country houses and estates will also be useful. All this together will form a composite picture, which, coupled with a willingness to make that imaginative leap, will provide ample material.

The next exercise gives a chance for the imagination to engage.

SPIRIT JOURNEY

Ask participants to lie on the floor on their backs, eyes closed, and to relax while you talk them slowly through this imaginative journey: Imagine that you are an invisible spirit hovering at the gates to the Gayev estate (where *The Cherry Orchard* is set). Start to travel through the estate to the front door of the house, noticing in as much detail as possible the landscape, the buildings and the atmosphere of the place.

It is impossible for people to get this exercise wrong! Encourage them to concentrate on what works for them and not to worry about what is incomplete or difficult to visualize. Tell people to imagine they can fly up in the air to get a bird's-eye view of the landscape, and of the relationship of the cherry orchard and the river to the main house. In their imagination they can go through the front door to the hallway, and look at its furniture and decoration. They are invisible, and can see people in the house who might hurry past them on some errand. They take a tour through the house, ending up at the nursery, and notice three interesting details about it. From the nursery suggest they look out to see the cherry orchard.

Most people find this exercise enjoyable when they get over the initial obstacle of starting the journey. It stimulates the resource of personal experience coupled with the imagination in order to substantiate the world of the play.

Having opened up the pathways to past experience, the imagination can be engaged to graft selective real-life experiences on to the particular circumstances of the character you are portraying. Ranyevskaya talks about sleeping in the nursery and looking out to the orchard. Your own childhood bedroom might have had a view that was special to you, and blending that memory with the given circumstances of the play provides a strong emotional connection. Justification is connecting everything a character says or does to yourself and a tangible experience. It provides a structured way for us to encounter our past and use it to inform and stimulate our creative present.

Leading the work, you can choose to keep the concentration going and to let the next stage flow out of the imaginative location by allowing the character to step into it. 'If' I was Ranyevskaya, what would I be doing?

CHARACTER ACTIVITY
i) Still lying on the floor on their backs, ask people to continue their journey as the invisible spirit. They should locate Ranyevskaya somewhere in the house where she is on her own, perhaps in her bedroom or in the nursery. The time is at the beginning of the play, when she has just returned from Paris. She is engaged in some solo activity, such as dressing, unpacking or reading a letter. They should observe her carefully and then, in their mind's eye, make the imaginative leap and become Ranyevskaya, in that place.

ii) The next stage is for people to get slowly to their feet and *be* Ranyevskaya in her room, engaged in her activity, which should keep them physically active and engaged in the present, and keep going like a looped tape.

iii) As they work, ask questions of the Ranyevskayas to stimulate their imaginations and sense of place. What time of day is it? Where is the light coming from? Is it warm? Cold? What does the air feel like against your skin? How are you dressed? What are you standing on? If you look out of the window, what do you see? What can you hear? Are others near by? Can you hear voices? What can you smell? Are you hungry? What did you last eat and when? etc.

If you have the time and resources (e.g. if you are a teacher working regularly with the same group), it can be helpful to set up this last exercise by using whatever appropriate furniture and objects you can find to build a congenial environment. The simple use of a couple of chairs, a sofa, a table and certain selected objects can provide a stimulus and help to lock the actor into the realm of the character. For example, Ranyevskaya may also have in her room a picture of her drowned son Grisha, a necklace that used to belong to her mother, a childhood doll. These significant objects help to keep the character physically engaged, to lock in her concentration and to keep her rooted in the imaginative world. The character's emotional responses will be fired as they encounter the personal objects in their room.

Finding the rudiments of costume, such as a shawl or a long skirt, will also help create an identity. A suitable choice of shoes can be particularly helpful. Costume can make the actor feel and move differently, and that physical reality has a direct effect on character behaviour.

It is important at this stage to encourage people to work on their own rather than being tempted to interact with other characters. It will be more challenging for the individual, and it is important to spend the time to establish a sense of who the character is and how she exists on her own, before thrusting her into the dynamic of relationships. Encourage participants to explore being the character in the environment they have created. Ask them what they have discovered and how they feel? It is important that the actors surprise themselves and don't pre-plan what will happen, but allow themselves to play and genuinely to find out how the character functions when they are on their own. They should take the exercise moment by moment and discover where it leads them. You are hoping that people will discover interesting details, rather than great revelations. For example, someone might have imagined Ranyevskaya to be alone in her room, arranging her private possessions. In becoming the character she might pick up a jewellery box she was given by her mother when she was a girl. Picking it up, what does she recall about the time it was given to her? It was her seventeenth birthday, she had a party, who came? They talked about her future . . . Her mother hugged her and looked sad . . . There is no particular reference to this in the play and it is the kind of possibility to explore, in order to fill in the character's background.

Are they now 'in character'? Yes, they should be, having crossed over and engaged in the magic 'if' of Ranyevskaya. It should feel an organic process, in which they have built up the identification layer by layer rather than diving in unprepared. A commitment to the journey will carry them forward rather than the need to see an end result. This workshop has effected a gentle act of transformation, in which they have stretched beyond themselves to take on the life of someone else. The character is firmly rooted and made out of the raw material of life-experience combined with the blueprint from the text. The transformation is not achieved by disguise or trickery but by a structured process of engagement that gives a powerful sense of being.

Driving Objectives

Having studied drama at Exeter University I was the fortunate recipient of a scholarship to train as an actor in the very different world of the University of California, San Diego. Acting classes were an exotic mixture of Stanislavsky and West Coast pop psychology. Working on a Chekhov play, I remember being thrown by my acting teacher demanding of me whether my character was a 'Poor Me' or a 'Now I've Got You, You Son of a Bitch' – a NIGYYSOB in shorthand?

The route of investigating the psychology of a character can easily be diverted down a blind alley. A teenager once said to me at the end of a Stanislavsky workshop that she was very relieved, as she had thought that I would be trying to break them down and make them cry! Emotion memory exercises can become self-indulgent or stray into the separate world of therapy; but working with responsibility and sensitivity to the group, and keeping the work focused in the arena of the character, it is useful for the participants to gather further information and experience. A platform for the character having been made, it can now be tested by a concentrated improvisation. The same Californian acting teacher had a helpful catchphrase to sum up any character discoveries – 'Put it in the bag, put it in the bag!' – conjuring up an image of the actors coming on stage with sacks over their shoulders full of their rehearsal goodies.

Information needs to be gathered by letting the character react to different situations. The key question Stanislavsky sets for the actor is:

What do I want? (What is my objective?) This is the key question for most of us for most of the time, and how we react to it shapes our lives. Life is a series of objectives; objectives cause action. You want to be a doctor: you go to medical school. You attend classes. You catch the train to school. You get up in the morning and so on. Objectives drive us forward and have a profound effect on our behaviour and attitudes. Imagine next time you are with a group of people that you are intent on stealing someone's wallet, and see how that would dominate your every moment if you had a real intention to do it. Recall being in the same room as someone you were strongly attracted to and wanted to ask out for the first time, and how that objective took you over.

Continuing on from the Character Activity exercise above, each Ranyevskaya is still existing in the environment she has created for herself, occupied in her solo activity. The purpose now of the outside voice is to put the character under pressure while individuals discover how she reacts.

FOLLOWING AN OBJECTIVE

i) Ask the participants to continue to explore the private world of Ranyevskaya. Ask them to think of something the character wants. It can be something momentous, such as 'I want to be in Paris with my lover', or something small, such as 'I want a cup of coffee'. This objective could be something that might happen in the next five minutes or five years. Ask them to focus on it as they carry on with their physical activity. As it goes on, encourage them to make the objective more and more important. Keep raising the stakes, causing the want to become obsessive, so that it takes them over and drives them forward. It now overwhelms them; all they can think about is how to achieve it, and what steps are needed to make it happen. Keep increasing the pressure.

ii) Suddenly, at the peak of intensity, you give it to them: 'It's there, it's happened, it's yours; whatever you wanted, it's happened . . . How does that make you feel?' Allow them to indulge in these feelings for a short while before saying: 'It's an illusion, a dream, it's gone; you haven't got what you wanted, and there you are in your room all alone, still wanting this thing, and it is further away than ever . . . How does that make you feel?' They continue in their private world, going about their activity. A short time later you ask them to stop and to let go of the character.

This process gives new information and deepens identification with the character. Like it or not, each time any of us enters a room we bring our life experience with us and reveal it in some way, in how we move, speak, dress and behave. The actor's need is to fill in as much of the life and history as possible of the part (s)he is playing to make the construction convincing. What the audience eventually see on stage is the tip of the iceberg. The actor must fill in the substance below the water line, so that the audience perceive the history and experience the characters carry with them.

With the introduction of the objective there will be a mixture of responses as it takes hold of them, causing action, which causes emotion. Whatever the activity they were carrying out as Ranyevskaya, it will change in rhythm and tempo as the drive for the objective takes over. The simple act of dressing will take on a physical intensity as she focuses on what it is she wants. The change of the physical rhythm stirs thoughts and emotions within the body.

During this exercise people will discover the difference between wanting something and getting it, a state in which being in active longing is often more absorbing than reaching your goal. Whatever people choose, if they invest the objective with strong desire, the journey towards it will trigger an emotional response. The objective might be 'I want Anya to marry someone rich.' Ranyevskaya starts to plan it, and becomes carried away, putting all the pieces of the jigsaw puzzle together in her mind; only to be disappointed, when the objective is granted, at the letting go of her remaining child. Then it turns out to be a fantasy, and she is despondent at the thought of her financial problems and the task of finding a way out of them. This is all speculation, but useful material to substantiate the character and her state of mind.

After the Character Activity exercises and following an objective, ask people to consider what they have discovered. Including the discussion, allow a minimum of forty-five minutes for this stage.

Up to this point could be a day's work, and now would be a suitable time to conclude. The workshop has:
• Opened up the topic with acting exercises.

- Prepared resources with exercises of memory and imagination.
- Established the character information from the play.
- Developed and tried out the given circumstances.
- Used the magic 'if'.
- Engaged with the strong need for an objective.

The character should feel prepared and launched. Character discoveries are valuable and need to be stored away; the important thing in performance is not to be tempted to stop every few moments to keep getting them out to show the audience! You have to trust that they are there and that they make a difference. Character background works like a hovercraft: it gives characters buoyancy that the actors can ride, secure in the knowledge that it will support them.

The methodical exercises and approach we have looked at in this chapter are only of any use if they release people into play. Actors have to find a way to feel secure enough to begin to take risks, to be playful and creative. The detailed work is only the start of the process, which can be used as a platform to dive off into the unknown.

One of the most playful and inventive actors I have worked with is Mark Rylance (presently Artistic Director of Shakespeare's Globe in London). He works incredibly hard examining the detail of the text and researching the background of the play and his character. He uses that grounding to feed his imagination and creativity, so that in rehearsals he has a ready stream of inventive ideas with which to animate each moment. What is also noticeable is his willingness to discard ideas in the belief that fresh ones will arrive. One day in rehearsal he picks up a newspaper, enters the scene and sits himself down in a chair. He stays put, using the newspaper in various ways to ignore, dismiss and attack his opponent, who is questioning him. It works brilliantly for the scene and is very funny to watch. As onlookers, we assume he has cracked that scene and the newspaper will continue to feature in it. The next time the scene is rehearsed the newspaper is abandoned, and the scene is equally funny and effective, but completely different, as he finds ways of evasion and defence based on his unpredictable movement and flexible use of the text. His ability to be playful and keep the work fresh and alive also continues into performance, so that each show is within a tightly controlled structure, different and specially made for that occasion.

Character Relationships

For the intense period of formulating a character it can be profitable
to encourage the actor to establish a journal. Start with an autobiog-
raphy written in the first person by your character, detailing the major
events of his or her life, based on and moving out from the information
established by the facts written down in the earlier exercise of The Four
Lists. This is followed up with diary entries, also in the first person,
exploring in detail any events in the history of their life, such as
their twenty-first birthday, first trip abroad, the death of a parent,
relationships with friends and family. Also take a reference from the
play, such as the day six years ago when Ranyevskaya fled abroad, and
write about it from her point of view. At the other end of the book the
actors can write as themselves, noting any thoughts, ideas, associations,
images, barriers and breakthroughs.

Active research is also useful to build up knowledge of characters
and their worlds, and might include travel, interviewing people, looking
at films, pictures and books, and listening to music. This can be
broadened out to a collective approach, in which different people lead
workshops based on their research to explore aspects of the social
background, which will share information and allow people to interact
off the direct demands of the text. It will give people a greater investment in the material and increase their commitment to the project.
For instance, practising dances of the era, even if they are not called
upon in the play, is a way of learning about the style and physical
movement of the time. Images are direct and useful, and you might
cover the walls of the room you are working in with pictures that help
visualize the environment of the play.

Previous sections establish a strong and secure base for building up
work on an individual character. If you are working with a particular
group or company of actors for an extended period, and you have been
able to do the preparation work on a number of characters, you could
now put them together to explore their relationships.

Our relationships with people are defined by our common history
and experience, none more so than in families. I worked with a colleague, and one weekend he invited me back to visit his parents' house.
We left the urban centre where we worked and travelled by coach into
what seemed the back of beyond. On arrival at his parents' house a
very different person emerged, as my friend let some of his acquired

sophistication slip and fell back into familiar patterns of behaviour as he interacted with his parents and sister. Their exchanges were superficially minimal, but carried with them layers of history. The body language and what was left unsaid revealed how they felt in each other's company. In relationship to his father my friend became defensive, dismissive and sarcastic, and his father seemed to feel frustrated, hurt and inadequate.

Different people allow us to feel different things about ourselves, and this next exercise provides a framework to explore the history and relationship between characters.

EXPLORING RELATIONSHIPS

Ask people to work in pairs. They should choose partners based on linking up with another character whom they have a significant relationship with in the play. Together they will prepare for an extended improvisation.

Decide on a location where it would be suitable for the two characters to spend time together without the need for other people to be present (e.g. one person's house rather than a café). As before in the individual work, use whatever furniture, props and costume can be found to help build a useful environment. Decide when this meeting takes place. It will be at some specific time before the play begins, as the concern is to fill in the history of the characters and their relationship. The choice might be aligned with some specific reference in the play (e.g. two months ago, just after the divorce). Decide the time of day. Decide on an activity that will provide physical engagement (e.g. sorting out some family possessions).

Each character must have a simple objective for the improvisation that is known only to him or her. Encourage the actors to prepare and agree the background based on what they know from the text. They should also decide on three characteristics that the other person makes them feel about themselves, which can be known to each other: for example, you make me feel sad, angry, decisive. (In the example of my friend, he became defensive, dismissive and sarcastic in relationship to his father.) They should not pre-plan what will happen in the improvisation, but rather set up clear given circumstances in which it may occur. The improvisation can take place between the two characters while the rest of the group watches.

Continuing with our character work on Ranyevskaya, let us look at an example of how we might develop her relationship with her brother

Gayev: Let us say the meeting takes place in the nursery of the house. It would be useful to have two upright chairs, a sofa and one armchair, a coffee-table with a cloth, a bookcase, a sideboard and perhaps a wooden rocking-horse. The time is six years before the play begins. It is a Wednesday mid-morning in May. It is the time before she went to Paris. Her husband died twelve days ago. Ranyevskaya and Gayev are drinking coffee together.

Asking the actors to choose straightforward objectives is important because it gives the improvisation some shape. It is advisable to keep them simple, otherwise the improvisation will become dominated by the objectives, which will detract from the opportunity to allow the relationship to develop openly between the characters. Keep each objective known only to its character, as that will provide direction and tension for the scene.

Ranyevskaya could choose: 'I want Gayev to take more responsibility for Anya' (Anya is her eleven-year-old daughter). Gayev could choose: 'I want to go into town for lunch.'

The two actors should discuss and agree the background to this meeting, such as the circumstances of the husband's death. When was the funeral? Where have they both just come from? For the three characteristics Ranyevskaya might say that Gayev makes her feel impatient, childish and bored. Gayev might want to explore that his sister makes him feel naughty, deficient and pained. The choice of characteristics can give a useful structure to the improvisation as markers around which the relationship can develop.

In all this preparation they should not allow themselves to decide what will take place. The ground having been prepared, the most important elements are the actors' ability to play, to take risks and see what happens. Allow a good amount of time for the improvisation, probably fifteen to thirty minutes. At the beginning it can almost be an extension of their previous individual work, where they get accustomed to being in the space; encourage them not to rush into language, more to co-exist and see where it goes. Throughout try to steer them away from an overreliance on words and towards discovering an active physical life, where the furniture, objects and the other actor feed them with a tangible reality. This physical life can keep going, existing from moment to moment, and will stimulate their imaginations to be free and creative. If the actors come in with preconceived intellectual ideas of how they want to conduct themselves, the work is likely to be lifeless and dull.

Working on character relationships with the students at the Royal Academy of Dramatic Art in London, the improvisations would sometimes meander along and it was plain to see the actors were struggling to keep them going. We were working with two characters from Maxim Gorky's *Children of the Sun*. Pavel, a scientist, and Dmitri, an artist, had been friends since being at school together and then at university. Some fifteen years later Dmitri has reappeared and is falling in love with Pavel's wife Elyena, which Pavel chooses not to notice. The improvisation was built around the two men having some tea together in Pavel's home-made laboratory, while he attempted to interest Dmitri in doing some drawings of his scientific equipment. It started slowly and a certain amount of self-consciousness was appropriate to the circumstances. They talked stiltedly about the 'old times' of their youth; but as the scene continued, both actors looked lost and awkward and were sending out signals that they wanted to stop. Pavel had said Dmitri made him feel childish, while Dmitri had said Pavel made him feel spiteful, but at the moment there was little evidence of either.

Coaching from the sidelines, I encouraged them to keep going and to respond in the moment to what the other one was doing. Dmitri chose to poke fun at Pavel's experiments, and Pavel responded by mocking his 'dabbling' with painting. Again I intervened, telling them to stay with that, to raise the stakes and go further. Pavel tried to light a flame as part of his experiment, but it wouldn't ignite, so Dmitri sneered at him, grabbed the matches, lit the flame and threw the box back at Pavel. The matchbox was now flying between them as they ducked behind the table and chairs, shrieking and jumping around the room as teaspoons, books and anything to hand became ammunition in their battle which mixed childish humour with a competitive tension. It concluded with a mini-explosion as Dmitri poured sugar on to the naked flame!

Fire regulations apart, it became interesting when the actors locked into each other, established real contact and worked to pull each other into the moment. They finally succeeded in playing, being responsive and free to discover where it could go. An idea was established and then it was the physical interaction, not the words, that took it further into an area that no one could have predicted, in which we started to see some of the history and life of the relationship.

When leading the work it is important to coach the actors, encouraging them to take risks, suggesting different directions to pursue and, most of all, getting them to make it more important. Drama is conflict and that is where personality is put to the test. Most people can appear balanced when little is demanded of them, and much more is revealed when they are pitched into a challenging situation. It is when whatever they are doing matters to them that their actions reveal the essence of their relationship.

Character relationship exercises can go on indefinitely: putting different pairs together, and moving up to threes, fours and so on, until some grand improvisation, which could be Ranyevskaya's birthday party, with everyone invited. The idea is to build up the world of the play so that you get a spider's web of interrelationships, and the audience will believe that the world they see on-stage comes from a world that exists off it.

Play Acting

The demands of acting can be very different and can require a different process. It is important that the performers have a practical way to approach work that demands the investigation in detail of what it is they have to do. What is also vital is to know when to let go of the work you have done. Every good piece of theatre has its style, and as you get closer to performance you will let go of your personal process in order to fit into the style of the production. Acting is a personal journey; it is also the ability to be part of a machine that is bigger than you are. The actors have to be able to perform whatever it is that they are required to do by the production with truth, energy and commitment.

Whatever the demands of the piece, some actors will explore questions about the characters' history and experience. Others will choose to concentrate on the external definition. An actor told me that, when he was in a Brecht play, he did all the character research as he would have done for a play by Chekhov, because that was how he approached his work and made himself feel secure in what he was doing. As he got closer to performance, he realized that what was really required of him was to wear his costume and large hat with presence, and perform his function in the narrative. However, he couldn't have trusted to that before he started, and quite rightly he had to follow his personal process.

As a student I saw Ralph Richardson in *The Wild Duck* by Ibsen at the National Theatre, a brilliant performance as the Grandfather, which combined a wonderfully rounded character with the unmistakable presence of that actor. Both were displayed as if he held out his creation in front of him for us to watch and enjoy, while simultaneously sharing his delight with us at this act of make-believe. Was this a performance from the inside or the outside? What process did he use? I don't know. To me it was simply great acting that had its own truth.

The different approaches to playing character all have the same goal: to break the content down into ever greater detail, examine it and put it back together again. The task in performance is always the same: to be present, fully engaged and connected to what you are doing. To achieve this enviable state involves an endless journey; however, a willingness to investigate what acting is, and the playing of character, is essential for anyone studying theatre. As an extended workshop, these exercises also offer an opportunity for anyone interested in developing their personal resources in a creative way to learn about themselves in the meeting of a new challenge.

Working on character is only half the picture and it has to be undertaken in conjunction with exacting work on the text, which is covered in the next chapter.

6 Working on Text

Speaking Out

It is impossible for an Englishman to open his mouth without making some other Englishman hate or despise him.

George Bernard Shaw

There was a research project at Harvard to find out what people were most afraid of; top of the list was speaking in public. Standing up to make an announcement at a meeting, a presentation at work, a speech at a function can all fill people with dread, making them feel self-conscious and uneasy. The voice is personal and revealing, associated with ideas of class and education. In workshops when people are asked to free their voice and commit to sound and words is often the time they become their most inhibited and vulnerable.

Speaking your own words can be problematic, but speaking somebody else's is full of potential pitfalls. They can stick in the throat and feel awkward in the mouth, and there is always the potential embarrassment of misunderstanding or mispronunciation. Memories may surface that haunt us of standing up at school to recite a poem, or giving a reading in church, when we hear the words coming out but they sound disconnected and fall flatly into space.

Of course, public speaking is not confined to actors: politicians, newsreaders, business executives, teachers, priests, salesmen – all speak a text, which may be written down or improvised. All need to hold the attention of their audience by delivering the text with energy and clarity. To be convincing with a text, whether it is written down or improvised, you have to know what it is you want to say.

The ability to handle spoken language is a potentially powerful and extremely useful skill. Politicians and business executives employ coaches to help them become more effective in public speaking. Confidence with language makes an impression on the listener and implies a person of capability; but that confidence comes from ownership of the text. When we speak about something we know and feel passionately about, our voice is animated, responsive and holds the attention. When we mouth words that have little relation to us, the voice flattens out and we sound hollow. So how do we encounter someone else's text in such a way that we can start to own it?

In this chapter we will cover a series of exercises that build up to a detailed approach to working on extracts of text. After some preparation work we will continue using *The Cherry Orchard* as an example, as well as looking at two texts by contemporary writers: *The Birthday Party* by Harold Pinter and *Amy's View* by David Hare.

Workshops can explore all sorts of areas to do with self, play, movement, characters, themes, improvisation. Sometimes that is where they stop, because the next stage – dealing with language and acting text – is often perceived as difficult. As in all good workshop practice, it is useful to start with some exercises that involve the basic skills and vocabulary, which can then be applied to the task. To work on text, it is important first to get people comfortable with using language and committing it towards a specific purpose. The model here is for a workshop lasting one day, which will show a systematic approach used in current theatre practice and based on Stanislavsky, which gives participants comprehensible strategies for working on a script.

Wordplay

Before looking at a specific piece of text it is helpful to provide a bridge by investigating language through wordplay and creating simple dialogue. Drama teachers often feel that their students are good at improvising scenes and that their confidence and animation disappear when they have to pick up a written text. It is vital with speaking any text that it should continue to have the freshness of a good improvisation, and that it should be just as much about giving and responding.

This first exercise in pairs insists that participants listen and work off each other in order to create a dialogue.

YOU/ME

In pairs: each person can only say one word at a time and the dialogue has to go backwards and forwards, A→B→A→B, etc. The total text available consists of the words 'you' and 'me'. Each person can choose whichever word they want. For example:

A You.

B Me.

A You.

B You.

A You.

B Me.

As it goes on, the participants will become more inventive in playing with the language and batting the variations of meaning between them. After about forty-five seconds or so add in the use of 'maybe'. Then follow that with the use of 'yes' and 'no'. The whole conversation will then consist of only these five words, one at a time, in any order. For example:

A Yes.

B You?

A No.

B Me?

A Maybe.

B Yes!

A No!

The dialogue becomes animated as the participants, deprived of an extensive vocabulary, rely on sound and nuance to create meaning. People become fully involved in their conversations and the energy flows between them. The exercise is like keeping a ball up in the air with neither person wanting to be responsible for letting it hit the floor.

In the course of their daily lives most people speak thousands of words each day. However, as soon as any of those words are to be heard in public, speaking becomes a very different prospect and people can easily become self-conscious and inhibited. Certain basic skills are needed to communicate in any public situation, from addressing a handful of people in a meeting to speaking to a full auditorium.

The following exercise highlights the skills needed for clear communication.

SPEAKING APART

Take a line across the middle of the room. Ask people to stand in pairs facing their partner across the line, eyeball to eyeball. Everyone must simultaneously start a conversation with their partner about anything at all. On the signal of a clap from the leader, they must all keep their conversations going while taking two steps backwards. Continue with people taking two steps backwards, until everyone ends up speaking to their partner across the whole length of the room. It will become very noisy as everyone fights to keep their conversation going.

When they reach opposite sides of the room, stop the exercise and ask people what changed in their communication as they moved further apart. They are likely to say: they spoke more loudly, slowly and clearly, held eye contact with their partner, used hands and bodies more, and found easier things to say. These responses can be summed up as: projection, articulation, focus, gesture and simplification.

I was running a 'Behind the scenes at the National Theatre' workshop for the general public, and I conducted the above exercise as a way into rehearsing a text. One dignified older lady looked most put out at being expected to participate in this type of activity. After a few steps she gave up and made elaborate arm-waving gestures to her partner to indicate that she didn't want to carry on, and looked at me with a disapproving expression. The exercise continued and she moved back in silence, still indicating her refusal to participate, until her frustration overwhelmed her and she said, clear as a bell above all the other voices, straight across the space to me: 'This isn't working you know!' Projection, articulation, focus, gesture and simplicity brought together in a perfect moment!

If you really need to communicate, you will find the voice to do it. A parent seeing her child about to run in front of a car doesn't do a voice warm-up before the strong, open sound of 'Stop!' comes out. Speaking over a distance to someone else is like any form of public address used in teaching, presenting, acting, speech-making, training, coaching, although hopefully in none of these are you having to overcome nineteen other voices at the same time! All of these roles involve the need to project the voice, articulate words clearly, focus on who you are addressing, use gesture in order to be animated and expressive and – maybe the most important element of all – simplify what you are saying so that it can be understood.

It is easy in an intimate chat for two people in a bar to speak in a mixture of sentences, phrases and sub-phrases, which can allow for all sorts of twists and turns in the conversation. As soon as this opens out and the speaking is over a distance, the communication has to become clear and concise or the listener will start to lose the thread. This applies to any type of venue, from a large hall to an ordinary-sized room, where there will be a distance between speaker and listener.

More than Words

In the predominantly oral culture of Elizabethan England people were used to giving and receiving information by speaking and listening. The plays of Shakespeare and his contemporaries employ a richness of language, and the thought is on the word, which is to say that the acts of thinking and speaking happen at the same time. When Hamlet steps forward and says, 'To be or not to be, that is the question', the thought occurs to him right at that moment and there is no subtext with it; he is talking directly to the audience, asking, 'Should I live or die?' Moving forward 300 years to the time of Ibsen, Strindberg, Chekhov and, contemporaneously, Freud and the development of psychoanalysis, we delve into the area of 'subtext'.

Language plays along on the surface and all sorts of other meanings can be made around and underneath the words. Language is malleable and is there to be shaped, bent and twisted in order to communicate meaning. Try contrasting a page of Shakespeare with a page of a Pinter play or one of many contemporary writers (see pages 146–7). In the Shakespeare the print is dense, the page crammed full of richly textured words and thought structures. The actor's primary job is to investigate those words and to mine them for all the available information. The Pinter page may have a minimal number of words with pauses, silences and lots of blank spaces. The actor's job is to fill in all those blank spaces, to understand the character's psychology in order to be able to speak the text with an inner conviction.

This simple improvisation will introduce the idea of objectives and subtext. Have three people doing the exercise while the remainder of the group observes.

EATING BREAKFAST

Three people sit on chairs: Louise, Martin and Natalie.

Tell them they are three friends who share a house and are having breakfast together. They can talk about anything at all so long as it is to do with breakfast.

Let the conversation, about toast, tea and semi-skimmed milk or whatever, run its course, being sure not to let anyone stray on to another subject, such as being late for work, or last night's television.

Then take Louise out of the improvisation to tell her in private that she wants to tell Martin that she is in love with him, but that she can only talk about breakfast. The improvisation then continues with all three still only able to talk about breakfast.

The improvisation will change. Ask the observers to comment on what they see. Before they say, 'Louise fancies Martin,' they may also say that Louise has been told 'to do everything for Martin', or that she is trying 'to freeze out Natalie'. All of this information comes from giving one of the performers a strong objective: 'I want to tell you I love you.' Ask the spectators to say which was the more engaging of the two improvisations to watch, and they will invariably say the second. The objective gives the scene structure and the spectators are drawn in. They may not necessarily know what the objective is; it is just more interesting to watch somebody in pursuit of something.

Natalie quickly tends to feel left out of the improvisation, and it is interesting to note how the space between Louise and Martin becomes charged. In a fully rehearsed scene, Natalie would have an objective too, and there would be a network of objectives between the performers that would balance the dynamic. Without an objective to play, Natalie is adrift.

Take a single exchange from this improvisation, for example:

MARTIN Have we got any marmalade?

LOUISE Yes, I got some yesterday when I went shopping. I'll get it for you.

Ask them to say it as they did above, where Louise wants to tell Martin she loves him. Highlight the shaping of the words and the space around the language in the attempt to achieve the objective. Notice also the eye contact and body language. Then ask them to repeat exactly the same words with Louise now having the opposite objective: 'I want to tell you I despise you,' imagining that Martin is lazy and selfish, and she wants him to leave the household. Hear how the same words will come out very differently in tone and texture, and note the contrast in the body language.

From Tokyo to Prague to Boston this improvisation works; only the names and what they eat for breakfast change! We play with words all the time, meaning one thing and saying another. The student who has not done his or her assignment immediately plays the objective of wanting to be excused and given more time, and uses his/her language

King Lear

Fool. A spirit, a spirit: he says his name's poor Tom.

Kent. What art thou that dost grumble Come forth.   [there i' the straw!

Enter Edgar, *disguised as a madman.*

Edg. Away! the foul fiend follows me!—Through the sharp hawthorn blows the wind.—Humph! go to thy cold bed and warm thee.

Lear. Didst thou give all to thy two daugh-And art thou come to this!   [ters!

Edg. Who gives anything to poor Tom! whom the foul fiend hath led through fire and through flame, through ford and whirlpool, o'er bog and quagmire; that hath laid knives under his pillow, and halters in his pew; set ratsbane by his porridge; made him proud of heart, to ride on a bay trotting horse over four-inched bridges, to course his own shadow for a traitor.—Bless thy five wits!—Tom's a-cold,—O, do de, do de, do de.—Bless thee from whirlwinds, star-blasting, and taking! Do poor Tom some charity, whom the foul fiend vexes:—there could I have him now,—and there,—and there again, and there.

    [*Storm continues.*

Lear. What, have his daughters brought him to this pass!—   [them all!

Couldst thou save nothing! Didst thou give

Fool. Nay, he reserved a blanket, else we had been all shamed.

Lear. Now, all the plagues, that in the pen-dulous air   [daughters!

Hang fated o'er men's faults, light on thy

Kent. He hath no daughters, sir.

Lear. Death, traitor! nothing could have subdued nature

To such a lowness, but his unkind daughters.—Is it the fashion, that discarded fathers Should have thus little mercy on their flesh! Judicious punishment! 'twas this flesh begot Those pelican daughters.

Edg. Pillicock sat on Pillicock hill;—Halloo, halloo, loo, loo!

Fool. This cold night will turn us all to fools and madmen.

Edg. Take heed o' the foul fiend: obey thy parents; keep thy word justly; swear not; commit not with man's sworn spouse: set not thy sweet heart on proud array. Tom's a-cold.

Lear. What hast thou been!

Edg. A serving-man, proud in heart and mind; that curled my hair; wore gloves in my cap; served the lust of my mistress's heart, and did the act of darkness with her; swore as many oaths as I spake words, and broke them in the sweet face of heaven: one, that slept in the contriving of lust, and waked to do it: wine loved I deeply, dice dearly; and in woman out-paramoured the Turk: false of heart, light of ear, bloody of hand; hog in sloth, fox in stealth, wolf in greediness, dog in madness, lion in prey. Let not the creaking of shoes, nor the rustling of silks, betray thy poor heart to woman: keep thy foot out of brothels, thy hand out of plackets, thy pen from lenders' books, and defy the foul fiend.—Still through the hawthorn blows the cold wind: says suum, mun, nonny. Dolphin my boy, my boy; sessa! let him trot by.

    [*Storm still continues.*

Lear. Why, thou wert better in thy grave, than to answer with thy uncovered body this extremity of the skies.—Is man no more than this! Consider him well. Thou owest the worm no silk, the beast no hide, the sheep no wool, the cat no perfume.—Ha! here's three of us are sophisticated! Thou art the thing itself: unaccommodated man is no more but such a poor, bare, forked animal as thou art.—Off, off, you lendings!—Come, unbutton here.—   [*Tearing off his clothes.*

Fool. Pr'ythee, nuncle, be contented; 'tis a naughty night to swim in.—Now a little fire in a wild field were like an old lecher's heart,—a small spark, all the rest on's body cold.—Look, here comes a walking fire.

Edg. This is the foul fiend Flibbertigibbet: he begins at curfew, and walks to the first cock; he gives the web and the pin, squints the eye, and makes the harelip; mildews the white wheat, and hurts the poor creature of earth.

St. Withold footed thrice the old;
He met the night-mare, and her nine-fold;
    Bid her alight,
    And her troth plight,
And, aroint thee, witch, aroint thee!

Kent. How fares your grace?

Enter Gloster, *with a torch.*

Lear. What's he!

Kent. Who's there! What is't you seek!

Glo. What are you there! Your names!

Edg. Poor Tom; that eats the swimming frog, the toad, the tadpole, the wall-newt, and the water-newt; that in the fury of his heart, when the foul fiend rages, eats cow-dung for sallets; swallows the old rat, and the ditch-dog; drinks the green mantle of the standing pool; who is whipped from tything to tything, and stocked, punished, and imprisoned: who hath had three suits to his back, six shirts to his body, horse to ride, and weapon to wear;—But mice, and rats, and such small deer, Have been Tom's food for seven long year.

Glo. What, hath your grace no better com-pany!

Edg. The prince of darkness is a gentleman; Modo he's call'd, and Mahu.

Glo. Our flesh and blood, my lord, is grown so vile,

That it doth hate what gets it.

Edg. Poor Tom's a-cold.

Glo. Go in with me: my duty cannot suffer To obey in all your daughter's hard com-mands:

Though their injunction be to bar my doors, And let this tyrannous night take hold upon you,

The Dumb Waiter

GUS. Ben.

BEN. Away. They're all playing away.

GUS. Ben, look here.

BEN. What?

GUS. Look.

BEN *turns his head and sees the envelope. He stands.*

BEN. What's that?

GUS. I don't know.

BEN. Where did it come from?

GUS. Under the door.

BEN. Well, what is it?

GUS. I don't know.

They stare at it.

BEN. Pick it up.

GUS. What do you mean?

BEN. Pick it up!

GUS *slowly moves towards it, bends and picks it up.*

What is it?

GUS. An envelope.

BEN. Is there anything on it?

GUS. No.

BEN. Is it sealed?

GUS. Yes.

BEN. Open it.

GUS. What?

BEN. Open it!

GUS *opens it and looks inside.*

What's in it?

GUS *empties twelve matches into his hand.*

GUS. Matches.

and delivery to achieve it: 'I'm sorry, the dog was sick and . . .' Likewise, when two people meet at a party and one says to the other, 'Would you like to come back to my place for a cup of coffee?', the sentence is shuddering with subtext.

A playwright may similarly choose to restrict the language that a character uses, leaving him to talk about travel arrangements when he intended to propose marriage. The subtext is left between the characters, and the audience read it underneath the words they hear. Confining the improvisation to being only about breakfast takes the emphasis away from the choice of words and puts it on to how the body and voice convey meaning. It helps us to break down how communication works. Research conducted by Albert Mehrabian showed that communication is 55 per cent body language, 38 per cent tonality and 7 per cent words. The words we choose to speak are the smallest part of the total effect. We give out the strongest signals through our physicality, followed by the way we shape and use the sound of language.

David can stand up in front of the sales force and say, 'I'm really excited about this new product and I'm sure with the great team we have here we can meet our targets.' But if he leaves his hands in his pockets, slumps his shoulders, looks at his shoes and mumbles his words, no one will believe a word he says. His body language and voice need to be congruent with his purpose, which is to motivate his colleagues. He has to be clear about what his intention is; then his body and voice will follow along with his words.

Does this mean that in a Shakespeare play what the audience receive is only 7 per cent to do with the words on the page? Perhaps the clearest way to think about it is that the stage presentation and what the actor does with his body and voice are the 93 per cent that are there to support the 7 per cent. So the actors have to be clear what it is they want to communicate, and ensure that their body and voice are flexible enough to accomplish it.

To focus communication we need a clear intention – an objective.

Using Objectives

Making Contact

In rehearsal the director sits like a statue on his chair all day long, watching and listening intently as the actors work. With razor-sharp concentration he watches the run-through of the scene. He uses his words sparingly and quietly, puts some questions, makes some suggestions, and asks for the scene to be run again. The actors hang on his every word. On to the next scene, and slowly through the day. Suddenly, late in the afternoon, he stops the run-through and asks one of the actors, 'What are you doing?' The room freezes; the actor mumbles something incoherent. 'What is your objective?' The actor's mind goes blank. The director explodes, 'Don't come on the f***ing stage without a f***ing objective. Start again.'

Objectives root you into what you are doing and make sure that you come on to stage with a purpose. They also ensure that you make contact with the other actors on-stage, that you want something from them and that what you do affects them.

Performance training is centred on concentration and focus of energy. These qualities enable actors to be present and in the moment, and that is where they are at their most creative and most available for interaction. In preparation for working on text it is necessary to have opened up the facility to make contact with fellow actors and to be available to give and receive.

THE HYPNOTIST

In pairs.

i) A focuses from ten centimetres away on the palm of B's hand. B moves slowly around the space, varying his/her physical pattern and shape; A follows, keeping the ten-centimetre distance constant between his/her eyes and B's palm. And change over.

ii) Now drop the hand and make eye contact. Move around the space together, A leading, then B; then no one leading, just moving together, keeping the steady focus and becoming bolder in the use of space and physical movement.

This establishes a circle of concentration where the two players are focused on each other. It also creates the effect of the fourth wall, where the audience are not acknowledged and the players are locked into each other, helping them to keep in their shared reality. It requires the actors to be open and able to respond to each other.

Teachers and parents of young children are particularly good at doing several things at once. So should actors be; it is the equivalent of remembering your lines, using the space and playing your objective all at once. If you do the following exercise, you have no room left to think about what is for lunch or to feel self-conscious as you are made to concentrate by the task in hand. Being mentally alive and alert, able to respond lightly and quickly, is how you aim to be as a performer.

THREE AND ONE

Four people, one of whom is Ella, who will be the focus of this exercise.

Ella sits on a chair with Freddie sitting opposite. Freddie leads Ella in a simple mirror exercise. At the same time Grace and Harry alternate asking Ella questions.

Grace asks simple personal questions, such as 'What is your favourite film?' Harry asks simple mathematical questions. Grace and Harry can overlap their questions and insist on getting answers.

How well can Ella keep the movement going while at the same time continuing to answer the questions? It requires strong yet flexible concentration.

Objectives Cause Action

To communicate clearly, you have to know what it is you want to say. An actor has to have a firm objective. Once a choice is made, it must be played for all it is worth. Playing the objective causes action, and action causes emotion. The following exercise takes people through the progression of given circumstances: an objective, action, obstacle and emotion.

RAILWAY STATION

i) Ask people to walk quickly in the space. Vary it: walk on tiptoes, heels, the insides and outsides of their feet, take large steps. The space will be full of people moving, making different shapes and patterns.

ii) Now ask participants to work on their own and to imagine that they are at a large railway station to meet a friend in whom they have a strong interest. They have in their pocket two expensive tickets for a sell-out show, which starts in half an hour at a venue next door to the station. They have spoken on the phone with their friend and gone over the arrangements, and the time to meet is now, on the station concourse.

iii) Each person is in the space, playing the objective: 'I want to find my friend.' It is rush hour and there are lots of people, and so it is difficult to find someone. They keep active in the attempt to find their friend. Move the time forward: twenty minutes to go and the friend still isn't to be seen ... Ten minutes to go ... Eight minutes to go ... Additionally, each person ought to be at an important work meeting this evening, but they phoned in, feigning illness in order to be able to go to this special occasion; and for some inexplicable reason they spot their boss coming across the concourse, heading in their direction ... What do they do? Five minutes to go ... The boss has gone and still 'I want to find my friend.' Bring the exercise to an end.

The looking for the friend will cause the space to be full of people moving in different shapes, similar to the initial walking on the toes, heels, etc. What is the difference? Both sets of instructions produce movement in broken patterns. The first is a physical objective – 'I want to walk on my toes' – which is carried out. The second is a psychological objective – 'I want to find my friend' – which causes action. People start to act by moving in the space in different ways to look for their friend. It was never stated that people should start to act; it is that a strong objective causes action.

The psychological objective causes action, which causes emotion. The given circumstances were such as to give the situation some value, and it is the physical action of looking that generates the emotion. This is an important point: that emotion comes out of a want and an action to achieve it. As Uta Hagan, the American actress, said neatly in her book *Respect for Acting*: 'MOOD spells DOOM.' You cannot play a scene on mood, with a generalized feeling that you are sad or angry or in love. I may shuffle on-stage believing I am awash with emotion, but unless I am playing action, I will be giving nothing to my fellow actors and it will be mere self-indulgence. In the exercise above the participants had to play a strong objective – 'I want to find my friend' – which caused action; and as they failed in their objective, that perhaps generated the emotion of worry or frustration.

As you read these words, stop, close your eyes and think of being angry. Now try the same thing while gripping the book as hard as you can, or banging your fist into your open hand. The action makes it much easier to generate the feeling of anger. In the Railway Station exercise the emotions are generated by the action of moving in a quick, fractured pattern pressurized by the given circumstances of time and the desire to find the friend.

This is the link between our physical action and our psychological response, which is the basis for working methodically on text: that taking a physical action into our bodies releases attendant feelings. If you wake up in the morning feeling terrible and then spend the day slouching around, the chances are you will continue to feel terrible. Taking a brisk walk wakes us up.

In the exercise above the objective of finding the friend was made even more difficult at one point by the boss's untimely appearance at the station. This is the introduction of an obstacle. Life is a series of objectives that would be straightforward enough if it were a case of just going ahead and achieving them. However, life is also full of obstacles, and attempting to overcome them generates friction and energy. For instance, Robbie wants to tell Suzy that he is in love with her; the obstacle is that Suzy is going out with Tom, and Tom is Robbie's best friend. The objective is strong and the stakes are raised by the obstacle.

An objective serves to focus both the actors and the audience, as in the following quick example.

HAIR AND CUFF

i) Ask three people to stand on one leg. They must hold a lock of their hair between the thumb and forefinger of one hand, and with the thumb and forefinger of the other hand hold on to the cuff of the trousers of their raised leg. Ask them to hold the position while everybody else looks at them.

ii) Then ask them to repeat the same position, but now to feel the difference in texture between their hair and the material of their trousers.

The second time they will be more focused, steadier on their one foot and less self-conscious. They now have an objective to root them in the action: 'I want to feel the difference in texture . . .' and they will be absorbed in attempting to achieve it. The audience will also be drawn in by the second version, as they are interested to watch them pursue an objective. The first time they watch sitting back, amused, because it is not they who are standing on one leg feeling foolish.

The potential for feeling self-conscious and awkward in front of an audience is infinite, irrespective of it being in a grand theatre or a tiny church hall. Acting in a play, giving a business presentation or making a speech, when you don't know what you are doing, are all the stuff of nightmares. Who are you speaking to and what is your objective? They all require preparation and a clear strategy to be successful.

The objective is a hook to hang on to. As an actor you stand in the wings, ready to go on-stage, waiting for your cue. Any number of critical voices will be competing for attention inside your head, spurred on by the lowered resistance of your nervousness: 'I look terrible.' 'I can't act.' 'The audience won't like me.' It is like being on the phone. You are making a telephone call and someone comes into the room to ask you a question. Well, it is impossible to carry on two conversations at once, so you have to put the phone down, answer the question and then resume the phone call. Yet this is what we do constantly in our own heads, allowing a conversation to take place with ourselves that is usually negative and critical, while we attempt to carry out some other activity. At this moment, by the side of the stage, the one thing to concentrate on is your first objective, which will focus you and take you forward, such as: 'I want you to come away with me.' You repeat it over and over as a way of pushing away the negative thoughts, and then you are catapulted on to the stage – contacting the other actors, speaking the lines and shaping the words as you concentrate all your efforts on achieving your objective.

Including a warm-up, these specific exercises on the use of language, concentration, interaction and objectives should take ninety minutes to two hours. Together they prepare the ground, and we can move on to applying them to a piece of text.

On the Text

Actors love to be praised. At the bar after the show a member of the audience floats over to offer their admiration and congratulations. The actor, all humility, swells with pride, until the question 'How do you learn all those lines?' punctures the cosy atmosphere and somehow devalues the currency of the accolade. Learning the lines is the easy bit; it is what to do with them that is the hard part.

Building a workshop around taking a short section of text and breaking it down into fine detail is a microcosm of the whole process of making theatre. Every part of the work has to be deconstructed in order for it to be crafted into shape. It requires collaboration, negotiation, analysis and creativity. How do you do it? Unstructured rehearsals can easily descend into practising the moves, punctuated by generalized discussions about what it all means.

We are going to continue to use Chekhov's *The Cherry Orchard* as an example to work on, in a translation by Michael Frayn. Here is a short extract from Act 1, in which Ranyevskaya, Anya her seventeen-year-old daughter, and the footman Yasha have just arrived back from Paris. Varya is the adopted daughter and housekeeper, aged twenty-four. Firs is the old footman. Dunyasha the chambermaid is preparing coffee in the nursery.

Enter YASHA *with a rug and travelling bag.*

YASHA (*crosses with delicacy*): All right to come through?
DUNYASHA I shouldn't even recognize you, Yasha. You've changed so abroad!
YASHA Mm . . . And who are you?
DUNYASHA When you left I was so high . . . (*Indicates from the floor.*) Dunyasha. Fyodor Kozoyedov's daughter. You don't remember!
YASHA Mm . . . Quite a pippin, aren't you? (*Looks round and embraces her. She screams and drops a saucer.*)

Exit YASHA, *swiftly.*

VARYA (*in the doorway, displeased*): Now what's going on?
DUNYASHA (*through her tears*): I've smashed the saucer . . .
VARYA That's good luck.
ANYA (*coming out of her room*): We should warn Mama – Petya's here.
VARYA I gave orders not to wake him.
ANYA (*reflectively*): Six years since Father died, and only a month later that Grisha was drowned in the river. My brother . . . Seven years old, and such a pretty boy. Mama couldn't bear it. She escaped – fled without so much as a backward glance . . . (*Shivers.*) I understand her so well, if only she knew!

Pause.

And Petya Trofimov was Grisha's tutor. He may remind her . . .

Enter FIRS, *in jacket and white waistcoat.*

FIRS (*goes to the coffee-pot, preoccupied*): The mistress will be taking it in here . . . (*Puts on white gloves.*) The coffee ready? (*To* DUNYASHA, *sternly*) What's this, girl? Where's the cream?

DUNYASHA Oh, my Lord . . . (*Rushes out.*)

FIRS (*busies himself about the coffee-pot*): Oh, you sillybilly! (*Mutters to himself.*) Come from Paris . . . The master went to Paris once . . . by post-chaise . . . (*Laughs.*)

VARYA What are you going on about, Firs?

FIRS What do you want? (*Joyfully*) My lady has come home! I waited for her! I can die happy . . . (*Weeps with joy.*)

The first thing to do is to read out loud the section to be worked on. When people are asked to read a piece of text in a workshop, some will be terrified and read in a halting, broken manner. Some will be overeager and, in their desire to please, they will start 'acting' by jumping straight in to give a full-blown interpretation of the words based on very little. It could instinctively be interesting, but the chances are it will overwhelm the playwright's words and crowd out other possibilities. As in the character work of the previous chapter, it is important to start from neutral and to take in the information given. The work on text is about opening up what is possible, not about rushing into decisions. There should be no requirement to give any kind of performance here – quite the opposite, where you try to efface yourself so that we can simply hear the words.

The following exercise is an opportunity for people to listen and make contact.

SPEAKING AND LISTENING

Set up five chairs for the five characters of this extract. Dunyasha sits on one chair, as she is in the scene already. As Yasha enters he sits down so that he can make eye contact with Dunyasha. Reading the text, each person will take a line in before looking up from the page and making eye contact. They then speak the line neutrally and slowly to the other person. Continue with characters coming in and out.

The aim is not to colour the words at all, but simply to let the words be heard. The rest of the group should sit and listen rather than reading their scripts. This is the equivalent of the Four Lists exercise in the character work in Chapter 5: mining the text for all the available information before starting the process of interpretation. The words will have an impact of their own and, as an actor, you are a vessel for the language. It is said that one of the most important basic skills of acting is the ability to listen, because that is when you really give your concentration to the other person.

Breaking into Units

Presented with a plate of food, however hungry you are, you cannot eat it all at once. You cut up the food and digest it in mouth-sized bites. A play is too big to digest in its entirety, and it has to be broken down so that it can be worked on in detail. The playwright usually divides it into acts and scenes, and it will require further division into units. A traditional novel is written in parts, chapters and paragraphs, and the process of breaking a text down into units is the equivalent of putting in the paragraphs. All practitioners – Stanislavsky, Brecht, Grotowski, Brook, through to directors such as Max Stafford-Clark and Katie Mitchell – have a methodology to achieve the process of breaking the work down into ever greater detail.

A unit is a paragraph of narrative. If you wanted to describe the narrative of your day in detail to someone else, you would probably do so logically as a series of units: out of bed/get washed/get dressed/ eat breakfast/leave the house/walk to the station/catch the train/walk to work, etc. Unit breaks in a text are distinguished by the entrance or exit of a character, a change of subject or a change of stage action.

UNITS

Take the section of text we have chosen to work on, and as a group break it down into units. The chosen section could break down into four units. For example:

UNIT 1

Enter YASHA *with a rug and travelling bag.*

YASHA (*crosses with delicacy*): All right to come through?
DUNYASHA I shouldn't even recognize you, Yasha. You've changed so abroad!
YASHA Mm . . . And who are you?
DUNYASHA When you left I was so high . . . (*Indicates from the floor.*) Dunyasha. Fyodor Kozoyedov's daughter. You don't remember!
YASHA Mm . . . Quite a pippin, aren't you? (*Looks round and embraces her. She screams and drops a saucer.*)

Exit YASHA, *swiftly.*

UNIT 2

VARYA (*in the doorway, displeased*): Now what's going on?

DUNYASHA (*through her tears*): I've smashed the saucer . . .

VARYA That's good luck.

UNIT 3

ANYA (*coming out of her room*): We should warn Mama – Petya's here.

VARYA I gave orders not to wake him.

ANYA (*reflectively*): Six years since Father died, and only a month later that Grisha was drowned in the river. My brother . . . Seven years old, and such a pretty boy. Mama couldn't bear it. She escaped – fled without so much as a backward glance . . . (*Shivers.*) I understand her so well, if only she knew!

Pause.

And Petya Trofimov was Grisha's tutor. He may remind her . . .

UNIT 4

Enter FIRS, *in jacket and white waistcoat.*

FIRS (*goes to the coffee-pot, preoccupied*): The mistress will be taking it in here . . . (*Puts on white gloves.*) The coffee ready? (*To* DUNYASHA, *sternly*) What's this, girl? Where's the cream?

DUNYASHA Oh, my Lord . . . (*Rushes out.*)

FIRS (*busies himself about the coffee-pot*): Oh, you sillybilly! (*Mutters to himself.*) Come from Paris . . . The master went to Paris once . . . by post-chaise . . . (*Laughs.*)

VARYA What are you going on about, Firs?

FIRS What do you want? (*Joyfully*) My lady has come home! I waited for her! I can die happy . . . (*Weeps with joy.*)

It is useful to give the units titles to help clarity and understanding. People opt for different approaches with titling units, varying between tabloid newspaper headlines, such as 'Dunyasha's a smasha for Yasha!', and itemizing each part of the content, which ends up being longer than the text itself. We will aim for something in between.

Working with a group, someone might suggest for unit 1: 'Yasha and Dunyasha fancy each other and enjoy flirting.' This should be rejected, as it is too interpretative for this stage of the work. If you write this at the side of your text you may be stuck with having to act it like that for ever more. It may be a good choice; but you want to leave the possibilities wide open at this point. The aim is to give a clear outline of the narrative of the text and save the interpretation for later. A more useful title for unit 1 could be: 'Yasha enters, meets Dunyasha. They talk of recognition. Physical contact. Dunyasha screams. Saucer dropped. Yasha exits.' This tells you what happens, so that the story can keep moving forward. Yasha has to come in. He has to make physical contact with Dunyasha, in order for her to scream and drop the saucer, which causes him to leave. If Dunyasha does not scream, Yasha does not have a reason to leave, and Varya does not have a reason to enter.

Title for unit 2: 'Varya enters, questions Dunyasha.'

Title for unit 3: 'Anya enters, talks to Varya about Petya, the past and effect on Mama.'

Title for unit 4: 'Firs enters. Coffee. Cream? Dunyasha exits. Paris. Mistress has come home . . .'

These are only suggestions and there are no right or wrong answers. Dunyasha's exit in unit 4 could be made into a separate unit, but it seems to be contained within Firs's narrative. Deciding on units is like those science experiments at school with iron filings and magnets: you have to find the core of the unit and then all the lines are drawn to it. The only rule is that it has to be useful to the actor. Break it down too much and you will move towards each thought structure being a new unit, which will merely replicate the punctuation. Divide it too little and understanding of the narrative will remain too generalized to be helpful.

Read the text through again out loud, noticing the placement of the units; you will hear how it starts to make clearer sense and become the telling of a story. A good way to test the efficacy of the work on units is to do a follow-up improvisation. This will be the group's first time up on their feet working with the scene.

UNITS IMPROVISATION

Ask for five people to play the five characters. Make a rough approximation of the playing space you are going to use with its entrances and exits. Ask the actors to put down their texts and improvise the section, using their own words, or some or all of Chekhov's, if they can remember them.

This should show that through the units there is a common understanding between the actors of the progress of the basic narrative of the section. If they had just read the section a few times and not divided it into units, the improvisation would probably be inaccurate and generalized, with moments missed out and jumps in the narrative. For instance, Yasha might enter, be caught there by Varya and, before he has a chance to leave, Anya might enter to talk about her mother. Following the units should mean the actors have a clear grasp of the sequential course of the narrative, before they go on to learn their lines.

It is necessary for the actors to be clear about the story they are telling before moving on to the interpretation of it. It is like getting the base line of a song worked out before you go on to layer in the harmonies. In rehearsals some directors divide the play into units with the whole company discussing and agreeing the divisions. Some directors may have prepared it before rehearsals began; others never mention it at all. An actor needs to have a way of breaking down the text to enable him or her to work on it in the detail it will require. The aim is not for the audience to be leaving the theatre many weeks later after a performance and turning to one another to say, 'My goodness, their units were good!' It is part of the process, and when the audience see the play it will appear as a whole structure.

Applying Objectives

Speaking text can be daunting, and it can also be liberating. A workshop on the play *Billy Liar* by Keith Waterhouse and Willis Hall was offered to a boys' school in the East End of London, where the students were mostly Bengali, with English as a second language. I thought we had made a big mistake: the play is set in an industrial town in the north of England in 1959, and the page of dialogue I had chosen contained references to British Army Desert Troops in the Second World War, a funeral, garden gnomes and fishing. As well as this, it was all written in strong Yorkshire dialect. Sure enough, the boys looked completely bemused and humiliated as they painfully attempted to read their way through it. It was incomprehensible to them. Sticking to the plan, we divided the extract into units, discussed what wasn't clear and, as we did so, they began to understand the narrative. We then got to our feet and started to make choices about objectives, discovering the needs and wants of the characters. The words started to take on shape and colour as the dialogue became animated and the characters came to life. Their speaking of the dialect was lively and unforced, and they completely understood the situation of the three young characters, who are hanging around on a Saturday night, wondering what to do. It is captivating to release a writer's well-written dialogue and to feel the rhythm and texture of the words interacting. The boys were empowered by their ability to bring this alien text to life and enter into another world.

Objectives are particularly effective with inexperienced actors, as they give them something definite to hold on to, and provide a clear structure to help creativity. In the limited time available they can move the participants forward quickly, enabling them to see the advantages of making clear choices and playing them with commitment. As in the 'Eating Breakfast' improvisation earlier, the objective immediately gives the scene a shape, and the participants can see the potential for making performance.

Workshops at least carry with them the idea of exploration, whereas rehearsals can sometimes get confused with practice. Rehearsals should not be about staging the play and repeating it. They are about clarifying, trying things out, experimenting and building up the possibilities that lie within a text, so that in performance you are buoyed up by the experience and information of a creative rehearsal period. A productive way to explore the potential of the text in a workshop or rehearsal is to try out different objectives. By testing objectives against the text you start to discover what the possibilities of interpretation are.

OBJECTIVES

Take unit 1 between Yasha and Dunyasha. The two actors need to choose an objective each. It is helpful to make people phrase their objectives and declare them out loud: 'I want to . . .' Otherwise it is too easy for people to be vague. Get them to be specific. Remember, the objective has to move the character forward and cause action; for example, for Yasha: 'I want to unpack the luggage'; for example, for Dunyasha: 'I want to make the coffee.' Using the text, perform the unit only, playing these objectives.

Played this way Yasha would be most interested in passing through with the luggage and Dunyasha in arranging the coffee-table – possible, useful and not terribly exciting. Try it again. Someone suggests for Yasha 'I want to seduce her,' and for Dunyasha 'I want to impress him.' Just as in the 'Eating Breakfast' exercise, you have to play the objective for all it is worth, moulding the language and the action to try to achieve it. A participant once said, 'Oh, you mean OTT!' No, it is not to do with being over the top; it is all to do with making the objective important, letting it affect you and change you. We found this in the character work with Ranyevskaya when she was alone and wanting something strongly. You must play the objective right through from the first moment to the last.

Play the unit again with these new objectives – Yasha: 'I want to seduce her'; Dunyasha: 'I want to impress him.'

Now the situation and the language start to come alive. The objectives are more immediate and they are to do with each other. Yasha's eyes fix on Dunyasha, she moves quickly in front of him, and they lock into playing together. It is being made in the moment and they are discovering where it can go. Yasha surprises himself by dropping the bag and advancing on Dunyasha, who spins and moves back to the coffee-table. They are projected into creative choices by the strength of their objectives.

Make sure the actors have absorbed the earlier exercise of Speaking and Listening (page 155) and that they still really talk and listen to each other. The words will now be more energized, but that does not mean that they should shoot past each other in some exaggerated manner; they still have to connect and be spoken to the other actor. It is about giving and responding.

The actors should enjoy trying things out, allowing anything to happen within the confines of the text and the unit. Yasha has to enter and exit; there has to be physical contact, and a saucer has to be dropped – otherwise you can ignore the stage directions and any idea of 'blocking', the process of deciding in rehearsal the most effective stage positions of the characters. George Bernard Shaw achieved the zenith of writing stage directions with good reason: to help those people unlikely ever to see a performance of the play to visualize the action. As an actor you need to discover the stage action for yourself rather than having it prescribed for you. Yasha may indeed end up 'embracing' Dunyasha, as suggested in the text, and it is also worth exploring what else that moment of physical contact might be? A squeeze of the arm? A pinch on the bum? 'Blocking' is a terrible word, as solid and deadening as it suggests. Some parts of the stage action, probably including entrances and exits, will eventually need to be fixed. Meanwhile, keep the possibilities of play and discovery as wide open as possible.

A good quick game to introduce at this point to illustrate how objectives should be played is:

BACK-HAND TAG

In pairs: each player puts his/her left hand behind their back, and their right hand up in the air. The aim is to score points by tagging your opponent's back hand while protecting your own. The game is usually played with high energy, with both players on the front of their feet dancing around each other. That is how playing objectives should feel: you are on your toes, aiming hits at your partner and responding to what comes at you.

The actors playing the roles of Yasha and Dunyasha, with their objectives of 'seducing' and 'impressing', will now be having such a good time flirting and playing off each other that when Dunyasha screams, Yasha will not want to leave. He would rather stay to pursue his objective further. So what takes him out of the room? It is the hierarchy of objectives. His immediate objective might be 'I want to seduce her'; his overall objective for this section might be 'I want to unpack the luggage'; his main line of action for Act 1 might be 'I want to keep in favour with Ranyevskaya'; while his super-objective might be 'I want to get back to Paris.' They are appropriately like Russian dolls, one inside the other. His most important need is 'to get back to Paris'. In order to achieve this he has 'to keep in favour with Ranyevskaya', and 'unpacking the luggage' is part of that. At the moment he arrives at the door with the rug and travelling bag he is playing his overall or scenic objective: 'I want to unpack the luggage,' until he spots Dunyasha, when he changes to 'I want to seduce her.' When she screams and he is in danger of being discovered alone with Dunyasha, his brain clicks into Paris! Ranyevskaya! Unpack the luggage! And he hurriedly leaves Dunyasha until later.

Seducing Dunyasha still fits with his super-objective. He still intends to return to Paris in order to feel he is moving up in the world, and meanwhile an affair will feed his sense of self-importance and status.

Objectives should always be broadly moving in the same direction. They may go off at a tangent, but they should not be in opposition. The important point is to make bold, clear choices, as the objective has to excite and stimulate you so that you enter the scene with an energy and commitment to play it. It is your drive through the text, and causes you to shape and mould each line to achieve it. Everything in acting has to be urgent – that doesn't mean it has to be fast. The objective has to motivate you to take action. It has to be precise and alluring, to engage your character's passion and your actor's creativity.

Immediate objectives usually change with the unit. They can also change for a character within a unit. An objective may last for two or more units. There are no rules. Objectives are not written in stone; they provide a framework for the actor to play within. Use a pencil to write them on your script, for practical reasons and to acknowledge their changeability.

Try out different immediate objectives to explore other possibilities – for example, Yasha: 'I want to assert my superiority'; Dunyasha: 'I want to puncture your stuck-up manner.' See how different the unit becomes. It will help the actors to discover the range of their characters and the text. It will all provide useful information that will not be wasted, as it will make you brim-full of the possible choices the character might make. The text should never become preordained, as if it were fate being played out. It should always retain the spark of improvisation, where characters make moment-to-moment choices, unaware of their final destination. They play their want, which maybe different from what they eventually achieve.

If you are moving towards performance, you will probably make choices about which objectives to play. Whichever you choose, there are still many different ways to play it. If you stay with 'I want to seduce her,' you can still feed your fellow actor at every performance with the ways you choose to achieve it. The text between you has to be reinvented each time to make it fresh and real: an improvisation within a tight structure of the lines and the objectives, made for that audience on that particular occasion.

When a workshop or rehearsal process leads to performance it is vital, even under the pressure of scrutiny and repetition, to keep the freedom of invention alive. Some directors come to see performances and then ask that the actors come up with some different choices next time, in order to shake up the set patterns and cause the performances to be reinvented. One director moves the set about in small ways to throw the actors slightly, and to prevent the performance from becoming comfortable or mechanical.

To work through this chapter up to this point would provide plenty of material for a one-day workshop. You will have covered playing with language, improvisations to explore objectives and subtext, as well as dividing the text into units and applying objectives to it. The next section provides an opportunity to develop the work further in a specific area.

Physical Actions

Stanislavsky was the stage name created to hide the real identity of Konstantin Alexeyev who, as a young man of a wealthy Moscow merchant family, had to hide the fact that he acted in makeshift theatre groups in the city, as it would have been thought improper and lower class by his family. The family fortune was made from the manufacture of gold and silver thread for the civil and military uniforms of Imperial Russia. By day the young Alexeyev worked in the family business, and by night he was a dedicated amateur actor. As Jean Benedetti points out in his biography of Stanislavsky, he would have been familiar with the breakdown of complex manufacturing processes into a sequence of simple actions on a production line, and there is a connection with the step-by-step system he evolved to create high-quality acting.

In this section we will further break down the text to examine each line or phrase and attach an action to it. It is painstaking and detailed work. At this point in a workshop participants can start to look troubled, and to feel that this is all some way from the 'get up and do it' acting that all of us comprehend. It all seems intensely logical and dry.

It is logical and possibly particularly male in its sequential, left-brain approach. What is of paramount importance is to remember that it is a means to an end, and that the end product should be anything but dry and lifeless. The detailed investigation of the text is only intended to provide a platform for work that will be free, inventive and creative. In order to enjoy the liberation you have to do the hard work first.

The spark of improvisation in playing a scene allows the actor's movement to change: a different physical pattern will stimulate a different creative response and open up new possibilities. The body leads and the brain follows. Acting is action towards an objective, and that action has a physical impulse, which causes an emotional release. Stanislavsky's later work focused on 'The Method of Physical Actions'.

Taking Action

This next exercise can be played in two ways – firstly, with a new group at rehearsals or workshops to break the ice and to introduce people; secondly, as an introduction to the challenging task of delving into our personal memories and resources.

MAP OF THE ROOM

i) The whole of the floor space is an imaginary map of the country that you are in, e.g. Britain. You agree which direction is north. Everyone has to go and stand on the map where they were born. This requires negotiation and some knowledge of geography. People born outside Britain can place themselves at the appropriate edge of the map. Each person in turn announces his/her full name and where they were born. Then you can do the same again with everyone at ages five, eleven, twenty-one, and whatever you choose, saying where they were and what they were doing. You will notice a great shift of location and activity for people generally between the ages of eighteen and the mid-twenties. It is a good way of building up information of each other's history and how that has shaped them (just as you might go on to build up the history of a character), and also of asking people to present themselves to the group.

ii) A variation is to play the game with everyone having to become themselves as they were at five years old, to say their names and addresses as they would have done aged five if asked by a friendly adult. This is not about 'acting' in the sense of putting something on; it is about stripping away to reveal the five-year-old within you, being as truthful and real as possible. Allow for a strong concentration to develop to give people the chance to connect back with their own past. Try again at eleven and eighteen. Conclude with people saying their names and addresses as they are today.

It is an affecting and difficult exercise. That five-year-old is there within you – you are still the same person – it is just difficult to reach down to it. In a similar way, all the emotional resources we need to act a part are within us, and the task is to reach into that reservoir of stored feelings and experiences to activate them. Consideration of the play and the given circumstances will start to unlock our feelings, and a more physically active approach is also needed to release them.

This next exercise aims to clarify how a physically expressed activity causes an emotional release.

ACTIVITY AND EMOTION

Ask people to stand still, close their eyes and think of FEAR, then of LOVE and then of ANGER. Now ask them to move in the space. When you call out each of the words, FEAR, LOVE, ANGER, they must use a physical activity to express it. What you expect to find is that it is much easier to feel the emotion of the word when it is combined with a physical activity than when you are standing still. Start to alternate quickly between the three words, so that participants have to change their physical activity fast. The faster you get, the more chance there is for the body to take over and the brain to follow. People move into the physical activity without thinking, and achieve a direct connection between the activity and the feelings generated within the body.

We touched on this in the earlier exercise of the Railway Station (page 150). The physical activity calls up the emotion. FEAR is easier to experience if you are moving agitatedly from foot to foot, looking behind you, imagining someone following you in the dark. LOVE is easier to experience as you open your arms to pick up a small child or to embrace a lover.

We are now going to move on to establish what we mean by an action. It is not to be confused with a stage action, or blocking, as in 'He moves to the French windows.' Actions, like objectives, are things we use every day. An action is a strategy to achieve an objective. An objective might be: 'I want to win the argument.' The actions I might employ to achieve it might be: 'I persuade you', 'I bully you', 'I deride you', 'I flatter you', 'I convince you' and so on . . .

The following exercise makes it clear how an action moves towards an objective.

ACTIONS

Split people into pairs.

   i) B lies on the floor, where (s)he wants to stay. A's objective is to get B to stand up by any means except physical contact – e.g. they trick

them that there is a spider about to crawl over them; they plead with them that they need their help urgently; they bribe them with an offer of a drink at the pub. Allow this to run for about a minute.
ii) Swap over the active role and try this variation: B's objective is to get £20 from A. B can use any means except physical contact. Give them about a minute to attempt to achieve their objective.

After the exercise ask people how they attempted to achieve their objective. A might start by 'asking' B to stand up and, when that does not succeed, A 'tricks', then 'pleads', then 'bribes', all different actions towards the objective. B might 'beg' for £20 and when this fails go on to 'cajole', 'intimidate', 'persuade' and 'blackmail'.

From that you can write down a list of the actions that were employed, and this starts to build up a bank of verbs that may be useful when going on to work on the text.

An action can be expressed physically in a specific gesture, which the next exercise demonstrates.

PHYSICALIZE THE ACTIONS
  i) Ask people to walk in the space. They have an objective towards an imagined person in the room: 'I want you to leave the room.' When you call out the word 'command' they have to use a physical action to express it. Their action is: 'I *command* you to leave the room.' This might mean they stamp their foot and point with their arm and forefinger. Do the same for 'beg'. They might clasp their hands together and go on to their knees. Do the same for 'dismiss'. They might use the arm to reject the person. Keep calling out the words in a random order.
 ii) Add in that they can use sound coming from the breath with the action.
iii) Add in that they can use a few words coming out of the sound. Keep calling out the actions, speeding up so they have to change from one to the other quickly.

This encourages people to be specific in their choice of gesture for a physical action, and the fast rate of change should make the action stronger, so that the verb ceases to be a mental thought and becomes located in the physical body. Connecting the movement to breath, sound and words prepares the actors for using the actions with text – the next stage.

This has explored a physical action. A verb is not just a word; it is an action. And the action stimulates a response within the body. We 'jump for joy', we 'squirm with embarrassment', we 'shake with rage'.

Actioning the Text

Jacques Tati, Buster Keaton, Charlie Chaplin: possibly the most satisfying and engaging performers to watch are brilliant comic clowns. From childhood to adulthood we are swept along in the delight of their invention and laughter. Marcello Magni, founder member of Théâtre de Complicité, playing Launcelot Gobbo in *The Merchant of Venice* at Shakespeare's Globe Theatre in London, had the audience hanging on his every moment. His performance appeared effortless and to flow in a stream of creativity. It was, of course, the result of meticulous rehearsal, where each part of a particular sequence was broken down, examined and put back together. Some of it was maybe inspired improvisation, but it sprang out of the foundations of hard work.

The key is in the detail. Having established what individual physical actions are, we can now apply them to the text. It is worth having a thesaurus available to extend the range of possible verbs. It is good to be imaginative in the choice of transitive verbs that can be done to somebody else, favouring those that already have a physical dimension. For example: slap, batter, poke, nudge, massage, crush, caress and tease all contain an inherent physical action. In rehearsal the actors will literally try out the actions on each other, to experience what they will end up doing metaphorically. We tend to think of good acting in terms of star performers, who become much admired. Every individual (excepting the one-man show) needs somebody to act with, and that is where good acting takes place: in the space between people. Acting is action, the doing of something to somebody else – a continuous chain of giving and responding, proposal and resolution.

To continue working with our example of the first unit from the section of *The Cherry Orchard*:

ON THE TEXT

Ask people to sit down in pairs and write in an action for each sentence or thought structure of the text. Encourage them to be bold and playful in their choices. For example:

UNIT 1

Yasha's objective: I want to seduce her.

Dunyasha's objective: I want to be noticed.

Enter YASHA *with a rug and travelling bag.*

YASHA (*crosses with delicacy*): [I grab you] All right to come through?

DUNYASHA [examine] I shouldn't even recognize you, Yasha.

[admire] You've changed so abroad!

YASHA [taunt] Mm . . . And who are you?

DUNYASHA [hook] When you left I was so high . . . (*Indicates from the floor.*) [offer] Dunyasha. Fyodor Kozoyedov's daughter. [challenge] You don't remember!

YASHA [squeeze] Mm . . . Quite a pippin, aren't you? (*Looks round and embraces her. She screams and drops a saucer.*)

Exit YASHA, *swiftly.*

These are suggestions for actions. What is important is that the verb means something specific to the actors and projects them into action. Each action has to go towards the objective. So Yasha grabs, taunts and squeezes Dunyasha in order to seduce her. Dunyasha examines, admires, offers, hooks in order to be noticed. As in the game of Back-hand Tag, each thrust aims to hit the target. It is a duel between two people.

Now the two actors playing Yasha and Dunyasha can get to their feet and experiment with playing the actions.

PLAYING ACTIONS

This exercise is removed from any idea of staging the scene, so no attention need be paid to 'blocking' or location. The actors are free to move wherever they want, playing off each other. You will run the unit three times:

i) They *say* and *do* the action, and *say* the text. They *say* the action out loud. Then they *do* the action, which means making a strong physical gesture to the other person that best expresses that particular action. It will probably involve physical contact. Then they *say* the text. For example, Yasha says, 'I grab you.' Action of physically grabbing hold of Dunyasha. 'All right to come through?' Dunyasha replies, with *say*ing and *do*ing her action, and *say*ing her line: 'I examine you.' Action of physically examining Yasha. 'I shouldn't even recognize you, Yasha.' And so on through the unit.

ii) *Do* the action and *say* the text. Repeat the unit but this time without needing to say the action.

YASHA Action of physically grabbing. 'All right to come through?'

DUNYASHA Action of physically examining. 'I shouldn't even recognize you, Yasha.'

And so on.

iii) *Say* the text. Repeat the unit but this time without needing to say or physically do the action.

YASHA 'All right to come through?'

DUNYASHA 'I shouldn't even recognize you, Yasha.'

And so on.

Having experienced the action by saying it and doing a strong physical gesture, the actors are then reducing it to a trace element. In the last version of only *say*ing the text – 'All right to come through?' – Yasha will probably not touch Dunyasha or even be near her, yet by the way he says the line he is grabbing her attention in order to seduce her. Dunyasha will examine Yasha with her line – 'I shouldn't even recognize you, Yasha' – as a way of being sure he notices her.

Having been expressed in an exaggerated physicality, the chosen actions are then reduced to a level where they could be used in the performance of a 'realistic' text. The trace element is left of the physical action 'to grab', and the language is moulded to achieve it. The line is specific and the subtext is alive.

Only Connect

Students and teachers of theatre are often eager to gain access to rehearsals to see what goes on behind closed doors. It is a specialized activity made even more intriguing for being hidden away, and a difficult request to satisfy because often the actors do not feel ready or willing to be looked at. The truth is also that if people did come into rehearsal, they would often be stunned by the tedium of it. So much of the time, especially early on, is spent going over the text in minute detail. Some directors will go through the entire text with the actors physicalizing each action. It is rigorous work and takes time. Much of any rehearsal process is about exaggerating and extending the content of the play so that the actor can experience it at a heightened level. That experience lodges itself in the actor's brain and body, and the essence of it can be retrieved to give the later performance validity and truth.

The enemy of good acting is generalization. Unlike playing a musical instrument, acting is something anyone can get up and do. Instinct is involved with acting, so that sometimes people can hit it right and produce something that works with little conscious preparation. Watching young people work, I have seen some wonderful individual performances that have had little to do with technique and much to do with good instinct. Sometimes a performance might be unremarkable, and then a line will suddenly jump out of it because it is spoken with total conviction and truth.

The process of identifying units, objectives and actions gives a structure to use and forces the actor to be active and specific. There is always the temptation to be lazy and to put your trust in instinct, somehow believing it will all magically happen . . . Yes, it possibly might, and it probably will not. The best policy is hard, structured work, knowing that this does not add up to acting. Instinct and inspiration are vital, and all this process is doing is preparing the ground where those qualities may flourish.

If actors go through their entire parts, dividing the play into units and giving themselves a series of objectives and actions to achieve, they will have a firm grasp of their characters' journeys. Having physicalized each action, the actor's body will have experienced each impulse, and that will be stored in their physical memory. The actions stir the reservoirs of memory and experience and feed the psychological richness that will underlie the character's creation. In performance the actor will still be playing the essence of each individual action. It is still an improvisation, as each action can be played in myriad different ways. At times the specific action will be barely conscious, as the actor allows the character to play the situation and the scene to unfold. At other times, especially if a scene is seeming awkward, the actor may consciously recall the actions and play them strongly so as to get back on purpose with the objective and the means of achieving it.

The approach to text in this chapter involves a gradual process of breaking it down into detail, and building up information layer by layer. As part of that process, physicalizing the actions makes the performer commit fully to each moment. Acting or meeting any challenge successfully is about putting yourself and your resources into the task – opening up and connecting.

Working with Texts

For many people, drama workshops will often mean drama games leading to an improvisation exercise. This is a popular activity and a good way to structure a one-off workshop. Often people are drawn to a drama workshop because they have been to the theatre and seen a play that they have enjoyed, and they are interested to try out acting a script. Yet picking up a play text is often the last option a workshop leader considers. It is hard to find extracts from plays that stand up on their own out of context of the whole play, that make sense quickly, and are short enough to be worked on yet have a shape to them. It also involves the participants in acting a text, which will be challenging to make work in the space of a short workshop. Workshop leaders often also feel that they need to know the play backwards and forwards before they can lead a session on it. Rather than being experts on the play, it is important that they choose a manageable extract to work on.

In this section we will look at two twentieth-century extracts of text that are self-contained and could be approached in a full- or half-day workshop. They give good opportunities to put into practice some of the devices we have already covered as well as some new ones.

The first extract is from *The Birthday Party* (1958) by Harold Pinter. It is short, with a beginning and an end, and on the surface it is straightforward. It also has a great deal of scope for developing work.

The scene is set in the living-room of a house in a seaside town.

There are three characters: Petey, a man in his sixties; Meg, a woman in her sixties; and Stanley, a man in his late thirties.

Stanley is the only lodger of a boarding house run by Meg and Petey. The extract is from early on in Act 1.

PETEY *reads the paper.* STANLEY *enters. He is unshaven, in his pyjama jacket and wears glasses. He sits at the table.*
PETEY Morning, Stanley.
STANLEY Morning.

Silence. MEG *enters with a bowl of cornflakes, which she sets on the table.*

MEG So he's come down at last, has he? He's come down at last for his breakfast. But he doesn't deserve any, does he, Petey? (STANLEY *stares at the cornflakes.*) Did you sleep well?

STANLEY I didn't sleep at all.

MEG You didn't' sleep at all? Did you hear that, Petey? Too tired to eat your breakfast, I suppose? Now you eat up those cornflakes like a good boy. Go on.

He begins to eat.

STANLEY What's it like out today?

PETEY Very nice.

STANLEY Warm?

PETEY Well, there's a good breeze blowing.

STANLEY Cold?

PETEY No, no, I wouldn't say it was cold.

MEG What are the cornflakes like, Stan?

STANLEY Horrible.

MEG Those flakes? Those lovely flakes? You're a liar, a little liar. They're refreshing. It says so. For people when they get up late.

STANLEY The milk's off.

MEG It's not. Petey ate his, didn't you, Petey?

PETEY That's right.

MEG There you are then.

STANLEY All right, I'll go on to the second course.

MEG: He hasn't finished the first course and he wants to go on to the second course!

STANLEY I feel like something cooked.

MEG Well, I'm not going to give it to you.

PETEY Give it to him.

MEG (*sitting at the table, right*) I'm not going to.

Pause.

STANLEY No breakfast.

Pause.

All night long I've been dreaming about this breakfast.

MEG I thought you said you didn't sleep.

STANLEY Day-dreaming. All night long. And now she won't give me any. Not even a crust of bread on the table.

Pause.

Well, I can see I'll have to go down to one of those smart hotels on
the front.

MEG (*rising quickly*) You won't get a better breakfast there than here.

She exits to the kitchen.

The first strategy for approaching this piece of text is to use two
exercises previously outlined.

The first two stages of the Triangle Improvisation in Chapter 2 (page
21), where the scene between three people is cut down to five lines,
will give participants an experience of using dramatic language and
investigating the space around and underneath the language, and will
feed well into an exploration of this short scene.

The second exercise is Eating Breakfast in this chapter (page 144),
which investigates objectives and subtext, and (neatly) is built around
the same situation as the extract.

These two exercises together will give participants a reminder not to
skate over the language, but to start using the text to reveal what is
going on within the scene.

Following on from these two exercises we can start work on the text
itself. Set up some simple staging for the scene:

• A table and three chairs.
• An entrance from the kitchen.
• An entrance from the stairs.
• Provide a few simple props: i.e. a newspaper, a bowl and spoon.

Using three people from the group to play the characters, ask them to
walk through the staging of the scene, so that they have a sense of the
entrances and exits and the basic stage action.

You could now use the units and objectives work described above;
and if you had time, the work on physical actions.

The following exercise is good for getting around the problem of
people not knowing the lines and being hampered by holding scripts
in workshops.

FEEDING THE LANGUAGE

You have three people to act the parts and three people who are their
'shadows'.

i) The actors in the scene are free to move in the space and are not
holding the text. Each actor has a shadow, who is at the edge of

the space. The shadows feed each line in neutrally to their actors. The actors listen, take in the line, then give it out to the other actors on stage. This allows them to be totally in the moment with each line of language. Taking in the line should be like holding a piece of paper, screwing it up into a ball, and then throwing it at the target. Encourage the performers to take the line and let it drop down into them, before giving it out to their fellow actors in the scene. They should try to let each line be specific, and shape and mould it as it comes back out of them, aiming it towards another character.

ii) In a workshop where several groups might be working on the same scene, as well as having someone feeding in the lines, you can also ask someone to feed in their choice of physical actions. The actor then has to *do* the action and *say* the line (as in the Playing Actions exercise above).

This can be very freeing, as individuals' choices of action will be different, and the actor has to respond in the moment and use the action (s)he has been given, with the line, to contact their fellow actor. It demonstrates how engaging a scene can become when it is broken down and specific. This work in fine detail allows each moment to be tasted.

The following exercise will work better if you have already done the work on units. It again allows people to work partly without scripts, and increases their physical understanding of the scene.

PHYSICAL STRUCTURE

i) Improvise the scene in the participants' own words, being very free with it.

ii) Improvise the scene using only key words or phrases.

iii) Improvise the scene using nonsense language, using only sounds and no recognizable words to communicate.

iv) Improvise the scene using no sound, with just action to communicate.

Notice how the shape and structure of the scene become well defined. It may end up resembling a telegram with the important points and the throughline standing out.

By taking away the words and then the sounds, the physical life of the scene will become more defined. The characters create between them a rhythm and a physical shape, and by concentration on that and experience of it, the situation and the emotions are released. The physical size of the performance achieved at the end of this exercise is useful, as it shakes up the pool of resources and the ways of responding, and makes the improvisation alive.

It also creates the need for words where the actors want to be able to express themselves. They will then find that the playwright has given them the best language with which to do it. When adding back the words, do not let the physical life shrink away. Keep the scene physically heightened, and this will feed the playing and the dynamics of the language.

v) Play the scene using the text.

You will find that this short scene has great potential for the actors to listen and play off each other. It may seem too short, but it is better to mine this extract for all it's worth, and for the actors to feel they are making detailed discoveries, than to approximate a larger section. Thorough work takes time.

This is a workshop, and the aim is not for a definitive version of the scene but to free up the creative process of bringing the text to life. When I was working with some teachers, they started the work with a received idea of 'Pinteresque': all brooding silences and clipped speech. Working with objectives and improvising around the physical structure of the scene made the work much lighter and more engaging. They chose to explore the relationship between Meg and Stanley having a sexual dimension (supported by the play), giving Meg the overall objective 'I want to flirt with Stanley', and Stanley the overall objective 'I want to wind up Meg'.

Immediately, with these strong objectives, the stage action became much more fluid and interesting. As soon as Stanley entered, he checked that Meg was in the kitchen and deliberately slumped down at the wrong place. The trading of the word 'sleep' from Meg's 'Did you sleep well?' took on a darker tension. A tussle developed over the rejected bowl of cornflakes, and the exchange with Petey about the weather became an attempt to freeze Meg out. All these were good ideas worth trying and not ones to be dreamed up by a director or workshop leader. They were found organically by the actors when they followed a strong choice.

Moving on to the Physical Structure exercise, the teachers became very free in their physicality and movement, as they reduced the amount they could rely on the words for their communication. They became fully committed and engaged with their choices, which was in complete contrast to their 'cool' acting style of the first 'Pinteresque' version. Adding back the text made the words together with the physicality very rich. It was great to watch and gave the participants a strong sense of accomplishment. They had picked up the scene, made it their own and found a bold acting style that took risks and felt comfortable.

The choice of the sexual relationship between Meg and Stanley is indicated by a background knowledge of the characters. A workshop is always helped by the participants knowing the play, so that you can start to pull together information that impacts on a particular moment, as in the second choice of text from *Amy's View* (1997) by David Hare.

The scene is the living-room of a house in rural Berkshire, not far from Pangbourne. The year is 1979. It is past midnight, midsummer.

There are four characters: Esme Allen, aged 49, an actress; Amy Thomas, aged 23, her daughter; Dominic Tyghe, aged 22, boyfriend of Amy; and Evelyn Thomas, late seventies, mother-in-law to Esme.

The extract is from early on in Act 1. Dominic has been mending a puncture on an old bicycle in the middle of the room.

AMY Is that the sound of a car?

EVELYN Did you say she's coming?

AMY Dominic, I think it's my mother.

EVELYN I'll put her food in the oven. The pub sends something round.

DOMINIC I'll move the bike.

EVELYN It's usually disgusting.

AMY My goodness, she gets her food from the pub?

> EVELYN *has gone. Seeing* DOMINIC *about to move the bike,* AMY *stops him.*

There's no need. You musn't be embarrassed. She's terribly easy, I promise you that.

DOMINIC It's all right. It's not me that's embarrassed.

AMY No.

> DOMINIC *kisses her lightly. They wait a moment, their backs to us, like children. Then we see Amy take his hand.*

ESME (*off*) Hello. Is there anyone there?

AMY (*raising her voice*) Yes. Yes. We're in here.

ESME *comes in wearing a simple dress and carrying a big bag.*

ESME Amy, how are you? How good to see you. Are you all right?
You don't look very well.
AMY No, I'm fine.

ESME *kisses and hugs her daughter warmly.*

Mother, I promised I'd introduce you. This is my friend with a bike.
ESME We've never met.
DOMINIC No.

They shake hands. There is a slight hiatus.

Dominic.
ESME How are you?
DOMINIC Thank you. I'm very well.

They both smile at their own awkwardness. EVELYN *comes in and starts laying a place.*

ESME I got your message. I'm thrilled at this privilege.
DOMINIC Just let me move this.
ESME Don't move it please, on my account. I quite like it there.
What've you been doing? Rallying?
AMY No, Mother, he's just been mending the tyre.

DOMINIC *has turned the tyre upright and is leaning it against the wall.*

ESME I see. Is he freelance? Does he do fuses and plugs? The tank in
the attic's in a terrible state. Why did he start with the bike?
AMY Very funny . . .
ESME I don't need to bother with supper, Evelyn.
AMY He fancied the pub for a beer.

Again this extract would follow on well from the first two stages of the
Triangle Improvisation in Chapter 2 (page 21). In preparation you could
request the three characters in the improvisation to be a mother,
daughter and boyfriend, which will open up the territory that Hare
explores in this scene.

It is interesting how Hare handles this first meeting between the mother and the daughter's boyfriend, with two devices that heighten the situation. The mother enters her own house to meet her daughter and the boyfriend, reversing what would be the normal format of such a meeting. Moreover, the boyfriend Dominic has a bike upside down in the middle of the room, having mended a puncture.

To facilitate the group's appreciation and use of these devices in the playing of the scene, it would be appropriate to precede the work on the text with the Ten-line Scene from Chapter 2 (page 29). The exercise heightens the awareness and importance of a given location.

The location for this scene is Esme's house, where Amy grew up and is now returning for a visit with Dominic, who is here for the first time. They all have a different relationship to the environment that will affect their confidence, ease and familiarity, all of which will be reflected in their physicality and movement. The bike also works like a given location; it is there and you have to play the reality of it. Using either a bike or a couple of upturned chairs, the actors can exploit it as a displacement that heightens the dialogue and the tension of the meeting. It provides Dominic with a physical activity, and feeds Esme's sense of humour and performance, with Amy left in the middle between them.

The group having read the play in preparation, there are three exercises that are useful in workshops to bring character and text work together.

PRELIMINARY CIRCUMSTANCES

Before they enter a scene the characters are to improvise a monologue out loud. It is about where they have been and what they have been doing in the time immediately before their entrance. It must be in the first person, be specific and have a dramatic energy. It has to be important to the character. For each person the last word of their monologue should be followed by the first word of their text, so they get launched into the scene.

So in this example Esme might say: 'I finished the play, felt tired and left as quickly as I could. The taxi was waiting. I got in, had a chat with the driver Eric about his mother still in hospital. Then I dozed intermittently, and looked out of the window, thinking about Amy. How is she? Is she all right? Is she happy? How does she cope with London and the publishing business? She's still so young. I was lost at her age. Will I know if she is all right? And the new boyfriend. The last boyfriend Tim was sweet enough, but completely clueless. That was ages ago. Wonder what this one will be like? Maybe it's not serious. Finally arrived at the house. I felt excited to see Amy. I haven't seen her for about three or four months, and that was just briefly at the theatre between shows. I feel nervous. I wish it was just me and Amy, and we could have a good chat and a joke. I feel awkward to meet this new boyfriend. I'm tired out, what will I have to say to him? I hope Amy is all right. Why has she come down to see me now? There is always something else, isn't there? It can't just be a visit. Oh God! Christ she's not going to say she's engaged or something? No people don't get engaged now, do they? I hope she's all right, she's so precious. I hardly seem to see her any more. Oh well! Put on a brave face . . .'

ESME (*off*): Hello. Is there anyone there?

The monologue will project Esme into the scene and give her an energy to play the opening exchanges. It fills up the life of the character and gives her some substance from which to enter. She has to bring her world on with her.

Amy, Dominic and Evelyn can read the preceding part of the scene. They can also improvise the arrival of Amy and Dominic earlier in the evening, and what they have been doing up to the opening exchanges of the play.

Amy's View is a play that uses the theatre as a metaphor for changing values in Britain over a period of eighteen years. It also comments on actors and acting:

ESME 'Give me five thousand pounds.' As a way of getting my attention, it would take some beating. Well, wouldn't it?

AMY Yes. I don't know. Oh perhaps. I'm confused.

ESME After all that is the basic skill. That *is* my profession. You have to get that right or you might as well give up. You say one thing but you're thinking another. If you can't do that, then truly you shouldn't be doing the job.

Saying one thing but thinking another is subtext, where one seeps into the other. The next exercise is particularly good with inexperienced actors to encourage them to slow down and to think through the thoughts that exist underneath the language, to realize that the lines spoken are a result of all the things the character chose not to say.

STREAM OF THOUGHTS

Each actor speaks their subtext out loud, followed by their actual text. The actor has an internal monologue running as the character, and this exercise allows it to be voiced.

So following on from Esme's entrance (with the stream of thoughts in brackets):

AMY (I'm desperate to see her.): Yes. Yes. (Oh please let her like Dominic!) We're in here.

ESME *comes in wearing a simple dress and carrying a big bag.*

ESME (Amy, my love, I'm so pleased to see you, you're so precious.) Amy, how are you? How good to see you. (Something is wrong.) Are you all right? (Of course that's it, she's pregnant!) You don't look very well.

AMY (Whatever happens I won't tell her I'm pregnant.) No, I'm fine.

ESME *kisses and hugs her daughter warmly.*

(I must include Dominic.) Mother, I promised I'd introduce you. (Oh God! He looks like a little boy standing next to his bike.) This is my friend with a bike.

ESME (I can't stand him.) We've never met.

DOMINIC (I won't be intimidated by you.) No.

Go right through the scene, filling in all the subtext. Repeat the scene, allowing the monologue to be still running but this time unvoiced, and being aware of how the subtext impacts upon the lines.

Amy is pregnant, which she attempts to conceal while asking her mother for five thousand pounds. Later Esme says she knew the moment she saw her. There is a lot going on underneath the language and this exercise helps the actors to be specific about what it is. In turn they will find the scene much more involving and satisfying to play, in contrast to what might happen when they first pick it up and assume superficially that there is not much to it.

An exercise like this serves to give an insight into some of the processes of acting and rehearsing a play. *Pygmalion* by George Bernard Shaw was playing at the National Theatre. A secondary school a stone's throw from the theatre was offered a workshop on the play and reduced-price tickets as part of an education scheme. They were local kids, who were as likely to step through the doors of the National Theatre of their own volition as they were to fly to Mars, it not being a place they considered to be 'for them'. The workshop was viewed with suspicion. We took the beginning of the scene where the flower girl Eliza Doolittle first visits the grand house of Professor Henry Higgins.

The students read the scene as if it was written in a strange language. We then told the story and explained the background: that Eliza felt intimidated at visiting the Professor, but that she also had her pride and was determined to be listened to. We read the short extract again and it started to make more sense. We put the scene up on its feet and started to play some objectives. The students started to recognize what was going on and to enjoy the tension and conflict between the characters.

We then tried the Stream of Thoughts exercise detailed above. One girl playing Eliza took hold of this idea. She had been sullen and detached at first in the workshop, and slowly she had become interested in what was going on. She wanted to have a go at this exercise – and the floodgates opened. Out of her mouth flowed a stream of abuse aimed at Mrs Pearce, the stern housekeeper, followed by an equally energetic and inventive stream of justification to Higgins as to why he should give her speech lessons. It was hard at times to get her back on the text. However, the next time through, using the text only, all that energy and anger was focused on Shaw's words and she was thrilling to watch. She was focused, full of life and completely engaged in the situation.

The following week they all came to see the show at the theatre. They really enjoyed it. They loved the story and the spectacle of it. The workshop had served its purpose as an introduction to the play and a window into the detailed work that an actor has to do to make the words lift off the page. They met some of the actors afterwards and were full of questions. The girl from the workshop, showing bravado worthy of Eliza herself, asked for a job. Possibly the whole experience had made her see that the theatre is not just for someone else.

Running Scenes
In a single workshop it will probably be enough work to explore units and objectives in a small section of text. Working over a longer period of time and having done some of the other exercises suggested, it is then possible to run whole scenes. In a rehearsal process, as the opening

performance approaches, scenes, acts and the complete play will be run through many times to achieve what should appear a seamless flow. The detailed examination of each constituent part only takes place so that it can be put back together again as a satisfying totality.

At first when running scenes the actors will be sufficiently engaged keeping their objectives and actions clear and precise. Rather than letting this become comfortable and safe, add in a point of concentration.

POINTS OF CONCENTRATION

The actors, while playing their actions and objectives, are also given a point of concentration: something they all agree to focus on during the running of the scene. It will affect them, and they will discover more about their character and the situation.

In the example from *Amy's View* a point of concentration could be that it is late at night, or that it is hot and humid, or that people are tired. Any of these will build up the layers of reality and may free the actors to make interesting discoveries in the scene.

The point of concentration can also usefully be created by choosing one of the characters. You can run the scene four times with a different character being the focus each time. So the first time through, the focus is on Esme and how people respond to her. Then change it to Evelyn, to Amy and to Dominic. See how the emphasis and undercurrents of the scene shift with the different characters. It also helps establish the network of relationships and needs that constantly exists between the individual characters, and substantiates the world between them.

This work refers back to the Three and One exercise described earlier (page 150). As an actor, your brain is so full of playing your objective, your action and your point of concentration that your restless mind has nowhere to wander; and the effort of spinning these simultaneous thoughts can have the effect of freeing your creativity, so that unexpected choices spring up to surprise you.

Richness

All this textual analysis serves to free up the actors. Without it they are thrown back on to bluff and luck. If they work at the process with commitment and diligence, they may be fortunate, being rewarded with creativity and inspiration. At the very least they will have a bank of information on the play and their characters.

For most actors, their script becomes their bible. It is best to have a script in A4 format with plenty of space to write in units, objectives, actions, and personal notes and references that may be intelligible only to them: a word, a phrase, a drawing, a picture that sparks a memory or thought. In this way the script becomes the score, consisting of a series of notes that together contain the life of the part. This is the key. Somehow, however you choose to do it, every moment of a performance has to be given some personal connection, so that what you play is specific and truthful.

The work starts simply and builds up to give a richness of texture. The work on units, objectives and actions starts to fall away from conscious consideration and to become the secure foundation that allows creativity to flourish. Freeing up the movement or a point of concentration can spark a moment of inspiration, where the character and the text are revealed through small details riding on the back of all the busy work of homework and rehearsals.

In performance the actors should tread lightly from moment to moment, confident that they are supported by the work they have done. It is the same with any form of public speaking. A process of detailed preparation is required that gives the speaker the confidence to be focused and fully present at the point of delivery. Knowing how to prepare is the best way to ensure that inhibitions and self-consciousness do not sabotage the moment.